MW00879864

TWO WAYS TO DIE
A Java Jarvis Thriller
by Erin Wade
Edited by Katherine Fleming
Copyright 11/2019
ISBN: 9781708223939

Covers by Joolz & Jarling
Julie Nicholls & Uwe Jarling

©11/2019 Erin Wade
www.erinwade.us
Independently published
By Erin Wade

Two Ways to Die
A Java Jarvis Thriller
by Erin Wade

DEDICATION

To the one who has always supported me in everything I have ever undertaken. You have encouraged me and have always been my biggest fan. Life is sweeter with you.

Erin

Two Ways to Die
A Java Jarvis Thriller
by Erin Wade

Acknowledgements

A special "Thank You" to my wonderful and witty "Beta Master," **Julie Versoi**. She makes me a better storyteller.

~~~

A heartfelt "Thank You" to **Laure Dherbécourt** for agreeing to beta read for me. She has added insight and an incredible knack for catching incorrect homophones.

~~~

A huge "Thank You" to **Julie Nicholls & Uwe Jarling** for our beautiful cover.

~~~

A special "Thank You" to **Kathryn-Ann Nourse**
Empangeni, KwaZulu-Natal, South Africa
for the voodoo doll artwork at the end of the chapters.

Two Ways to Die
A Java Jarvis Thriller
by Erin Wade

Someone

If you are lucky, in your lifetime someone will come along who takes your breath away. Someone who gets into your head and touches your every thought. Someone who makes the time fly when you are with her but makes it crawl when she is away from you. Someone who only needs to hold your hand to turn a thunderstorm into the brightest sunshine. Someone who makes you wish for snow so you can snuggle with her in front of the fireplace. Someone who makes you laugh. When she comes along, don't lose her. Do whatever it takes to have her in your life.

. . . from "Two Ways to Die"
by Erin Wade

I'm the One You Need

You don't scare me
I've ridden a lightning bolt.
You can't hurt me
My heart is too remote.
So, bring your pain and doubt
to my doorstep, we will work it out.
At the end of the day after you share
your disappoints and unsavory deeds
I'll hold you gently in my arms and
you'll know that I'm the one you need.

> . . . from "Two Ways to Die"
> by Erin Wade

Two Ways to Die
A Java Jarvis Thriller
by Erin Wade

CONTENTS

Two Ways to Die
A Java Jarvis Thriller
by Erin Wade

Two Ways to Die
A Java Jarvis Thriller
by Erin Wade

Two Ways to Die
A Java Jarvis Thriller
by Erin Wade

CHAPTER 1

Classy slumped onto the stool as the bartender pushed an Irish coffee to her. She sipped it and marveled at the taste as it warmed her throat and insides. "Thanks, Randy."

"You through for the night?" Randy asked.

"The sun's up isn't it?"

"Yeah, I just wondered," Randy ignored her querulous answer. "Pender was in here looking for you. Said he had a whale."

"Yeah, that probably means he wants me to do a four-hundred pounder."

"Jesus Classy, why don't you get out of this business. A looker like you, you could find a decent job."

"You think Pender would just let me walk away," Classy huffed. "I'm his biggest meal ticket right now."

"Yeah, and he's using you up. How many last night? Ten johns in twelve hours."

"Look, Randy. I told him I wanted out. He said the only way I was leaving this job was in a body bag."

"He's just trying to scare you. Pender's all bark and no bite. That's why he runs girls. He can intimidate them.

"Just take your money and run, Classy. Get the hell out of Orleans."

Classy studied Randy for a long time. "Maybe you're right. Maybe I should leave. Go back home and start over. This certainly isn't what I had planned for my life."

Another customer entered the bar. "We're closed, sir," Randy advised him.

The man asked for directions and Classy closed out the sounds around her. As she always did, she withdrew to a place where no one could reach her. A place where Classy didn't exist. A place where . . . where . . . she couldn't even recall her own name.

"Hey, you deaf?" Pender shook her elbow. "I swear. Classy. Sometimes I think you go into a trance or something."

"Sorry, Pen. I'm just exhausted." She drained her coffee cup and slid from the bar stool. "I'll see you tonight."

"Wait, I need you to take care of one more john."

"Seriously, Pender. I can barely stand up."

"Thousand bucks. Twice your usual take," Pender dangled the carrot in front of her. "He's waiting for me to call him. He'll pay with PayPal."

"Like I'd ever see that," Classy snorted.

"I'll pay you cash, right now. Just . . . please Classy. He requested you. Look!" Pender pulled a wad of money from his pocket and started counting out hundred-dollar bills. "Your five thousand from last night and another thousand for this fellow."

Classy licked her lips as she recounted the money. *With this and what I have saved I can get out of this town,* she thought.

"Okay, but he's the last one today." She slipped the greenbacks inside her bra and took the note with the address of her client.

Barron Windom drove his Mercedes through the gates of his thriving business, Mulch & More Landscaping Supplies. His daughter was getting married tomorrow and he needed to move some money around in his accounts to cover the expenses that had skyrocketed.

"Boss, you'd better come look at this," his manager skipped from one foot to the other. "I've never seen anything like it."

11

Two Ways to Die
A Java Jarvis Thriller
by Erin Wade

Barron laughed. "What's so exciting you can't stand still, Willie?"

"At the back of the lot, where the road dead ends." Willie's wide-eyed glare made Barron pay attention.

"Is it something bad?"

"Yeah, boss, really bad." Willie sprinted a few feet ahead of Barron as if checking out things before his boss proceeded.

"There," Willie pointed a shaking finger toward something half buried in the mulch pile.

Barron pushed past Willie for a closer look. "Oh, dear Jesus," he exclaimed before he threw up.

CHAPTER 2

Java Jarvis half listened as the Director droned on about the purpose of the new task force. She was more interested in the brunette at the other end of the conference table.

They were introducing themselves, their name, rank and serial number. Each talked about their specialty, areas in which they excelled.

"I have a license to . . ." the redhead's voice faded away as Java wondered which of her own licenses would be required for the assignment they were undertaking. Java had a driver's license, a commercial driver's license, a pilot's license, a concealed carry license, a license to perform weddings, baptisms and funerals, a license to kill, a license from Microsoft declaring her a computer genius— to go with her degree from MIT, a notary license, a license to practice law in Louisiana, and a liquor license. Her weapons of choice were a Glock, a knife, and her bare hands in that order.

"Java, it's your turn," the director repeated. "Would you like to share your areas of expertise with us?"

"Umm, I have a driver's license and I love computers."

"That's it?" The brunette smirked.

"Oh, and a concealed carry license," Java added smirking back.

"You look like a girl scout," the brunette taunted her.

"That's my other specialty," Java grinned. "I look harmless." She wiggled her eyebrows at the brunette. "Trust me, I'm not!"

13

The brunette gave her a sultry look, smiled slightly, and shrugged.

She's flirting with me, Java thought. *Yep, she's flirting with me.*

"Your base of operation is a restaurant called Java's Place, or as the locals refer to it, Java's." the director continued. "Java actually owns it and has operated out of it for several years. It's amazing how much information one can glean from a tongue loosened by booze. As always, Java will run the operation."

"Barbie, you'll do your dumb blonde waitress routine." The Director addressed a cute little blonde with dimples to die for, who was anything but a dumb blonde.

"I need a better cover than a waitress," the brunette demanded.

"Oh, we have a better cover for you," Java grinned. "You're the head dish washer."

The brunette didn't rise to the bait. She knew she'd be front and center in the operation. That was why she was here.

"Chris you'll take over as head cashier and part-time hostess. Kat, you're the resident blues singer during this maneuver."

The brunette raised a perfectly arched Belizean brow and gave Java an "I told you so" look.

Katrina Yvonne Lace was one of those breathtaking beauties that drove both sexes mad. Brown bedroom eyes with a permanent "think you can handle this" look and a right cross that would lay low anyone who tried, made her irresistible.

"You'll report to Java," the director concluded.

Java locked gazes with Kat. "That means you'll be working under me," Java's devilish grin made Kat blush and scowl.

Two Ways to Die
A Java Jarvis Thriller
by Erin Wade

"It means I'll file sexual harassment charges against you if you even glance at me sideways," Kat threatened.

"Oh, she scratches," Barbie giggled. "I see claw marks and blood in your future, Java." Everyone laughed.

"Ladies," the Director quieted them. "We're after a killer—or killers—that travels between Louisiana and Texas. Java, you want to bring us up to speed?"

##

Java pushed a remote control that raised a panel exposing their electric white board.

"I miss chalk," Barbie spouted.

Java zipped a "Z" across the electric whiteboard with her finger. "I don't know," she grinned. "I rather like fingers, don't you Kat?"

"Director, must I work with her?" Kat glared at Java.

"You four were handpicked, Kat," FBI Director Karen Pierce quipped. "You know Java's just trying to get a rise out of you. This is one of the goriest cases I've ever worked. Before we finish, I think you'll welcome Java's attempts to distract you."

"Personally," Barbie laughed, "I'm looking forward to working under Java. She's a legend in the world of—."

"Bedrooms," Kat butted in.

"I was going to say criminal investigation," Barbie smirked. "But maybe you know more about Java then I do.

"Thank you, Barbie." The smile disappeared from Java's face. "Each of you were selected for this assignment because you have special skills.

"Kat is one of our best profilers and although she looks like a sexy cream puff, her abilities in hand-to-hand combat are phenomenal. Trust me she can kill a man faster than you can blink an eye. Kat's married and I respect that. As far as I'm concerned that takes her off the market, which makes my teasing harmless. Have you noticed that I keep the table between Kat and me when I razz her?"

15

Two Ways to Die
A Java Jarvis Thriller
by Erin Wade

Everyone laughed, and the group relaxed. Beginning to meld into the cohesive unit they would need to be to survive their assignment.

"Although we're all licensed to carry guns, we won't during this operation. We were selected because of our hand -to-hand combat abilities.

"Chris Canton's weapon is pressure points. Let Chris get her hands on you and you can be dead or paralyzed within a few seconds.

"The newest member of our team, Barbie Wallace is as deadly as a rattlesnake. Her specialty is poisons. I'm guessing that Barbie has enough poison on her person right now to kill everyone in this room. Am I right, Barbie?"

"Maybe," Barbie blushed.

"Don't be fooled by her innocent, blushing. She's a blonde. Blondes can blush at will." Java demonstrated letting a slow redness creep up her chest to her face. "It's in our genes."

"How many women has that worked on?" Kat demanded.

Java cleared her throat. "I've lost count. Director Pierce will supply us with every gadget imaginable. If we need it Karen will get it for us." Java continued.

"In front of each of you is a large envelope with your identifications: driver's license, passports, birth certificates and a couple of credit cards in your alias.

"Drop the titles and ranks. Always call each other by your first names. Use the alias last names we've assigned to you. They're all backed up in every database imaginable. Beau Braxton will be our police coordinator with the local authorities. He's working another decapitation murder right now and couldn't make this meeting. He'll join us for dinner and drinks later tonight.

Two Ways to Die
A Java Jarvis Thriller
by Erin Wade

"This case has been turned over to us because we have the heads of four women and no bodies. We think we're dealing with one or more serial killers."

"Were all the heads found in Louisiana?" Barbie asked.

"No, two in Louisiana and two in Texas," Java answered. "All the details of this case are in the envelope in front of you. Read it all tonight and familiarize yourself with the photos of possible suspects and their background. You'll see those characters drinking and dining at Java's Place. Are there any questions?"

"I have one," Kat smirked. "Who came up with the name for our team?"

"Serial Killers Investigative Resolution Team," Java scowled. "I think the head of the FBI had to be the brain trust behind that title. I mean how insane is it to form an all-female serial-killer investigation team and give them an acronym like SKIRT?"

"I'll see if I can't get that changed." Karen frowned.

"Any more questions?" Java asked. "No. Then let's go to dinner. Beau will meet us there."

##

"May I buy you a drink, Kat?" Java asked.

"Why?"

"Because I'd like to," Java grinned her best little girl grin settling into the seat next to Kat. "Where's your husband? If I had a woman like you, I'd never get very far away from her."

"If you had a woman like me, you wouldn't know what to do with her."

"Try me," Java growled.

Kat leaned over and whispered in Java's ear. Java's eyes darted around the room as Kat's soft lips brushed her earlobe.

17

Two Ways to Die
A Java Jarvis Thriller
by Erin Wade

The team watched as the two sparred with each other. "Is that a controlled blush that just enveloped you," Chris laughed, "or is Kat setting you on fire?"

"I was just asking Java an innocent question," Kat purred.

Java cleared her throat and licked her lips. "There's no such thing as an innocent question."

The four talked and danced as they waited for Beau to join them. It was obvious Barbie was enamored of her new boss.

"I swear Java, I keep expecting you to rip open your shirt and expose a big S on your chest," Barbie giggled as she touched Java's arm.

"Yes, I'm sure she's had more than one big ass on her chest," Kat retorted.

"S a big S as in Supergirl," Barbie hissed.

Java smiled, enjoying the good-natured teasing going on between her teammates even if it was at her expense. Kat shot her a smoldering look and Java sobered. "Enough joking around ladies. We've got some nasty work to do."

Two Ways to Die
A Java Jarvis Thriller
by Erin Wade

CHAPTER 3

Slow dancing with Java was an exercise in self-control. Kat watched as Barbie almost climbed the lithe frame of their team leader. The smaller woman slid her hand behind Java's back and found the hem of her pullover. She slipped her fingers beneath the top and slid her hand up Java's back pressing skin against skin.

Java locked gazes with Kat and grinned sheepishly. *Time to save her ass*, Kat thought. She sipped one last swallow of her wine then walked to the dancers. "Cutting in." She dared Barbie to deny her request.

"It's about time," Java released her breath. "I thought you were going to let her seduce me." She pulled Kat into her arms and reveled in the feel of the brunette. "You on the other hand are welcome to succeed."

"You shouldn't ride me so hard in front of them," Kat whispered in her ear as their bodies melded, and Java moved her gracefully around the dancefloor. "It's a turn on you know."

"Meant for you and no one else," Java pointed out.

"Note to Java," the blonde grinned, "don't ride Kat so hard in public. What about in private?"

"In private, you can ride me as hard as you like." Kat bit Java's ear hard.

"Ouch," Java squealed jumping away from Kat. "That hurt."

"I'm going to the lady's room," Kat smirked. "Go charm our teammates."

19

Two Ways to Die
A Java Jarvis Thriller
by Erin Wade

Java ambled to the table where the others were laughing at her.

"She scratches and bites," Chris poked fun at her boss and the others laughed as Java continued rubbing her ear.

Java finished her drink then followed Kat into the foyer of the immaculate lady's room. The brunette was washing her hands at the sink next to the wall. She dried her hands and turned to face the woman that often made her heart race.

"You shouldn't be in here," she purred as Java backed her to the wall.

"I don't want to be anywhere else," Java whispered in her ear as she pressed her body against Kat's. "You drive me crazy."

Kat raised hands Java knew were lethal weapons. She caught Kat's wrists in her left hand and forced them against the wall above Kat's head.

"Someone is living dangerously," Kat mumbled.

"You know you've wanted this all day," Java kissed her neck and shoulder.

"Sometimes I could kill you," Kat threatened.

"And other times?" Java continued to kiss and gently suck Kat's neck.

"Other times I could fuc—," Soft lips pressed against Kat's— "your brains out."

"I'm hoping this is one of those other times," Java pressed her lower body harder against Kat and let her free hand edge under Kat's sweater.

Kat couldn't stop her foolish heart's acceleration as Java's soft hand moved closer to her breast. "I hate you," she mumbled as she sucked Java's lip between her teeth. "Hate you."

"Incoming," Kat whispered.

Java groaned loudly and braced herself for the inevitable.

Two Ways to Die
A Java Jarvis Thriller
by Erin Wade

Kat's movement was imperceptible. One-minute Java had Kat's hands pinned to the wall over her head and the next minute Java lay on the floor curled into the fetal position whimpering like a scared puppy.

"I won't be so gentle next time, Java," Kat kicked at her team leader as she headed for the door and their shocked team members.

"Oh, I thought we were alone," Kat shot a hot glance at her two teammates pretending to notice them for the first time. "You might want to help your boss; you know the one with five hands."

CHAPTER 4

Beau Braxton wished there was something he could put up his nose to block the stench of blood but that was just a myth, so he shook his head, held his breath then stepped into the bedroom of the middle-class home in Rayne, Louisiana.

The message Beau's eyes sent to his brain was far worse than the smell of blood. A mother and her three children were lined up on a king-sized bed that was now a blood-drenched resting place for them.

"Dear God," Beau exhaled glancing at his partner.

"Yeah," Lou Davenport snorted. "What kind of monster would do this? There are brains splattered all over the walls and blood is everywhere."

"Any witnesses?" Beau croaked taking shallow breaths.

"Not a soul so far," Lou said. "Penny just arrived. Her people are in the other rooms and she's pissed about the local authorities contaminating the crime scene. She's banned them from entering the house. She said the children were slaughtered in their rooms and moved in here."

"Good," Beau nodded. "Penny will go over this place with a fine-toothed comb. Do we have any idea how many killers there were?"

"At least two," Penny huffed as she entered the room. "I've got the prints from a man's shoe and a woman's boot. Looks like a couple, out for a little Friday evening massacre."

Penny Short was the forty-five-year-old medical director for Orleans Parish. A tough, no-nonsense woman

Two Ways to Die
A Java Jarvis Thriller
by Erin Wade

who had single-handedly straightened out the mess the Coroner's office had become after twenty years of neglect.

"Don't get too excited though. I suspect the woman's footprint belongs to that local officer standing over there."

Penny pointed an accusing finger toward a petite female wearing the police uniform of the local sheriff's department.

Beau groaned loudly as he looked at the officer's shoes covered in blood. "How badly have the locals contaminated the crime scene?"

"Enough that I'm going to be forced to fingerprint and check the shoes of everyone who arrived before I did," Penny groused. "It's not like I have time to waste clearing the local law enforcement officers. I should consider them all suspects and have them arrested, but that would just increase your workload."

"Please don't do that, Penny?" Lou pleaded.

"Why have we been assigned to this case?" Penny asked. "This is way out of our jurisdiction."

"You know we're part of the statewide metro squad," Beau snorted. "When the perps are classified as serial killers, it becomes ours and yours."

"Serial killers!" Penny smirked. "Since when?"

"As of this case," Beau informed her. "This is the third murder with the same MO."

"Damn," Penny cursed. "I hate serial killers. They're so frickin' crazy they tend to outsmart us normal folks."

"I'll need the other two cases ASAP so I can compare them to make sure this is the work of the same loon before we start a panic among our fellow citizens."

"The files have been sent to your office," Beau shrugged. "I had them sent to you as I drove to this location."

"So, you've already classified this the work of a serial killer?" Penny frowned. "What do you need me for?"

"Come on Penny," Beau flashed a smile, "tell me I'm wrong?"

Penny glanced at the tall detective. "You know you're right," she grumbled.

"Yeah, I'm headed to a meeting with SKIRT right now. Is there any chance you could brief us in the morning?"

"SKIRT!" Penny snorted. "What the hell is SKIRT?"

"Serial Killers Investigative Resolution Team," Beau laughed. "I'm the liaison between them and the rest of the law enforcement community in the state."

"Ah, yes, that's the new group Java's heading up," Penny shook her head. "How'd you get so lucky?"

"Java requested you and me," Beau grinned. "This should be fun."

"Yeah!" Penny chuckled. "Or at least a lot of kick-ass action. Do you have any suspects?"

"Not yet," Beau grimaced, "but believe me you'll be the first to know when I do."

CHAPTER 5

Beau Braxton stood in the doorway surveying the clientele of New Orleans' most elite supper club. He wondered how the FBI justified the expense of belonging to the members-only private club. His eyes focused on the four women across the room. They were laughing and talking.

Beau knew Java, Kat and Chris. He was pleasantly surprised by the beauty of the newest team member. He searched his mind for a name. *Barbie, yes Barbie Wallace. Geeze, I hope she's straight!* He thought.

Java caught his eye and waved him over to their table. He'd had a crush on the blonde during their first case together but soon learned that he wasn't playing on the same team as Java. Hell, he didn't even have the right uniform much less the game plan. Although she was every man's wet dream, Java was tough as nails and very much a woman's woman.

His eyes moved to Kat Lace. It was no secret Java was crazy about Kat, but the brunette rarely gave her the time of day unless one considered the fact that Kat had taken a bullet for Java during their last case. *Kat may hate Java but didn't hesitate to die for her. Both women are FBI through and through.* Beau thought.

The women greeted Beau warmly as he pulled out a chair to join them. Java introduced Barbie as Chris ordered him a drink.

Two Ways to Die
A Java Jarvis Thriller
by Erin Wade

"If I recall correctly," Chris smiled, "you're a Ragin' Cajuns Lager man."

"I am," Beau grinned like it was his birthday. He was pleased that the red-haired beauty remembered his beer of choice.

"Dance with me, Java," Barbie caught Java's hand and stood up.

"Not right now Barbie. My coffee will get cold." Java sipped her favorite drink.

"You and your coffee," Barbie huffed. "Does your coffee always come first?"

"I can think of only one thing I'd miss my coffee for," Java raised her brows at Kat who sneered back at her. "Besides, I'm pretty sure Beau has information we need."

Beau took a long drink of his beer and squinted his eyes as the red murder scene flashed in front of him.

"I know your team's top priority is the four women's heads found in Louisiana and Texas," Beau exhaled, "and I'm sorry to tell you that I have nothing on those crimes. Not a single lead.

"The thing I'm most disturbed over right now is the murder of thirteen people in the past five days. I know you've been following the murders and are aware of the debauchery involved."

"I've been following the reports," Java frowned, "but it's not our case. We're strictly serial killers."

"It is now," Beau rubbed his temples.

"The scene I just left is definitely number three," he tried not to gag. "Even more gruesome than the other two. Three children involved. Penny's going to meet with us in the morning and further validate it, but I'd bet my retirement it's the same perp or perps."

Java nodded solemnly. "We'll go over all the details in the morning. Right now, let's enjoy dinner and the excellent camaraderie."

Two Ways to Die
A Java Jarvis Thriller
by Erin Wade

##

The next morning Beau arrived as Java was unlocking the office door. She balanced two large styrofoam cups of coffee on a laptop bag as she turned the knob and pushed the door open.

"What the hell is going on, Beau?" She grunted as she placed the coffee and computer bag on the table at the front of the room. "We've got one case involving four women's heads and another case with three separate murder scenes where families are axed to death. Are the two cases related?"

"I don't think so, Java. The MO on the decapitations is completely different from the ax murders. I'm certain it's two different psychos."

"I'd like to visit the murder scene after Penny briefs us," Java informed him. "While it's still fresh."

"I thought you'd want to do that," Beau agreed. "I had the house sealed and posted two guards to keep out the looky-loos."

"I appreciate that. Thanks Beau."

Penny and Kat entered with the others following behind. Java shook hands with Penny. "It's good to be working with you again," she said.

"You know I'm up to my neck in dead bodies," Penny growled, "And I received a memo this morning that we're being assigned to the ax murder cases."

"You have to admit the case is a puzzler, Penny."

"I know, Java. I'm all in on it. This bastard has massacred thirteen people in five days. Most serial killers rest and savor their kill. Each kill just seems to make him want to kill again. It's like a shark on a feeding frenzy."

"So, you are calling it a serial killing?" Java grimaced.

"Oh, yes," Penny exhaled. "The Basher has a need to kill and kill again."

"The Basher?" Kat questioned.

27

Two Ways to Die
A Java Jarvis Thriller
by Erin Wade

"Yeah, he doesn't hack 'em like you'd expect with an ax. He uses the blunt side and bludgeons them to death. That bit of information cannot go outside this room," Penny cautioned. "It's the only way we will know when we encounter copycat killers and we always do."

Penny opened her laptop, plugged it into the projector, and waited for her slide show to load. "I can't believe we haven't caught him. He seems to randomly select his victims. I can't figure out how he kills so many without anyone putting up a fight."

"I've wondered about that too," Beau joined in. "Did toxicology show any barbiturates in their systems?"

"You will find this hard to believe," Penny shook her head. "The bodies from the first two murders haven't been worked yet. I've called for them to be delivered to my morgue as soon as possible."

"Penny, you're the best," Java complimented. "Everyone's here so let's get on with the show."

Penny flashed the presentation on the whiteboard and Beau turned out the lights. Java slid a cup of coffee to Kat. "Peace offering," she smiled as Kat took the cup letting her fingers linger around Java's longer than necessary.

"We believe the killer or killers' first victims were the family in West Crowley, LA," Penny started. "The Martins, a husband and wife and their small son, were murdered around January first. The second murders were four days later in Gonzales. The Dailey family consisted of two sisters and four children under the age of five. Our latest murder—the third—was yesterday in Rayne.

"I haven't had time to complete the autopsy on yesterday's kill and I'm waiting for the bodies from the first two murders, but from the written reports from local authorities, the mode of operation seems to be the same.

"In all three murders the victims were beaten to death with the blunt side of the ax not the sharp edge as one would expect. I've only the bodies in my morgue to go by but from the force of the blows I'd say we're looking for a strong man capable of crushing an adult's skull with a single blow.

"Although the victims were killed in various rooms of the house, all of them were lined up across the bed meaning the killer had to carry them to the bed to arrange them in his bizarre ritual.

"Until I can complete autopsies on all the bodies that's all the information I have. Any questions?"

"All the children were small," Kat thought out loud, "so a large, strong woman could have carried them, or two killers would have no problem moving the bodies."

"True," Penny nodded.

"At the recent murder in Rayne," Beau said, "the killer left the ax leaning against the headboard of the bed. Has the ax been left in all the murders?"

"Yes," Penny answered. "They probably didn't want to be caught with it. It wasn't wiped clean, but blood was intentionally smeared all over it effectively destroying any fingerprints."

"Are all the axes the same?" Java asked.

"No, each one is different and very common," Penny answered. "They could have been purchased anywhere."

"All three murders were committed close to the Amtrak stations," Barbie noted. "I'd think they were riding the train but that would mean they'd have to hide the ax in route to the crime. After the crime they'd be covered in blood and brains which would draw a lot of attention. So, I'm guessing they are using their own vehicle to get to the murder scene.

"Were there any tire prints?"

"None were pulled from the first two murder scenes," Penny huffed, "and the one we worked yesterday was overrun by the local authorities. Honest to God, they drove their vehicles right into the driveway and parked all along the curb. If there was any evidence, they wiped it out."

Java thumbed through Penny's report then asked a question. "Voodoo dolls. This says that voodoo dolls were left at each crime scene. Is that true?"

"Yes," Penny shrugged. "All identical. You know, the fancy-dressed ones that look like voodoo priests. The kind one can purchase at any high-end tourist trap in Louisiana."

"Can you shoot us over a photo of it—front and back?" Java requested.

Penny flashed a phone number on the white board. "My cellphone," she quipped. "Each of you text me and I'll set up a group text, so all of you receive info as I get it."

Penny's phone dinged five times as the team responded. "One voodoo doll coming up," she grinned thankful for modern technology. Everyone's phone dinged as the picture of the doll showed up on their screen.

"Hum, pretty cute," Barbie commented. "Most of the ones I've seen looked like a burlap bag. This one actually has on decent clothes."

"It looks like that priest that leads the Christ's Sanctity Church," Chris noted. "You know the mulatto fellow with the spikey hair."

"Handsome dude," Barbie added.

"Maybe we should pay him a visit," Java scowled.

"To summarize the similarities in this case," Penny raised her voice, "All the families were mixed. In each case the children's father was black, and the mother was white or visa-versa. All were killed with the blunt side of the ax. All the bodies were lying on their backs and lined up on the bed. All murders were committed sometime after midnight. Each victim's arms were crossed over a voodoo doll."

CHAPTER 6

Java was stacking drink glasses in the bar when Barbie Wallace arrived. "You're early, Barbie."

"I just wanted to get the lay of the land before others arrived." Barbie tied on an apron that said, "Java's Place." "Is it okay if I walk through the restaurant?"

"Sure. Do you need a guided tour?"

"No, I want to commit it all to memory," Barbie raised her brows, "and I'm pretty certain you'd be a distraction."

Java shrugged her shoulders and turned away. The last thing she needed was to get involved with a member of her team.

Chris Canton joined Java in the bar. "I wanted to thank you for requesting me," she said as she settled onto one of the bar stools.

"You might change your mind when you find out why," Java smirked.

"Do tell?" The redhead hid a smile.

"You fit the description of all The Decapitator's victims. You are the bait in our little trap."

"Ah," a thoughtful expression crossed Chris's face. "I assumed the bait would be Kat."

"Kat does seem to attract the crazies," Java chuckled.

"Does that include you?" A smile ghosted Chris' lip.

"We're all crazy," Java avoided the question. "Otherwise we'd have sane jobs instead of putting our lives on the line to catch psycho killers."

"Why don't you give me a quick run through of your system?" Chris nodded toward the computer used to run Java's Place financial activities.

Two Ways to Die
A Java Jarvis Thriller
by Erin Wade

"All the waitresses have hand-held devices similar to mini iPads," Java led Chris to the computer. "They enter the customer's order as they take it and it goes to the cooks in the back and into the processor here. At any point in time you can see how many orders are working and how many orders have been filled. It keeps a running total of daily sales so you will always be able to see how business is doing."

"Impressive," Chris said. "Did you set this up?"

"Of course," Java grinned.

"You've added a new stage and enlarged the dancefloor," Chris noted. "As I recall, the dancefloor was half this size."

"Yes, the band has developed a big following and you know how Kat packs them in when she's here," Java added. "And who knows how long this case will take. Our leads are nada."

"With so much blood and destruction," Chris shook her head, "one would think there'd be all kinds of evidence. I can't believe the perp could go unnoticed covered in blood and brain matter."

"That puzzles me too," Java agreed as she refilled her coffee cup. "Want a cup?"

"Sure," Chris smiled. "I remember you brew the best coffee in the South."

"This a nice place, Java," Barbie joined them in the bar. "How'd you manage this on an FBI salary?"

"I inherited it," Java explained, "from my parents about five years ago. A gang robbed them three weeks in a row and they decided it was time to retire. So, they signed it over to me."

"How many times have you been robbed?" Barbie giggled.

"Once," Java shrugged. "The same gang made a run at my cash register."

Two Ways to Die
A Java Jarvis Thriller
by Erin Wade

"What happened?" Barbie asked.

"I convinced them they didn't really want to tangle with me," Java grinned. "I never saw them again."

Kat entered the establishment followed by a couple of the band members. "Mm, I love the smell of your freshly-brewed java." She winked at Java as the blonde handed her a cup of coffee.

"Just one of the many perks of working with me," Java laughed as Kat took a seat on a barstool.

"What's on the agenda for today boss," Kat asked sipping her coffee.

"I thought we'd take a drive to Rayne after you finish rehearsing with the band," Java said. "I want to get a good look at the crime scene. Not that I think Penny missed anything. I just want to get a feel for it."

"It's about an hour's drive from here," Kat frowned. "I'd better get the band going if we're to get there and back before we open. Give me thirty minutes of rehearsal time."

Java watched the dark-haired woman as she sashayed toward the stage.

"Are we all going?" Chris asked.

"I think we should," Java answered without taking her eyes off Kat.

"Let's rehearse our new song first," Kat instructed the band. "Let Java see if she likes it."

Kat had the perfect voice for torch music. It could be full and throaty or soft and sensuous. Classically trained she could sing any style music but loved singing blues tunes.

The band gave her an intro and her silky voice caressed an old Julie London tune *Cry Me a River*. When the song ended Kat realized that she had sung it to Java. She pulled away from the blonde's gaze and began the next number in the set.

"What did you do to her, Java?" Barbie asked.

Two Ways to Die
A Java Jarvis Thriller
by Erin Wade

"Nothing," Java downed the last of her coffee and walked away.

CHAPTER 7

"Not a bad neighborhood," Chris commented as Java stopped the car in front of a three-bedroom, wood-framed house surrounded by crime scene tape. "Well kept."

The team sat in silence each getting a feel for the home and its former occupants. The recently edged sidewalk was still covered with bloody footprints of all sizes and the caliche drive had multiple ruts from various vehicles. The victims' two cars were still in the attached carport. A window screen was missing from the front window and the freshly mowed grass had been trampled relentlessly.

"Wow, I've seen better preserved crime scenes in a cattle barn," Barbie barked. "I'm assuming the locals let the news media have unfettered access to the scene."

"Yeah," Java grunted. "Penny said they were all over the place by the time she appeared on the scene. That's how those gory film clips appeared on the late-night news shows."

"We're probably wasting our time with a crime scene this contaminated," Kat frowned, "but let's give it our best shot."

"Kat, you and Barbie take the inside first. Chris and I will cover the outside, then switch places," Java directed.

##

The team spent the next three hours going over the murder scene inside and out. "Anyone find anything of interest?" Java asked as she started the car.

"I've never seen so much blood splatter," Chris commented. "It was almost as if the killer was furious and couldn't stop beating them. It was on the ceiling and all the walls—a real blood bath."

The others nodded in agreement. The ride back to the restaurant was a quiet one.

"Apparently the killer murdered the family then left through the front door," Barbie noted following Java into her office. "There's no blood on the window frame."

"I found a button," Kat held up a small, clear evidence bag containing a plastic button.

Java flipped through her crime folder and pulled out a photo of the voodoo doll found at the scene. "It's similar to the buttons used for eyes on the doll," she said holding the photo close to Kat's button. "But the dolls have both their eyes. Maybe it came from the killer's clothing or has a fingerprint. Let's get it to Penny."

A call to Penny's cellphone resulted in a meeting at Java's Place. "I'll come by later tonight," Penny agreed. "Can you lock it in your safe to preserve the integrity of the chain of evidence until I get there?"

"Sure," Java assured her. "Kat found it and is standing right here. She'll put it in the safe now. Oh, and plan on dinner here. On the house."

"All set for your opening night?" Java chatted as Kat remained when the others left Java's office.

"As set as I'll ever be," Kat shrugged. "How are reservations going?"

"Sold out. You really pack a house," Java chuckled. "That's the real reason I always insist on you working a case with me."

Kat laughed out loud. "Is that the only reason?" She teased.

"You know the only reason," Java said seriously.

"Umm, I thought so," Kat cooed. "Try not to follow me around like a love-struck teenager. It's unbecoming."

Two Ways to Die
A Java Jarvis Thriller
by Erin Wade

"You're a hard-hearted woman Kat Lace," Java growled.

The increasing hum of voices reached the office. "Your public awaits," Java tilted her head toward the club's dining room area. "Help me keep an eye on Chris tonight. Landers is coming in later to begin flirting with her. We want word to get around that Chris is dating the black police officer."

"Penny and you think the murders are racially motivated?" Kat frowned.

"It really looks like it," Java said. "Who would think that much hate still exists today?"

"There you are, my little cupcake!" Déjà vu LeBlanc wrapped her strong arms around Java and squeezed.

"I can't breathe," the blonde squeaked as Déjà tightened her grip.

"We need to talk," Déjà mumbled casting a wary eye toward Kat. "Right now! So, tell your pretty, little cream puff to run along. You can fool around with her later."

Java backed away from Déjà and held up her hands to ward off the rage she could see building in Kat's black eyes. She started to introduce the two women but decided the less they knew about one another the more likely their investigation was to succeed.

"I'll . . .uh catch you later Kat." Java opened the door and ushered her dream woman out of her office.

##

"She your latest squeeze?" Déjà teased.

"My personal life is none of your business," Java glared at the dark-skinned woman. "Tell me what's going on in the world of high priestesses?"

Déjà was tall, voluptuous, beautiful with glorious dark skin and wickedly funny.

Two Ways to Die
A Java Jarvis Thriller
by Erin Wade

"Nothing a little voodoo and vodka can't cure," Déjà laughed helping herself to Java's liquor cabinet. "You had another murder recently. Any leads?"

"Zero," Java dropped a pod into her Keurig, filled it with bottled water and pushed the button to start the magic that would fill her cup with fresh coffee.

"You know that stuff will kill you," Déjà lifted her glass to toast Java.

"And vodka won't?" Java laughed.

"Are you hearing anything on the streets?" Java inquired as Déjà settled onto the sofa.

Déjà patted the sofa beside her. "Why don't you set your little blonde butt right here and let Déjà whisper in your ear?"

Java retrieved her coffee and relaxed beside the black beauty.

Déjà dropped her voice to a low murmur. "Word I'm hearing is your multiple murders are some kind of ritual sacrifice—a cleansing of tainted blood."

"Seriously," Java snorted. "If that's the case our killer or killers will kill half of the people in America. Who even thinks like that in this day and time?"

"I'm just giving you the word on the street baby girl," Déjà smirked. "I love this Grey Goose Vodka. Déjà would like a bottle to take home with her."

"I might consider that," Java chuckled, "if Déjà would tell me something I don't already know."

"The murders are copycat murders," Déjà delivered her news with flair gesturing widely with her arms.

"Copycat? Déjà I've lived in Orleans all my life, I don't recall anything like this."

"Maybe they were killings before your time, sweetness." Déjà winked. "You know the world didn't just begin to turn when you were born. You're just a baby. Do I get my vodka or not?"

"Of course, you do," Java laughed. "If you want an unopened bottle, we'll have to get it from the bar."

"Lead the way, honey."

As they approached the bar, Java motioned for the bartender to give Déjà her usual bottle of Grey Goose. The two stood talking as Kat approached.

"I think she likes you," Déjà whispered.

"Humph," Java huffed.

"Kat I'd like you to meet our local Voodoo Priestess Déjà vu LeBlanc. Déjà this is Kat Lace. Kat will be performing here for a while."

"Open-ended contract?" Déjà raised her brows. "Until Java no longer wants you?"

Kat scanned Déjà up and down zeroing in on the bottle of vodka in Déjà's purse. "I shudder to think what you had to do for that."

Déjà reached into her purse and pulled out a pair of scissors holding them up for Kat to see. "Would you mind if I just snip a small piece of your glorious hair?"

"Hell, yes, I'd mind," Kat jumped back from the grinning Déjà, spun around on her heel and stomped off.

"Well thanks for that." Java heaved.

"I've found that a very effective way to end an argument is to ask the other person for a piece of their hair," Déjà smirked.

"I'm a believer," Java furrowed her brow wondering how she was going to explain Déjà to Kat.

Two Ways to Die
A Java Jarvis Thriller
by Erin Wade

CHAPTER 8

Java sat in the upstairs balcony of her supper club watching Kat sing the blues. Kat always aroused her, but she particularly made Java's insides flutter when she smiled her impish smile and sang directly to the blonde like she was tonight.

Kat finished her set and walked between the tables smiling and greeting diners. For the first time Java noticed a flashy dresser named Jody Schooley leering at Kat. "Damn," she whispered as she downed the last of her coffee and bounded downstairs coming to a stop behind Jody.

Jody yanked Kat down onto his lap. "Why don't you give me a lap dance, pretty lady?" Jody drawled. "And let's see what comes up."

Java grabbed a hand full of Jody's hair and yanked his head back, "Why don't I nail your privates to the chair with this fork?" She growled in Jody's ear as she buried the tines of the fork in the table beside Jody's arm.

"She would, you know," Kat hissed as she stood up from Jody's lap straightening her dress. "You're lucky Java intervened. I was going to kill you."

"Get out of my club, Jody," Java scowled at the man. "I don't want a pimp hanging around my place."

"Oh, come on, Java," Jody whined. "I was just having a bit of fun. You know how I love boobs and this little lady has some real nice ones."

"If you ever touch her again, I swear I'll rip out your heart," Java promised.

"She's your woman, ain't she?" Jody narrowed his eyes.

"No," Java hissed. "She's my employee and I won't allow you or anyone else to manhandle a woman that works for me. Now get out."

Jody stood towering over Java. "You think you can take me, little lady?"

Moving faster than imaginable, Java kicked Jody's legs out from under him sending him crashing to the floor. She planted the heal of her boot against Jody's Adam's apple. "Move and I'll crush your trachea," Java hissed.

Two bouncers appeared from nowhere, dragged Jody to the door and tossed him into the street.

"There you go making friends and influencing people," Chris joined Java and Kat. "You know he'll be waiting for you at closing time."

"Yeah," Java grunted. "He has no idea how close he was to dying."

"I can take care of myself," Kat glared at Java.

"I wasn't worried about you," Java smirked. "I was worried about Jody. You were going to kill him, weren't you?"

"Maybe," Kat shrugged.

"I saved his life," Java snapped.

CHAPTER 9

Jody Schooley sat in the bar and grill across from Java's Place and nursed a bourbon and coke. A short man with beady black eyes, a long-pointed nose and shoulder-length blonde hair sidled up to him.

"I saw what that woman did to you in Java's," the man mumbled.

Jody took a slow sip from his drink and glared at the man. "So?"

"I heard her call you a pimp." The man cleared his throat as if something were stuck in it.

Jody shrugged.

"Are you?"

"What's it to you," Jody snarled. "You lookin' for some action?"

"No! No," the man squeaked. "I'm looking for someone to take over my stable."

"Because all you've got left is a barn full of old nags?" Jody questioned.

"No, I've got nice looking fillies. Good producers."

"Who are you?" Jody demanded.

"Pender. Pender Crane."

Jody ignored the man's outstretched hand offering a handshake. "Yeah, I've heard of you. Can't say any of it was good."

Pender smiled as if he'd just had his ten seconds of fame. "So, you know I run nice ladies?"

Jody curled his lip indifferently thinking the man looked like his name—a whooping crane. "Why you wanting to get rid of them?"

Pender moved closer to Jody and whispered. "Someone is killing them."

"What?" Jody gasped.

"I'm pretty certain that's what's happening," Pender's eyes darted around the bar to make certain no one was listening to them

"Killing them," Pender rasped. "Decapitating them and leaving their heads all over Louisiana and Texas."

"The case the cops are so worked up about," Jody queried. "Those are your ladies?"

"Yeah," Pender released a deep breath. "I got a call from some dude who wanted my finest. Said he'd pay two thousand for one night with her. He paid through PayPal. I sent her to the address and I never saw her again.

"When I learned she never returned from the job I went looking for her. The address was an empty house in a nice part of town."

"How do you know it's empty?" Jody asked.

"I walked around back and looked in through the windows. It had no furniture in it.

"At first I thought my girl had taken her money and run," Jody continued. "I knew she wanted out, so I didn't think anything about it.

"A couple of days later the same dude calls for another girl. Same scenario, he pays on PayPal and my girl disappears."

"And you sent him two more girls knowing they would disappear?" Jody growled. "You weren't selling the girls as prostitutes you were selling them to be murdered."

"I . . . didn't know that for sure!" Pender sniveled. "Then I received a call requesting another girl and I told him I didn't have any. He said to send him a girl or he'd do to me what he'd done to the ladies.

"The next day I saw on the news about the heads. I knew they had to be my girls."

43

Two Ways to Die
A Java Jarvis Thriller
by Erin Wade

"Why didn't you go to the police?" Jody asked.

"Right! And tell them I run girls who just happen to fit the description of the heads they found." Pender squeaked. "I'd be their prime suspect."

"Good point," Jody shrugged. "Still, you have to do something. You can't just keep sending women to their deaths."

"I'm leaving town," Pender snorted. "I'm not hanging around here waiting for some psycho to chop off my head. That's why I'm offering you the opportunity to take over my stable. I'm not asking much. Say fifteen thousand for the entire operation."

Jody sneered. "Fifteen thousand for the opportunity to take your place in the crosshairs of some killer. No thanks."

"Look, my girls, they're all licensed and good workers. They get their shots regularly. They're healthy. I'm leaving town tonight. You want them or not?" Pender pulled a small brown book from his inside coat pocket along with his cellphone. "Everything you need is right here. The calendar and merchant's info to accept credit cards is on the phone and the girls and johns are all listed on my phone and in this book."

"You keep your girls, or do they live all over town?" Jody asked

"They're working girls," Pender snorted. "They have their own places. I just call them when someone contacts me. They work out of the Creole Hotel on Bourbon Street and all of them have steady customers. They pay all their own expenses. I just schedule them collect their money and provide protection for them for half of their take."

"I'm betting at least four of them would want their money back right now." Jody rasped.

"I had no idea they were being murdered until I saw the artist's composites on the news." Pender defended himself. "I'm not stupid. I wouldn't send my girls to their death."

"I gotta' take a leak and think about this," Jody mumbled. "I'll give you my answer when I return from the men's room. Order me another bourbon and coke."

Jody considered the pros and cons of Pender's offer. He needed more ladies, but something about Pender's anonymous customer gave him the heebie jeebies. He didn't want to be on the receiving end of death threats.

Jody snorted to himself when he saw Pender leaning his forehead on the bar. *What a wimp. He's probably crying, and the little twit didn't order me another drink,* Jody thought.

"I gave this some thought," Jody whispered in Pender's ear. "I'll take your stable off your hands for five thousand. That's my only offer. Not a penny more."

Pender ignored him. "Not a penny more," Jody huffed.

He caught Pender by the shoulder and pulled him upright so he could see his face. Pender slid off the barstool and crumpled onto the floor. The front of his shirt was soaked in blood.

"Jesus!" Jody exclaimed. "Somebody call an ambulance. This guy's been stabbed."

As the bartender raced for the phone Jody removed Pender's little brown book and cellphone from the dead man's pocket and slipped it into his own.

Two Ways to Die
A Java Jarvis Thriller
by Erin Wade

CHAPTER 10

The wail of sirens was nothing new on Bourbon Street and few noticed the ambulance or when the coroner's van backed up to the front door of Rochelle's Ale House to cart off the body of Pender Crane.

Java watched from the outside balcony of her supper club. The sight of Jody Schooley scurrying from the Ale House made her wonder what the man was up to.

Java scanned the throng of people writhing their way down the potholed street. Her eyes settled on two brothers she suspected were involved in most of the robberies in the French Quarter.

Tiny and Pierre Roché were exact opposites. Tiny was six foot four, two-hundred-fifty pounds and completely bald. Pierre was short and slender with a mop of unruly black hair.

"Why are you watching the Roché brothers?" Kat touched Java's back and let her hand slide down to the blonde's waist.

"The coroner just hauled off a body from Rochelle's. I have a feeling the Roach brothers had something to do with the death, but I'm not sure."

"You do know its pronounced Row-shay," Kat furrowed her brow at Java's insistence on calling the two men the Roach brothers.

"Roach brothers fits them," Java chuckled. "Look, they're going into Rochelle's now."

"Buy me dinner somewhere quiet and private and I'll find out for you." Kat promised.

Two Ways to Die
A Java Jarvis Thriller
by Erin Wade

"Umm, sounds like a win-win for me," Java agreed. "Turn on your earbud just in case you have any trouble."

"I can handle myself," Kat insisted.

"It's not you I'm worried about, love." A twisted grin crossed Java's face. "Don't hurt them."

##

Kat slid onto the barstool at Rochelle's and smiled sweetly at the bartender.

"You're on the wrong side of the street, pretty lady" Lindy Rochelle grinned at Kat, "but you're always welcome here. What's your poison?"

"Dubonnet over ice," Kat answered. She looked around the club and wasn't surprised to see it conducting business as usual so quickly after the coroner's extraction of a body.

"You had some excitement a while ago," Kat placed a twenty on the counter to pay for the drink Lindy slid toward her.

"No charge," Lindy grinned. "It's not every day one of Java's girls visits my establishment."

"I'm not one of Java's girls," Kat seethed. "I'm just here for the season."

"You do come and go," Lindy admitted.

"And do you keep track of my activities, Lindy?" Kat's brow went up.

"Oh, no! No!" Lindy declared. "It's . . . uh, who wouldn't notice you? That didn't exactly come out right."

Kat smiled to herself at the other woman's obvious discomfort. "Your excitement? I saw the authorities here. What happened?

"Someone knifed that pimp Pender Crane," Lindy fumed. "Wouldn't you know he'd die in my place. It'll be all over the news. I can see the tag line now, 'Pimp Stabbed to Death in Rochelle's Ale House.' It'll sound like he ran his business out of my club."

Two Ways to Die
A Java Jarvis Thriller
by Erin Wade

"Did he?" Kat's eyes danced. She knew he didn't but wanted to hear Lindy fume.

"Hell no! He didn't. You know . . . ah you're just poking me, aren't you?"

"Who stabbed him?" Kat took a sip of her aperitif.

"I have no idea. Someone yelled for me to call an ambulance, but the guy was already dead when they arrived. Knife wound in the side."

"Was he with anyone when he came in?" Kat asked.

"No, he came in alone. But he did sit down next to some guy at the bar. They struck up a conversation. A little later the other guy went to the men's room. When he came back Pender was bleeding all over the place."

"Did anyone approach Pender while his friend was in the men's room?" Kat queried.

"I didn't see anyone, but obviously someone did. I'm pretty sure Pender didn't stab himself."

Kat leaned her head toward the Roche brothers. "Do they frequent your establishment?"

"Yeah, but they give me the willies," Lindy volunteered. "I think they're trying to establish a protection operation along Bourbon Street. Have they tried to shake down Java?"

"No," Kat's short laugh ended with a sigh. "No one tries to shake down Java."

"Yeah, I didn't think so," Lindy chuckled. "I heard what she did to the gang who tried to rob her after her parents left Java's Place to her."

"What did she do?" Kat asked.

"You should ask her," Lindy shrugged. "That story has been retold so many times its more legend than truth. I don't want to add to the myth."

"Have the Roche brothers tried to shake you down?"

"No," Lindy frowned, "but I can feel it coming."

"You should tell Java if they do," Kat advised.

"What can she do?"

"If all the club owners ban together and file charges against the Roche's they'll do jail time. Don't let them get a foothold and form a gang," Kat advised. "That's when they really become dangerous.

"Were they in here when Pender died?"

"No, they came in later," Lindy said. "Would you like another drink?"

Kat checked her watch. "No, thank you. My show starts in fifteen minutes. I'd better get back."

Lindy walked around the bar and escorted Kat to the door. "I should catch your show sometime," She smiled. "I bet you're good."

"Of course, I am," Kat laughed. "You should come to our Valentine celebration. Java's pulling out all the stops."

"Maybe I will," Lindy beamed.

CHAPTER 11

Beau checked his calendar. Tomorrow was Valentine's Day. He didn't exactly have a date, but Chris Canton had invited him to Java's Place for their Valentine celebration. He knew the club had been sold out for months and was delighted to receive the invitation.

He thumbed through the two serial murder cases they were working. While the first week of January had presented them with enough deaths to last a lifetime, the rest of the month had been quiet—no murdered families and no bodiless heads. So far February was equally kind. Beau hoped the killers had moved on or had their fill of blood and death.

An anonymous letter to the police had resulted in identifying the four heads they had in cold storage. All belonged to local prostitutes managed by Pender Crane. Unfortunately, someone had murdered Pender in a busy club, but no one saw anything. Although all four women were from Louisiana, the heads had been scattered over Louisiana and Texas. Beau hated to think where the bodies might be.

Beau's phone announced a call from Penny. "This can't be good," he mumbled as he answered. "Penny, what's up?"

"I was wondering what the team is doing for Valentine's Day," Penny said.

Beau had a sudden pang of guilt that he hadn't included Penny in their plans. "I was thinking about going to Java's Place. Why don't you join me?"

Two Ways to Die
A Java Jarvis Thriller
by Erin Wade

"Sounds like fun," Penny laughed. "I'll meet you there."

"Kat's show starts at eight," Beau informed her. "Why don't you get there around six and we can have dinner with the team?"

"Sounds good," Penny responded. "See ya' tomorrow at Java's Place."

##

Java arrived at the club before sunup. Valentine's Day always stretched the supper club to its limits. All the reservations were filled, and they had been turning away customers for months.

A key turned in the door lock and Java prayed it was Kat. "Good morning," she beamed as the dark-haired beauty locked the door behind her. "Coffee?"

Kat nodded and followed Java to the kitchen.

"Did you sleep well last night?" Java asked.

"I did until I awoke in an empty bed," Kat smirked. "I don't really like—" Loud banging on the front door made both move to the front of the club.

Java looked through the small window in the center of the door to see Penny. "Penny, what's—"

"Another murder," Penny blurted as Java opened the door. "I just received the call on my way into the office. I tried to call you, but your phone went to voicemail."

"My team is en route and will meet me there. I'll swing by and pick up Beau. You get your team there as fast as you can. The locals roped off the entire area. We may actually be able to get some evidence from the crime scene. I'll text you the address in Lafayette."

"Happy Valentine's Day," Kat scowled at Java as the blonde held out Kat's jacket so she could slip into it. As Kat slid into the jacket, Java's arms wrapped around her.

"This is going to be ugly," Java mumbled into her ear.

Two Ways to Die
A Java Jarvis Thriller
by Erin Wade

##

"Do we know how many are in the house?" Barbie asked as they slipped on the blue morgue booties and disposable scrub caps Penny required at her crime scenes.

"No," Penny barked. "When the locals saw the bloody tracks leading from the house to the street, they immediately cordoned off the area."

"I like these people already," Barbie noted. "Judging by the amount of blood on the sidewalk, I'd say there is carnage waiting for us."

Java lightly touched Kat's arm trying to give her moral support. "Lead the way, Penny. We'll stay behind you and your people."

"Oh God!" Kat gasped as they entered the master bedroom of the house.

"Four bodies," Penny stated for the cameraman recording the scene. "One male, one female and two children." Penny motioned for the camera operator to zoom in on each victim's head.

"The skull of each victim has been split open by a blunt object. An ax—covered in blood and brain tissue—is leaning against the headboard.

"As in all the other cases the adult female's head has been pulverized by several blows. She is completely unrecognizable.

"The male and children died from a single blow to the head. Based on their size I'd say all are lined up on the bed in chronological order.

"Judging from the trails of blood the children were murdered in their separate bedrooms and carried into this room."

Someone handed Penny a card. She studied it then said into the camera. "According to the male's driver's license this is the Lane family."

Two Ways to Die
A Java Jarvis Thriller
by Erin Wade

Penny led the others from the room as the videographer filmed every inch of the room.

"We've photographed the footprints on the sidewalk," Penny's coworker informed her. "There's only one set of footprints. I can't tell if they're male or female but there is a brand on the sole so we should be able to pull that."

"That's more than we've ever had," Penny huffed.

The coroner's crew began wheeling the gurneys into the house. "A second van is on its way," someone informed Penny.

"I hate when it takes more than one van to clear the bodies from a crime scene," Penny shook her head and walked back into the house.

"Barbie you tag along with the fellow checking for the point of entry," Java barked orders. "Chris you make certain they cast any footprints or tire tracks on the place. Kat, you ensure that someone pulls water from the commodes for urine analysis."

Kat gave Java an exasperated look then stomped off to find the bathrooms in the house. "I'm going to shadow Penny," Java called after her.

Penny was taking blood samples from each corpse as it was placed on a gurney. Java watched as she meticulously labeled each evidence bag and each vial. "Just in case some idiot removes the vial and puts it back into the wrong bag," Penny grimaced. "I know it's overkill, but you'd be surprised how often it happens."

I'd kill for a cup of coffee, Java mused then regretted the thought others uttered a million times a day. She frowned when she realized how easily people integrated the phrase "I'd kill for . . ." into their thoughts and conversations.

"This case is baffling me," Penny grumbled as she swabbed a viscid fluid floating on top of coagulating blood.

"Is that what I think it is?" Java quizzed.

Two Ways to Die
A Java Jarvis Thriller
by Erin Wade

"I certainly hope so," Penny beamed. "If it is, we have the bastard. I have to say this is an incredibly large discharge."

"It appears the MO is the same as all the other slaughters," Kat joined them. "We took ample samples from the commodes and your men pulled the trap off all the sinks and collected gobs of unbelievable filth from them. He finally took the trap and all."

"Gobs?" Java raised her brow.

"Not a classy word, I know," Kat shot Java a scathing look, "but very appropriate. Gobs and gobs of filth."

Penny placed the tools of her trade back into her kit and snapped the clasps. "This is as thorough as anyone has ever been with one of these crime scenes. Hopefully we'll be able to pull some meaningful evidence."

"Did you find anything truly significant?" Kat asked.

"Semen," Penny beamed. "The DNA carrier every ME loves. I'm heading back to the lab now. Maybe I'll have a special valentine for all of you by tonight."

"The perp's ID," Java chuckled. "I can't think of anything I'd rather have for Valentine's Day." She openly appraised Kat. "Well, maybe there is one other thing."

"In your dreams, Java Jarvis," Kat snapped.

##

The ride back to the club was a silent one as each agent mentally sorted through the crime scene. It was Barbie's first introduction to mindless carnage and Chris' first encounter with pure bloodlust.

Java and Kat had seen a lot in their careers but nothing as senseless and evil as the murders they were now working.

"I hope Penny brings us something tonight," Java said. "We must stop this loon before he kills more families."

"Did anyone notice anything unusual at this scene?"

Two Ways to Die
A Java Jarvis Thriller
by Erin Wade

"There was a voodoo doll placed on each victim," Chris noted. "Do you think these murders are premeditated or spur of the moment?"

"Although they seem like some crazed killer giving into the urge to kill," Java said, "they must put a great deal of planning into each murder. No one has ever seen the culprit or even a vehicle and they take the entire family by surprise. It's almost as if they know their victims.

"They must case the house. They seem to know what window to break into to go unnoticed."

"I agree with Java," Kat added. "For all the blood and carnage, I think the killer knows when the family is most vulnerable."

"Oh my God! Look at the cars lined up at our parking garage." Barbie gasped. "Java, please tell me we have extra staff for tonight?"

##

Java surveyed the crowd from her usual table in the balcony. She wondered if any of them were The Basher. Most of the city council was dining in her establishment tonight along with the mayor, a couple of senators and house members.

From her viewpoint she could see diners as they walked to the hostess stand where Chris graciously directed her assistants to take them to their table. She was surprised to see Lindy Rochelle enter alone. She watched as Lindy was seated at a table for two and wondered who would join her competitor for dinner. Lindy often dined at Java's club, but she was surprised Lindy wasn't swamped in her own club. *What would bring her here?* Java thought.

Ah, of course, the lovely Katrina Lace has caught Lindy's eye. Java thought watching Kat sit down across from Lindy.

The two women chatted, Kat motioned the sommelier to their table and Lindy ordered wine. Java clinched her

55

teeth when Kat led Lindy to the dancefloor. *I hate it when she dances with others*, Java thought. She tamped down the urge to run downstairs and cut in on the dance. She knew Kat was only extracting information from the brown-haired woman.

Java raised a brow when Jody Schooley entered with Déjà vu LeBlanc. She wondered what the black beauty was doing in the company of a low life like Jody. Although Jody was with Déjà, he couldn't keep his eyes off Kat.

Kat and Lindy returned to the table and shared a glass of wine. The band announced they would take a fifteen-minute break and return with the lovely Kat Lace. The dinner crowd applauded, and Lindy beamed as if Kat belonged to her.

Penny and Beau arrived together and were taken to Java's table. Kat soon joined them. Everyone was anxious to hear what the medical examiner had discovered.

"This killer is now toying with us," Penny hissed. "The semen at the scene was bull semen. That means he or she intentionally planted it to mess with us."

"Damn," Java cursed under her breath. "Did you find anything Penny?"

"A hair was wrapped around one of the doll's buttons," Penny answered. "It didn't have enough root to pull DNA from it and everything else is so iffy about hair analysis, the only thing it is good for is checking for drugs."

"I thought forensics could match a hair to someone and prove they were at the scene of a crime," Barbie said.

"No! Cases are being overturned right and left where the convictions were based on hair analysis," Penny frowned. "Thirty-five people have been put to death based on hair analysis only to have DNA prove they were innocent. It's not an exact science."

"So, we're right back where we started," Kat declared.

"Not quite," Penny said. "I can give you an overall description of your killer and it is one killer. Based on the bloody footprints and length of the stride between steps, I'd judge our killer to be around five-feet-nine inches weighing about a hundred-ninety pounds."

"A man then?" Beau guessed.

"Not necessarily," Penny shrugged, "could be a tall woman about the size of Déjà vu LeBlanc."

"Surely you're not suggesting that Déjà is our—"

"No," Penny interrupted Java. "I'm just saying it could be a woman her size or a man her size."

"That's really not much help, Penny," Kat vocalized what the others were thinking.

"It's all I've got," Penny threw up her hands.

"When will the tox screens be back?" Java asked.

"Friday, maybe we'll find the family was drugged," Penny grimaced. "That would tell us why no one ever puts up a fight."

The band returned to the stage and played the music that was known as Kat Lace's introduction. "I've gotta go," Kat glanced at Java who stood to follow her.

"Aren't you going to watch me from up here," Kat asked as the private elevator opened and they stepped inside closing the doors on the rest of the world.

"Seriously," Java wrinkled her nose, "why would I sit up here when I have a table right next to the stage where I can see the perspiration in your cleavage."

"You are such a—" Java's soft kiss cut off Kat's name calling. "bad little girl."

"Just for you Kat. No one else has ever gotten into my head like you have."

"Wipe off my lipstick," Kat murmured as the elevator door opened

Two Ways to Die
A Java Jarvis Thriller
by Erin Wade

Java dragged her hand across her lips removing Kat's red lipstick along with her own. She followed the singer to the stage.

"Ladies and gentlemen," Java leaned into the microphone. "You demanded her, and we brought her back for your listening enjoyment. Java's Place is pleased to present the south's favorite blues singer Ms. Kat Lace."

The applause was deafening as Java offered her hand to assist Kat onto the stage. Kat could work a crowd like no one Java had ever seen. She kicked off with "Come Rain or Come Shine" then alternated between torch songs and singing the blues. She wrapped up her set with "That Old Black Magic Called Love." She left the stage to a standing ovation.

Java caught her hand as she stepped from the stage.

"Don't," Kat whispered pulling away from the blonde and smiling brilliantly at Lindy Rochelle.

CHAPTER 12

Chris locked the door behind their last customer and kicked off her shoes. "Geez what a night. I had no idea this place packed in the customers the way it does."

Barbie agreed with her as she rang up the daily sales report. "I don't know why Java works for the—"

"Fun of it," Kat said loudly as she led Lindy toward the door.

"Oh," Barbie gasped. "I thought all our customers were gone."

"All but one," Kat smiled at Lindy. "We'll chat tomorrow."

Lindy nodded and bid them goodnight as Kat collapsed into the nearest chair. "Where's Java?" She asked.

"In her office," Chris answered as Kat stood. "She's not alone."

Kat shot Chris a scathing look. "Why am I not surprised?"

Everyone turned toward Java's office as the door opened and she walked out with Déjà.

"Anytime tomorrow is good for me sweet cheeks," Déjà cooed. "Just give me a couple hours' notice so I can be ready for you."

"I will," Java promised. "Thank you for coming tonight. I hope you enjoyed it."

"Oh, I did," Déjà rolled her eyes, winked at Java, and walked out the door Barbie was holding open.

"I need to talk to you," Kat snarled as she followed Java back into the office and closed the door.

Two Ways to Die
A Java Jarvis Thriller
by Erin Wade

Java sat on the edge of her desk and smiled sweetly at Kat. "Hard night?"

"Yeah," Kat raised eyebrows that drove Java crazy.

"You know how that affects me," Java grinned mischievously catching Kat's hands and pulling her between her knees. "Why do you do that to me? You know how I love your eyebrows."

"Mm-hmm," Kat murmured as she leaned in for a kiss.

The sound of the door opening behind her sent Kat into action. She stepped back pulling Java forward and slamming her onto the floor.

Java began cursing loudly, "Son-of a- I think you broke my ribs."

"You really should think twice before grabbing me. Next time I won't be so nice," Kat threatened. She shoved past Barbie and Chris as she charged from the room.

"Are you alright, Boss?" Barbie knelt beside Java.

"I will be," Java gasped, "as soon as I catch my breath."

"Let me help you up," Barbie volunteered.

"Just let me stay here for a minute," Java mumbled. "Until the pain recedes."

Java moaned loudly as she rolled over on her side and pushed herself into a sitting position. "I've got this," she warded off offers of help. "Just let me take my time."

"We've locked up everything," Chris reported, "and here's the bank deposit. Do you want me to put it in the safe?"

"Please," Java caught the edge of the desk and pulled herself to her feet. "I don't want to carry that much cash after midnight on Bourbon Street."

"Good call," Chris agreed as she dialed the safe combination and tossed the bank bag into it. "Most of the business was on credit cards but there's still several thousand dollars cash in there."

Two Ways to Die
A Java Jarvis Thriller
by Erin Wade

"Come on, Boss," Barbie took Java's hand. "I'll drive you home and put some ice on your ribs."

"I'm okay to drive," Java assured her, "but it will be safer if we all walk to our cars together. I just want to get home and lay down."

CHAPTER13

The next morning Java parked her car behind the club hoping to grab a few minutes alone with a cup of coffee before employees arrived.

Penny pulled into the parking lot as Java unlocked the door.

"We need to talk," Penny shook her head as she followed the blonde into the club.

"This can't be good if you're making house calls," Java surmised. "What's up, Penny?"

"I got a partial off the button your team found," Penny informed her. "I have a pretty good match to a woman who floats into and out of the system. Arrests for petty thefts that sort of thing. Nothing like murder, but you should follow up on it."

Java held out her hand and Penny placed a sheet of paper in it. "What's her name?"

"Kallan Latour. She goes by Kally. I had Beau send you her file. It should be on your computer by now."

"First things first," Java grinned. "I'm making a fresh pot of coffee. Want some?"

"Do fish swim?" Penny quipped.

"I'll take that as a yes," Java laughed pouring water into the large Keurig.

Java studied the information Penny had handed her as the coffee maker made gurgling, gasping sounds.

"She's a big girl. Over six feet," Java noted. "There's no date of birth in the file."

Two Ways to Die
A Java Jarvis Thriller
by Erin Wade

"She's either eighteen or thirty," Penny shrugged. "It depends on who you talk to."

"She's a, um—"

"Half breed," Penny finished her sentence.

"That isn't acceptable language," Java reminded her.

"What do we call them?" Penny wrinkled her forehead.

"Mixed parentage, Creole, um . . ." Java struggled to find a socially acceptable word to describe someone with white and black parents.

"Anyway," Penny grumped. "Her father is white, and her mother is black. Budro Latour or Bubba is what he goes by. A real piece of work. Beats his wife and kids weekly. Stays drunk 365 days a year and has served time for car theft and assault with a deadly weapon."

"The girl's fingerprint is on the button?" Java clarified. "The old man sounds more like a killer."

"As I said, it's a partial but it's a close match to hers."

"Um, Penny you know Kat's of mixed heritage, don't you?"

"I figured as much," Penny nodded. "She's got the best of all worlds. Those glorious eyebrows and thick dark hair, nice white teeth, creamy skin and the cutest dimples I've ever seen. I wouldn't mind—"

"You do know she's married," Java reminded her.

"That's your problem, baby. I've seen the way you look at her." Penny followed Java into her office and took a seat across from the blonde as she turned on her computer and opened Kally Latour's file.

"She works for Déjà vu," Java jerked as she realized Déjà might be in danger. "I think I'll pay her a visit."

##

Chris and Barbie walked in together and the restaurant manager followed them. Java gave the manager a few instructions then opened the safe and handed Chris the deposit from the night before. "Do you mind taking this to the bank?"

"I'll do that first thing," Chris said.

"Barbie you and I are going to pay someone a visit. You want to tag along Penny?"

"No, I'm up to my waist in dead bodies. Besides you don't want to look like the local authorities storming Déjà's. You'll end up a voodoo doll."

Java laughed, "We'll just be old friends visiting."

"Thanks for taking me along," Barbie beamed as she fastened her seatbelt. "I've been dying to watch you in action."

Java chuckled. "I'm afraid you will be very disappointed. I'm just going to visit with Déjà. Ask how her business is going and tease her about scamming the tourists."

"But all the time, you'll be watching, won't you?" Barbie noted. "Looking for anything unusual or out of place."

"Maybe," Java laughed. "I think you give me more credit than I deserve."

Déjà vu was reading a tourist's palm when they arrived. Kally Latour led them to the parlor. "Can I get you something to drink?" the girl looked down at her feet as she spoke.

"What do you have?" Java engaged her in conversation.

"Sodas, coffee, tea." Kally mumbled.

"Is the coffee fresh?" Java asked.

"No ma'am, but I can make it fresh for you," Kally raised her eyes to Java's.

Java tried to hide her reaction to the way Kally's face looked. The girl had obviously been recently beaten. Her lip was split, and her right eye was black and swelled shut.

Two Ways to Die
A Java Jarvis Thriller
by Erin Wade

Java was certain the girl was missing teeth, but she never opened her mouth or smiled enough for anyone to see.

"Why don't I help you?" Java motioned for Barbie to check out the room.

Kally led the way to the kitchen, dragging one foot as she walked.

"Do you need to see a doctor?" Java asked casually.

"Oh, no ma'am. Pa would kill me if I wasted money on a doctor."

"I'm concerned you might lose your eye," Java lied. "It looks awful. Can you see out of it?"

"No ma'am, but I can see just fine with the other one and this one will be okay next week. This ain't the first time Pa blacked my eye."

"Is your leg okay?" Java inquired gently.

"Yes ma'am. I've got a club foot. Pa says I ain't good for much." The girl's hands shook as she filled the Mr. Coffee with water.

Java took the water from her hands and placed it on the cabinet. "Why don't you sit down, and I'll make the coffee? I like my coffee stronger than most people anyway."

"Miss Déjà vu won't like that."

"Déjà and I are old friends," Java reassured her. "She knows I like to make my own coffee."

"She won't like me sittin' down. She likes me to be working."

"Do you like coffee?" Java asked.

"Oh, yes ma'am. I surely do."

"Then I'd like you to have coffee with me." Java pulled two cups from the cabinet and filled them. "Do you want anything in your coffee?"

"Just black, ma'am."

Two Ways to Die
A Java Jarvis Thriller
by Erin Wade

"How old are you Kally," Java made conversation as she placed the cups on the small kitchen table and took the chair next to Kally.

"Eighteen. How old are you?" Kally asked

"Fair enough," Java laughed. "I'm thirty-six."

"You own Java's Place, don't you?" Kally sneaked a peak at the pretty blonde over the rim of her coffee cup.

"Mmhmm. My parents left it to me. They founded the club when I was small and named it after me."

"Did they name you Java?" The incredulous expression on the girl's face indicated her disbelief that anyone would name a child Java.

"No, Jaquelyn," Java laughed. "They started calling me Java because I loved coffee even as a baby. Honestly, I prefer Java to Jaquelyn or Jackie."

"I like Java," Kally said shyly. "It fits you."

"Then I'm glad my parents nicknamed me Java. Kally, who did this to you?" Java gently touched the tips of her fingers to the girls swollen cheek. "Did your daddy do this to you?"

Tears ran down Kally's cheeks as she nodded.

"Why?" Java whispered.

"Cause' I asked him why he was gettin' home just before sunup. He slapped me then punched me with his fists. He was covered in blood. Please don't tell him I told. He'll kill me."

"When did this happen?" Java asked.

"Um, Valentine morning," Kally recalled. "I remember because he . . . he had sex with me and said, 'Happy Valentine's Day'."

Java fought the urge to find Budro Latour and choke the life from him. "Kally can you show me the clothes your daddy had on when he came home?"

Two Ways to Die
A Java Jarvis Thriller
by Erin Wade

Kally shrank back from Java and her good eye darted around the room as if looking for a place to hide. "I can't do that Miss Java. He'd beat me to death."

"Is he home now?"

"No ma'am. He works at the shipyard. He's there today."

"It would mean a lot to me, Kally," Java urged, "if you'd take me to your house and give me those clothes."

Kally's face contorted into a hundred emotions as she tried to decide what to do. "Can we go right now? Before he comes home early or something."

"Sure, I'll tell Déjà you're going to help me with something. She'll be okay with it."

Java informed Déjà that she was taking Kally to the doctor and the three walked to Java's car. Barbie slipped into the backseat as they always did when someone else was in the vehicle. *Never let anyone sit behind you* was an unspoken rule.

"We don't live in a very good part of town," Kally apologized as they drove past rusted vehicles and old washing machines. The ragged rear seat of a car was home to a mongrel with a litter of puppies. It looked more like a dumping ground than a residential area.

"That's my house," Kally pointed to a clapboard house that had long ago lost all its paint. Broken windows and a screen door hanging by one hinge completed the look of dilapidation. Old tin cans and other garbage were scattered over the yard.

"My folks ain't much for cleanliness," Kally lamented.

"We're just fine," Java assured her. "Is anyone home?"

"No ma'am. My brother is in school and Mama works at the drycleaners."

Kally pushed open the knob-less front door and led the way into the house. Java had to control her urge to step back from the stench in the shack. Barbie had no such self-control and stepped back outside to breath.

"They're in here in his bedroom," Kally led the way to an even filthier and more repugnant room at the far side of the house.

Java's eyes watered as the putrid odor filled her sinuses with an odor she knew she'd never forget.

"There," Kally pointed to a pair of overalls and a white wife-beater shirt covered in dried blood. Java cursed herself for not bringing a plastic bag along.

Overcoming the urge to puke and the aversion to touching the fetid clothes, Java pulled on a pair of gloves, shook a pillow from a frayed pillowcase and stuffed the bloody clothes into it.

##

"I'll take you back to Déjà's," Java said as they pulled away from the house. "It would be best if you don't tell your father we took his clothes."

"He'll never miss them," Kally shrugged. "He'd just bury them like he does all the clothes he messes up."

"Have you seen other clothes like these?" Java asked.

"Yeah, many times."

"Do you recall the dates or anything that would help you remember a date?" Java hid her excitement. She was certain Budro Latour was The Basher.

"No ma'am," Kally shook her head. "Not right at the moment."

"It's okay Kally," Java patted her hand. "You've been a tremendous help to me."

Java pulled her vehicle into a parking place in front of the local emergency clinic. "Humor me Kally. I'll feel better if you let a doctor check your eye."

Kally nodded reluctantly.

Two Ways to Die
A Java Jarvis Thriller
by Erin Wade

CHAPTER 14

After the doctor treated Kally's eye Java and Barbie drove her back to Déjà's shop. The priestess was gone but Kally had a key. "If anyone asks," Java advised, "Déjà insisted on you seeing the doctor."

"Are you thinking what I'm thinking?" Barbie asked as Java sped away from the curb.

"Yep," Java grinned pushing the call button on her steering wheel. "I'm calling Penny right now."

"Penny, Java here. Are you in your lab?

"I am," Penny responded.

"Barbie and I are on our way to you. We have something that's going to make you very happy."

"I could use some good news," Penny coughed. "Actually, what I really need is a day off."

"Barbie this should break this case wide open," Java said as she disconnected the call with Penny.

"Good," Barbie breathed. "We need to stop these mindless murders."

"We also need to get a handle on the heads," Java reminded her. "Four heads with no bodies and no leads."

"At least we know who the victims are," Barbie added. "My guess is that the women were targeted because they were prostitutes. Just like the families were targeted because they were mixed race.

"Is Kat's husband white?" Barbie blurted out.

"What difference does that make?" Java scowled.

"I was just thinking Kat's got several ethnic groups in her bloodline. If her husband is white The Basher might set his sights on her. She is beautiful and very visible."

Java's frown deepened. She hadn't considered that Kat might be a target. "I don't think so. She has no children. The Basher seems to be targeting families with children."

Beau was getting out of his car as Java pulled onto the parking lot. "Penny called me," he said as Java got out of the car. "She said you sounded excited."

"I am," Java beamed. "Come on, I don't want to tell this story but once." She retrieved the bundle from the trunk of her car and headed for Penny's lab.

Penny and Beau listened as Java and Barbie related the events of the morning. "We haven't broken the chain of evidence and I'm now turning it over to you," Java said.

"And I'm forwarding the video I took of Kally leading Java to the clothes and Java securing them." Barbie pushed the button and sent the recorded evidence to Penny.

"I'll make this my priority," Penny promised carrying the clothes to a sterile metal table.

"How long before we'll know something?" Java inquired.

"Around five this afternoon," Penny estimated. "I want to be absolutely certain before Beau gets an arrest warrant. This is a big deal. We can't afford any mistakes."

Everyone nodded in agreement.

"I could sure go for a burger and fries," Barbie said as they walked back to the car.

"That does sound good," Java agreed. "Drive through or sit down?"

"Sit down. You can get a good cup of coffee and we can relax a little. It's been a busy morning."

##

The waitress placed their drinks in front of them and took their orders.

"How long have you and Kat worked together?" Barbie asked as she tore the paper from her straw.

70

"Almost ten years," Java shrugged. "She's one of the best in the business."

"Yeah, the two of you are legends," Barbie grinned. "I heard about you in the Academy. You received the Director's Leadership Award and all the Top Achievers awards in firearms, physical fitness and academics. You swept all the awards. The next year Kat followed in your footsteps."

"That was a long time ago," Java brushed off the praise. "A lot of water has gone under the bridge since then. I loved the Academy and I love being an FBI agent."

"It's your life, isn't it?" Barbie insisted.

"Yeah, it is," Java agreed.

"But you're willing to risk it all for Kat Lace!" Barbie's blunt statement shocked Java.

"I . . . Kat and I have handled some tough cases together. I admire her abilities. We have a lot of history."

"Are you in love with her?" Barbie pushed.

"You do know I'm your superior?" Java tried to change the subject. "My personal feelings don't matter as long as I do my job and manage this team, so it gets results. I'm sure you checked our case clearance record before you requested your transfer to join us."

"One hundred percent," Barbie beamed. "Pretty impressive."

"Why did you join our team, Barbie?"

"I want to learn from you," Barbie confessed. "I want to be the best so who better to learn from than the best.

"This morning for instance, I saw that girl had a black eye, but it never occurred to me to convert that into a tell all against her father. How did you know to go down that rabbit hole?"

"It made sense," Java explained. "We knew Kally's fingerprint was on the button Kat found at the murder scene. It stood to reason that the girl was somehow connected to the crime. Since she had a club foot that made walking difficult, I didn't suspect her, but I did suspect someone in her household. When she told us about her abusive father, I thought he might be our killer. We already knew he had a record for assault. I just put two and two together. Let's hope I'm right."

"My gut tells me you are," Barbie laughed.

"That too," Java grinned. "Always go with your instincts."

They stopped talking as the server placed their food on the table.

"You must know I have a girl crush on you," Barbie blurted out.

"You know the agency's rules about fraternizing," Java wrinkled her brow.

"I'd be discreet," Barbie insisted. "No strings. Kat's married. She'll never be in a relationship with you, even though she does tease you and string you along."

"Barbie, I'm very flattered," Java searched for words, "but I don't make a habit of sleeping with the members of my team."

"But—"

"No, Barbie. It's not going to happen." Java scowled. "I don't want to have this discussion again."

"But—"

"That's an order," Java growled.

Two Ways to Die
A Java Jarvis Thriller
by Erin Wade

CHAPTER 15

The late afternoon lunch business was in full swing when Java and Barbie returned to the club. Kat was dining with Lindy Rochelle and Jody Schooley was at a corner table with a pretty bleached blonde.

Java glared at Lindy then strolled to Jody's table. "You slumming today Jody, or trying to impress this pretty young thing?"

"Yes, to both questions," Jody snarled careful to stay seated.

"Umm, well, we appreciate your business," Java grinned. "Sorry about the other night. You understand?"

"Sure," Jody relaxed. "I was way out of line. Too much alcohol."

Java nodded and walked away.

"She's not at all what I expected," Jody's friend said. "She's beautiful."

"Don't be fooled by her looks," Jody grunted. "She's meaner than a rattlesnake and twice as dangerous."

"Story on the street is she took care of the gang robbing the businesses in the Quarter." The girl related.

"Yeah, she did," Jody puffed.

"Did they all go to jail?"

"No!" Jody whispered. "They all went to the cemetery."

"What do you mean?"

Blondes really are dumb, Jody thought. "All four of them were dead by the time the police arrived. I don't know how Java managed to do it, but it looked like they had a shootout among themselves."

"Whoa," the blonde watched Java walking across the room greeting customers. "She really is something!"

##

Java took the private elevator to the balcony and sat down at her usual table. She was anxious to hear from Penny. She hoped they had caught the bastard who had murdered so many in her state. Someone brought her a salad and coffee and she realized she was hungry.

"There you are my beautiful white girl," Déjà strutted across the upstairs dining room and joined Java. Her eyes followed Java's gaze to Kat. "You sittin' up here mooning over something you can't have, sugar?"

"I guess," Java chuckled.

"Why don't you look at other women," Déjà motioned to herself. "There are plenty of women in Orleans that'd treat you right, baby girl."

Java laughed out loud. "What's that quote from Emily Dickenson, Déjà? *The heart wants what it wants – or else it does not care.*"

"I don't know who wrote that," Déjà shrugged, "but it's the damn truth."

"Did you come up here to discuss my love life or lack thereof," Java sipped her coffee, "or do you need something?"

"Yeah, I need to talk to you about Kally. Her daddy will beat the hell out of her tonight if he finds out you took her to the doctor."

"Can't you do something?" Java teased. "You know stick a pin in the crotch of his doll or twist off its head."

"You know it don't work that way, sweetness. Can't you arrest him for something and hold him until her eye clears up?" Déjà tossed back. "I'd rather save my magic for someone more important and I'm sure there is some kind of arrest warrant out for his sorry ass."

Two Ways to Die
A Java Jarvis Thriller
by Erin Wade

"Why didn't I think of that?" Java laughed dialing Beau's number.

"Beau, are there any outstanding warrants on Budro Latour?" She waited while Beau ran a check.

"Two," Beau chirped. "You want me to have him picked up?"

"Yes, pick him up on one and hold him as long as you can. If we must release him before we want to, let him go then pick him up on the other warrant. I'd like to hold him at least a week."

"Consider it done," Beau replied.

"Happy now?" Java grinned at Déjà.

"Very. Déjà loves beautiful, powerful women," the black beauty smiled.

Déjà looked down at Kat and Lindy. "Why is she with that woman?"

"Don't ask me," Java shrugged. "I've asked myself that question a dozen times in the last two hours."

"It's your restaurant," Déjà reasoned, "Why don't you throw Lindy out? Send her packing to her own place across the street."

"Oh, Déjà if I threw out everyone who's enamored of Kat Lace, I'd have very few customers."

"She doesn't like me," Déjà stated flatly. "It's because my breasts are much larger than hers."

Java laughed. "Really?"

"And you haven't even noticed, have you?" Déjà scoffed. "You only look at her."

"Heads up. She's headed this way," Java beamed.

"You just compare us, baby. You'll see Déjà has a lot more to offer you."

"Mm-hmm," Java laughed.

The elevator door opened, and Kat glided into the room.

"Miss LeBlanc," Kat cocked a brow, "I didn't expect to find you here."

"I didn't expect you to care," Déjà countered. "I'm having dinner with this gorgeous hunk of woman. In case you want to know my intentions, they are wantonly wicked."

"Humph," Kat walked around Déjà and stood by Java placing her hand on the blonde's shoulder. "I was planning on dining with you after my set."

Déjà shoved her chair back from the table and stood. "Perhaps you didn't hear me," she hissed at Kat.

"Oh, I heard you, Miss LeBlanc," Kat faked a smile. "I just ignored you."

"Kat!" Java cautioned her partner. "The last thing I need in here is a cat fight."

"Sometimes, I hate you, Java," Kat stormed.

"You heard Java," Déjà continued standing with her hands on her hips and her breast thrust out farther than ever, "she wants you to leave."

"I didn't say—" Java started but jumped between Kat and Déjà as the brunette stepped toward the priestess.

"I do need to talk to Kat," Java said. "Please Déjà have dinner on the house. I'll have Barbie show you to a table."

"Miss LeBlanc," Kat drawled. "You should make an appointment with Dr. James Jonda. He's New Orleans' most accomplished plastic surgeon. He can bring your breasts into the same zip code as your chest."

Déjà lunged at Kat but Java caught her. "Don't even think about hand-to-hand combat with Kat," Java warned. "You wouldn't stand a chance. Come on. I'll escort you to your table." She moved the ebony beauty to the elevator and closed the doors.

"How can you be so weak where she's concerned?" Déjà railed at Java. "You eat out of her hand and she barely gives you the time of day."

Two Ways to Die
A Java Jarvis Thriller
by Erin Wade

"Déjà she took a bullet for me last year. If not for her I'd be dead." Java clinched her teeth. "I owe her." She didn't add *I'm desperately in love with her*.

Java seated Déjà at her favorite table, ordered her an expensive bottle of wine and told the waiter to put her tab on the house. She wondered why Kat was in such a foul mood. No doubt about it, Kat Lace was a complicated lady.

CHAPTER 16

Java grabbed a wine opener and the club's best bottle of Chateau Lafite Rothschild Pauillac and pushed the button that would take her to either heaven or hell depending on Kat's mood. When she reached the balcony, she turned off the elevator to assure no one would disturb them.

Kat was seated in the chair vacated by Déjà. Java opened the bottle of wine, poured it into their glasses and sat down across from her.

Kat held up her glass for a toast. "To us," she whispered, "and solving this horrific case."

Java smirked and lightly tapped her glass against Kat's.

"You do know you were rude to Déjà?" Java asked.

"Why was she dining with you?" Kat huffed. "I always have dinner with you."

"Which usually ends with me in the fetal position on the floor," Java pointed out.

"You didn't answer my question, darling," Kat leaned across the table. "What was she saying to you?"

"She asked me to arrest Budro Latour," Java answered. "She was afraid he would beat his daughter when he discovered she had gone to the clinic because of the beating he gave her Valentine's Day."

"Oh, I feel a little foolish," Kat shrugged. "Perhaps I jumped to conclusions. Did you have him arrested?"

"Yes, Beau took care of it."

"Catch me up on today," Kat said holding out her glass for more wine. "What did you find out at Déjà's?"

Java related the information about the bloody clothes and the beaten girl. "I'm waiting to hear from Penny now to find out if the blood on Latour's clothes matches any of the victims."

"The girl must really hate her father to turn him in like that," Kat mused.

"Kat, he rapes her." Java muttered. "She told me he had sex with her as if it was an everyday occurrence—no big deal. God only knows how long that's been going on. If I wouldn't go to jail, I'd slit his throat myself."

"And I'd help you," Kat declared.

"What's going on with Lindy?" Java asked.

"I'm not sure. I don't think she knows anything about who knifed Pender." Kat placed her hand on top of Java's. "Are you going to be here for my show tonight?"

"Have I ever missed one?" Java grinned. "Someone has to keep the lovesick fools off you."

"So, anyone attracted to me is a lovesick fool?" Kat purred.

Java's phone rang flashing Beau's name on the screen. She pushed the speaker button so Kat could listen.

"Hey, Beau! I have you on the speaker so Kat can hear too."

"We've got him in custody," Beau exclaimed. "Why don't you come over now? You can watch us interrogate him."

Java glanced up at Kat and was secretly delighted that the other agent's face registered disappointment as Kat looked away from her.

"Let him stew until morning," Java suggested. "I'd like to have Kat there when you talk to him. She's our best profiler. She'll pick up on things you and I might miss.

"She'll be singing in about an hour. Why don't you come over for dinner?"

"Good idea," Beau beamed. "Letting Latour stew and having dinner at your place. I'll be there in twenty."

"Thank you," Kat muttered. "I like you here when I sing."

"Kat why can't we—"

"Don't Java," Kat whispered. "I need to get ready for my performance."

"You have time for one more glass of wine," Java picked up the bottle desperately trying to extend her time with the woman who determined her happiness.

"One more," Kat smiled slowly.

CHAPTER 17

Java rode the elevator with Kat fighting the urge to reach out and touch her. "I love your eyebrows," she blurted.

"I know," a throaty laugh from Kat made Java's knees weak.

Penny and Beau entered the club as Java followed Kat off the elevator. The four met at the hostess stand. "We need to talk somewhere private," Penny shivered with excitement. "We've got him, Java."

"I must go," Kat caught Java's arm. "Will you fill me in later tonight?"

"Of course," Java agreed. "We'll be in the balcony watching you."

The three entered the elevator as Kat disappeared through the door leading to her dressing room.

As she always did when she wanted complete privacy, Java turned off the elevator. They gathered around the table and put their heads together. "Okay, Penny, what do we have?" Java asked.

"A DNA goldmine," Penny enthused. "There is blood from all four of the Valentine's Day victims and the insides of the overalls are covered in Latour's semen. The son-of-a-bitch really got off on crushing the skulls of others."

"I'm waiting for the search warrants for Latour's home and the shed out back," Beau informed them. "As soon as Penny called me, I started the process."

"Let's be sure we do everything by the book," Java exhaled. "We don't want to return this monster to the streets on a technicality."

Two Ways to Die
A Java Jarvis Thriller
by Erin Wade

"My forensic evidence is as tight as a virgin's—'

"Uh, Penny!" Java interrupted.

"Kat's right, you are a girl scout," Penny laughed.

"You weren't in that meeting," Java furrowed her brow.

"One doesn't have to be in a meeting," Penny smirked, "she talks about you all the time."

"Really?" Java beamed.

"I didn't say it was complimentary," Penny added.

"Oh, of course not," Java mumbled. "I didn't think it would be."

"What's Latour's status?" Java turned her attention to Beau.

"He's in a private holding cell," Beau replied. "We aren't going to delouse him until tomorrow just before we interrogate him. I want him to be as miserable as possible."

Beau's phone rang. "Braxton," he barked. "That's great. I'll pick it up first thing in the morning.

"We'll have our search warrants at seven in the morning," Beau informed them as he disconnected the call.

"Great!" Java couldn't hide her excitement. "Penny can your team meet Beau's at the Latour home at eight in the morning?"

"We'll be there with bells on." Penny exclaimed.

They turned their attention to the band as it started playing Kat's introduction. As the sensuous brunette sang the blues, everything else in Java's world faded away.

##

Chris bid their last customer goodnight, locked the front door of Java's Place and turned to face her team. "I can tell by the self-satisfied attitude of you three that something good is going down."

"Is the back door locked?" Kat asked.

Two Ways to Die
A Java Jarvis Thriller
by Erin Wade

"I locked it myself," Java answered. "Penny, since you have confirmed our suspicions why don't you take the lead?"

"The overalls Java and Barbie took from the Latour home were covered with the blood of all four of the Valentine's Day victims," Penny informed the team. "Budro Latour's semen covered the inside of the overalls. We have a search warrant and will do a thorough search of the Latour home in the morning. According to his daughter there are more clothes covered in blood buried in the back yard of the home. Hopefully we can connect Latour to all the crimes."

"Penny and Beau will take point on this and their teams will clear the Latour home at eight in the morning," Java explained. "It's best we keep a low profile, so we'll show up here for work as usual.

"As soon as Penny confirms there are more bloody clothes associated with the other murders Beau will interrogate Latour. We'll watch from the observation room.

"I think we've solved this case folks."

"I certainly hope so," Kat expressed everyone's thoughts. "This case has given me the jeebies from the very beginning."

"If you're scared, I could drive you home," Java grinned mischievously.

"I might be more scared of you," Kat shot back.

The sultry look Java gave her made Kat step back.

CHAPTER 18

The search teams uncovered bloody clothes from the three previous murders and Penny was able to provide a match to the blood samples taken from the scenes. The District Attorney's office wasted no time filing seventeen cases of homicide against Budro Latour.

Kally and her brother Raymond gave statements that their father often returned home covered in blood and buried his clothes in the back yard the next day. Marra Latour claimed no knowledge of her husband's murderous activities.

Latour swore he was innocent and claimed the law enforcement agencies were framing him to get the public pressure off themselves.

Java's team met with FBI Director Karen Pierce in the agency's review room. "It looks like you four will be up for all kinds of honors," Karen informed them. "Great job ladies. You make me proud.

"We have been over two months with no carnage. No families have been slaughtered and no women's heads have popped up anywhere. I'm beginning to think Latour may have been responsible for both crimes."

"I don't think so," Java commented. "The MO is too different. The women targeted were prostitutes. The families slaughtered were of mixed heritage. Two completely different reasons for murder."

"Why don't you just take the win, Java?" Karen grimaced. "There are plenty of other cases your team can work on."

Two Ways to Die
A Java Jarvis Thriller
by Erin Wade

"We could use a few days off," Barbie chimed in. "This case has been nerve-racking for all of us. I'd like to check out Harrah's. This is my first assignment in New Orleans. I'd like to see the fun side of the city. You could show me around, Java."

"Why don't we all go to Harrah's tonight?" Java suggested. "I'll make dinner reservations and we can try our luck at the seven card stud tables or Texas Hold'em or whatever your game might be."

"I've heard they have purple felt on their tables," Barbie laughed.

"You heard right," Java joined in her merriment. "You're going to love Harrah's, Barbie."

"I don't know much about poker," Barbie glanced at Java. "Maybe you can teach me."

"They have a quick-study gaming school you can go to, Barbie," Kat informed her nonchalantly. "Takes about thirty minutes to become a pro."

"Why don't you join us Karen?" Java suggested.

"I think I will. It sounds like a fun evening," Karen agreed.

"Are you going Kat?" Java asked. "Or do you have to get home?"

"I wouldn't miss this for the world," Kat smirked. "Besides I'd just be home alone tonight."

"Five of us for dinner at seven. Does that sound okay?" Java asked. "We'll meet in front of Ruth's Chris Steak House."

Everyone nodded. Life was good in The Big Easy.

##

Java folded. The last card had been dealt and she couldn't beat what was showing on the table. As usual Kat's poker face revealed nothing about her hand. Java wished the woman had a tell—anything that would help her know what was going on in the brunette's mind. Kat had a pair of aces showing but Java had no idea what her hold cards were, and the bid had reached five-hundred dollars by the time it got to Kat. Four players were still in the game including Kat and Lindy Rochelle who had taken a loser's place in the game.

Kat fidgeted with her stack of casino chips as if trying to decide to stay or fold. "Call and raise a thousand." Kat slowly slid her stack of poker chips to the center of the table. She gazed into Lindy's eyes and smiled slightly.

Lindy ran her fingertips over her chin. *A tell*, Java *thought. Now let's see what it means.*

"Umm, you look dangerous," one of the players said as he tossed in his cards. "I'm out."

"I call," the other man grinned passing the bid to Lindy.

"I'll see your thousand and raise you a thousand." Lindy cocked her eyebrow at Kat and slid in her chips.

"Call!" Kat covered the bid.

The third player tossed in his cards. "Fold," he muttered.

"Show me what you've got?" Kat challenged Lindy.

Lindy grinned triumphantly as she flipped over a full house—three kings and two sevens.

Kat inhaled deeply and Java realized she was holding her own breath. "You win . . . second place," Kat cooed as she turned over two more aces. "Four of a kind."

The onlookers who had gathered around the table applauded and whooped as Kat pulled in the pot and turned to Java. "Would you cash it in for me? I'm going to grab us a table in the Voodoo Lounge. I want to watch the new singer in town."

Lindy walked around the table and started toward Kat.

Java curled her lip at Lindy. "Don't even think about following her."

Two Ways to Die
A Java Jarvis Thriller
by Erin Wade

Lindy held up her hands in front of her and backed away. "She's not your woman," she hissed.

"She's married," Java barked. "She's off the market. You need to stay away from her."

"She wouldn't be the first married woman I've taken to bed," Lindy bragged.

"She'd be the last," Java threatened. "I promise you that."

##

Java cashed in Kat's winnings and walked to the Voodoo Lounge. She smiled when she realized the brunette was watching her. She ducked her head and conjured her best blush as she pulled out her chair and sat down beside Kat. "Penny for your thoughts!"

"Umm, my thoughts would only get us both into trouble," Kat cooed.

"When it comes to you," Java grinned, "I'm always looking for trouble and it is after midnight."

"Tonight?" Kat whispered. "I don't want to be alone."

"Now?" Java asked.

"No, not right now. I truly do want to hear their new singer," Kat explained. "I hear she is my new competition.

"You have no competition, Kat."

Kat reached under the table and took Java's hand pulling it into her lap.

The band began playing and a very attractive redhead walked onto the stage. She was good. Not as good as Kat, but acceptable. A few years of experience and she'd be very good.

As the performer sang Kat toyed with Java's hand, playing with her fingers and drawing circles in her palm.

"You're killing me," Java whispered in Kat's ear letting her lips touch the brunette.

The band finished their set and the lounge goers applauded appreciatively for the singer.

Two Ways to Die
A Java Jarvis Thriller
by Erin Wade

"What did you think of her?" Java asked motioning for their check.

"Not bad," Kat shrugged.

"But nothing to worry about," Java added.

"Umm, honestly I was too busy thinking about you and your strong hands and long fingers. And the scent of you as you leaned in to whisper in my ear."

"We're out of here!" Java tried to stop the tremor that passed through her body. "You're not going to deck me in the lobby, are you?"

"No darling," Kat murmured. "I have other plans for you."

Java tried to control her excitement as she paid their tab and led Kat to the front of the casino.

"There you are," Karen had Chris and Barbie in tow. "We've looked all over for you."

"We were just leaving," Java replied. "Kat has a wicked headache."

"She'll just have to live with it," Karen scowled. "We have another family slaughtered in San Antonio. It happened yesterday. The authorities there just realized the MO is the same as The Bashers. Beau and Penny have been notified. Both are tied up on that bombing this morning. The four of you must handle this."

"Noooo," Java almost cried. "There's nothing we can do tonight."

Karen looked at her watch. "If you leave now you can be in San Antonio before noon."

"We can catch a plane at nine in the morning and be there by noon too." Java argued trying to overcome the ache in the pit of her stomach.

Karen's eyes moved from Kat to Java and back. "Ok, but make sure you get there before noon. I don't want the locals screwing up the scene. If it is The Basher, then how does Latour figure into all of this?"

"Good question," Java huffed. "Barbie, you arrange for our flight and a rent car. Let's meet at the restaurant at eight and all ride to the airport together.

"Chris you contact the SA authorities and have them email you everything they have: crime scene photos, pics of the bodies, and the break-in point. You know the routine."

"Got it boss," the two chorused.

"I'll take you home, Kat," Java said. "Take something for your headache. We all need to be hitting on all cylinders tomorrow otherwise the press conference we held to announce the arrest of Latour is just going to be egg on our face."

As everyone went their separate ways Karen caught Java's arm and pulled her aside. "Java, you and Kat," she said. "You know the agencies rules."

"Yes Karen," Java sighed. "I know them all too well."

"Be certain you adhere to them," Karen insisted.

"I will," Java mumbled. "I'll report in tomorrow as soon as we have assessed the situation."

Java sprinted through the casino to catch up with Kat.

"What did Karen want?" the brunette asked.

"She cautioned me about getting involved with you," Java shrugged.

"So, you're taking me home?" Kat pouted.

"Yeah," Java grinned. "My home!"

Two Ways to Die
A Java Jarvis Thriller
by Erin Wade

CHAPTER 19

Java had been motionless during most of the flight. Kat had fallen asleep on her left shoulder shortly after Java opened the San Antonio murder file on her computer. To avoid waking the brunette beauty Java had been careful to move only her right hand in scrolling through the report. She knew Kat was exhausted.

She closed her laptop, turned her head and kissed the top of Kat's head loving the fragrance of Kat's hair. She wanted to bury her face in that soft dark hair and whisper her love in Kat's ear. Instead she leaned her head back and fell asleep.

##

Wheels touching the runway woke Java from her short nap. Kat jerked, opened her eyes and looked around.

"We've landed," Java murmured. "Did you get any rest?"

"Umm, yes, I did," Kat snuggled into Java's side. "But I should pull the seat arm down between us before Chis and Barbie see how I'm glued to your side."

As the pilot turned off the fasten seatbelts sign Java pulled their luggage and forensic kit from the overhead bin and stood back to let Kat move into the isle. She checked three rows back to make certain Barbie and Chris were behind them.

They waited until they were in the rental car to begin discussing the case. "Did anyone notice anything different about this case?" Java asked as she pulled onto the interstate.

"The family's name was Rogers," Chris noted. "This is the first time the killer has murdered a baby. The report says a six-month old was clutched in the mother's arms. I'm guessing he crushed her skull then the baby's."

"The husband was black and the wife white," Barbie added. "The other two children were eight and two. I hate to say this Java, but the MO is the same: crushed skulls, total debauchery and all the bodies placed in one bed."

"Rogers was a teacher at the local middle school," Chris added. "Well respected and very active in the community."

"Latour must be working with another person," Chris suggested. "That's the only answer. There's no doubt in my mind he committed the Valentine murders so he must have a partner."

##

They checked in with the local authorities and requested any fingerprints, DNA and blood tests be sent to Penny immediately.

A local detective named Trilton Joe White accompanied them to the scene. "I've been on the force fourteen years," Trilton Joe commented. "I've never seen anything like this.

"I can't believe the agency sent a bunch of women to investigate this."

"What's that supposed to mean?" Java demanded.

"Uh . . . er . . . I just meant this is horrific. Ladies shouldn't handle anything this gruesome."

"We've handled worse," Java smirked.

"I'm glad it's your case and not mine," Trilton Joe muttered. "It would take one sick son-of-a-bitch to butcher a family like that."

"Yeah," Java grunted.

Kat walked to the front door of the house. "Is this locked?"

Two Ways to Die
A Java Jarvis Thriller
by Erin Wade

"Yes ma'am" Trilton Joe dug into his pocket and produced a set of keys. "These fit the front door and the back door, but the killer broke in through that window on the front of the house. He pointed to a window whose screen was leaning against the house.

"Did they check this for fingerprints?" Java asked as she pulled on a pair of latex gloves.

"Doesn't look like it," Kat scowled. "There's no dust or anything to indicate it was printed. Can you get your forensic people back out here?"

"I'll try," Trilton Joe frowned. "I doubt it."

"Pop the trunk, Java so I can get the forensic kit," Kat instructed. "I'll take care of this myself."

The others watched as Kat brushed the fine white powder around the dark screen frame.

"We can go inside," Trilton Joe said. "She doesn't need our help."

"No, but we do need you to validate everything we find that your forensic people may have missed." Java noted.

"Um, yeah," Trilton Joe nodded, "I read that the fellow you've charged with the murders is swearing y'all are railroading him."

"Don't they all?" Java puffed.

"I've got three good prints," Kat declared dropping the fingerprint lifting tabs into the clear bags and filling in the required information. "Detective White, if you'd be so kind as to validate my findings?"

White signed the tag on the bag and handed it back to Kat. "Should I take the screen to our lab?"

"Probably not a bad idea," Java raised a brow. "I just sent you photos of where the screen was when we arrived. Your forensic folks will want that too."

"I'm going to measure and shoot these bloody footprints too," Chris commented. "I'm sure your people did that, but just to be safe."

Trilton Joe verified Chris' work then they entered the house.

"God, I hate that smell," Trilton Joe gagged as he pulled a small tin of Vicks from his pocket and stuck the jelly up each nostril.

"Um, you do know that only opens your sinuses and enhances your ability to smell odors," Kat pointed out.

He inhaled deeply then ran out the door. "He's puking on the sidewalk," Barbie informed the others.

"If he weren't such a good ole' boy I'd video it and put in on the Forensic Investigation's Gone Bad Facebook page," Chris laughed.

Standing where Trilton Joe had left them, the four looked around the room. "Same blood and gore," Barbie commented.

"It's as if this guy gets off on a bloodbath," Java thought out loud. "I wish we'd gotten here in time to see the bodies. I need Penny to see if she can pinpoint the order in which the victims are killed."

"How will that help?" Barbie asked.

"I bet the more he kills the more excited and vicious he gets," Java theorized. "These are thrill killings."

"God, I hope not," Kat shuddered.

"What does that mean?" Barbie encouraged her mentors to keep talking.

"It means the killings will escalate," Kat shivered. "Each killing excites him more than the last until all he wants to do is kill and kill again."

Trilton Joe entered the house wiping his mouth on the sleeve of his jacket. "You're standing right where I left you," he gagged again.

"We can't proceed without your presence," Java informed him. "We need your validation on anything we do or find."

Trilton Joe dragged his jacket sleeve across his nose and shook his head. "Okay, go ahead."

Java kicked the footboard of the bed scattering the hoard of flies covering the dried blood on the mattress stirring up the foul odor even more. "Your forensic people didn't take the mattresses?" She questioned.

"I guess not," Trilton Joe shrugged.

Java pinched the bridge of her nose with her thumb and forefinger. She wondered how some departments ever solved a case.

Bloody footprints of various sizes and fresh cigarette butts doused in the pooled blood told her any evidence still at the scene would be tainted.

"There's nothing here," Java barked. "Let's go."

"I'd like to walk through the house," Kat said.

"Why not?" Java sighed. "Everyone else in the world has."

They followed the brunette from the master bedroom to two other bedrooms. The vast amounts of blood and the trail of gore from the children's rooms to the master bedroom confirmed they had been murdered and carried to their parent's room.

"Is that a coin?" Kat gestured toward a round object covered in blood.

Java crouched and picked up the object. "A button." She held it up so everyone could see it. "It looks like the one we found at the last crime scene."

Kat opened an evidence envelope and Java dropped the button into it. "Java, there's a piece of thread or string there too."

The agent grasped the slimy red string and dropped it into another envelope Kat held open for her.

They walked into the bathrooms and kitchen looking under all the sinks.

"What are you looking for?" Trilton Joe asked.

"Y'all didn't take the P-traps," Java glowered. "The killer may have washed his hands and left some evidence."

"You know, I'm beginning to feel very embarrassed over the way our forensics folks handled this scene." Trilton Joe apologized.

"Um," Java hummed. "We're going to have dinner and catch the late flight back to Orleans. I think we've accomplished everything we can here."

CHAPTER 20

Their Monday morning meeting with Karen Pierce was anything but a happy one. Budro Latour's attorney had produced two witnesses who swore the man was with them the night of the Valentine's murders.

"Dammit," Java said under her breath as Karen informed them of the latest twist to their case.

Beau and Penny joined the five FBI agents and listened as Karen discussed alternatives.

"If we release him," Java argued, "he'll beat the hell out of his kids. They testified against him. We have their testimonies and blood evidence."

"Both his children have recanted their testimonies," Karen shook her head.

"What about his overalls?" Java asked.

"He swears he has no idea how the blood got on them. He does admit having sex with his daughter but says he wasn't wearing those clothes. "

"Of course, he was," Java insisted. "Her clothes were covered in the crime scene blood and his semen. How reputable are the guys alibiing him?"

"One of them is the foreman at the shipyards. The other is a fellow worker," Karen answered.

"I'm afraid it gets worse," Penny interrupted. "The button and string you found at the San Antonio murders match the string and button from the Lafayette murders. It's the same guy."

"What about the fingerprints?" Kat asked.

"No match in IAFIS," Penny answered. "Latour's fingerprints are in the Integrated Automated Fingerprint

Identification System. The prints were close on a few points but they're definitely not Latour's prints."

"I promised that girl we'd protect her," Java exhaled slowly. "When did she recant? After the attorney dredged up the two alibis?"

"Yes," Karen said softly.

"When she realized we'd release him and he'd kill her if she didn't," Java exploded. "How long can we hold him?"

"A week, maybe two," Karen said. "We can drag our feet process the attorney's request that charges be dropped."

"Two weeks," Java shook her head, "and we have no more to go on than we did three months ago. He's murdered a family a month and we're . . . We got nothing."

"I hate to heap on top of the dung pile," Beau interjected, "but we got another bodiless head while you were in San Antonio."

"Please tell me it was in San Antonio too," Java pleaded.

"Nope. Right here in our own backyard," Beau shrugged. "Found her head in an ally off Canal."

"You got pictures?" Chris asked.

"Yeah," Beau plugged his thumb drive into Karen's laptop and flashed the head of a pretty bleached blonde woman onto the whiteboard.

"Isn't she the girl Jody Schooley had at Java's Place on Valentine's Day?" Chris moved to get a better angle on the picture.

"Yes, it is," Kat added. "Not a redhead like his other victims. Looks like The Decapitator is expanding his victims base."

"I'll pick up Schooley," Beau said.

Two Ways to Die
A Java Jarvis Thriller
by Erin Wade

"Can you put a tail on him for a few days?" Java asked. "Let's see what he's up to before we let him know we suspect him."

Java dragged her hand down her face. "Looks like we're back to square one, team. Let's go eat lunch and coffee. Lots and lots of coffee."

##

Jody Schooley was in the bar at Java's Place when the four women walked in. His eyes followed Kat as she stepped into the elevator that would take her to balcony dining. Her blonde watchdog followed her. A few minutes later Penny and Beau followed them.

Jody's phone rang and he recognized the number of the gravelly voiced PayPal customer that was willing to pay any amount for the woman he wanted. Jody shuddered and didn't answer the call. The client had requested Lilly and now she had disappeared.

Jody thought about filing a missing person's report but knew the authorities would want to know what he was to Lilly and then the crap would hit the fan.

He wasn't worried. He was phasing out the girls he'd inherited from Pender Crane. That should stop the phone calls. He still wondered who had killed Pender.

Jody stood when the hostess led his real estate agent to his table. After the usual pleasantries Jody asked the question he was dying to get an answer to.

"Did they accept my offer?"

"Yes," the agent beamed. She laid the contract on the table in front of Jody. "Five million for the mansion on Esplanade Ave. Eleven bedrooms, Twelve baths and thirteen-thousand square feet. Signed, sealed and delivered, Mr. Schooley."

"Perfect," Jody breathed. "Just perfect. How soon can we close?"

"Friday," the agent smiled.

Two Ways to Die
A Java Jarvis Thriller
by Erin Wade

"Kat, I'm going to pay a visit to Kally Latour," Java informed her partner. "Would you go with me?"

"Can you behave yourself?" Kat chided.

"It's hard," Java couldn't help the crooked impish smile that danced on her lips, "but I'll try."

"If you don't keep your hands to yourself, I'll break your arm," Kat warned as Java followed her out the back door of Java's Place."

"Are they always like that?" Beau asked.

"Most of the time," Chris chortled. "They really should get a room and get it over with."

"Seriously," Barbie huffed, "you think Kat would go to bed with Java?"

"In a heartbeat, if she weren't married," Chris shrugged.

"No way," Barbie declared. "That's the point. She is married—a married, straight woman. Straight women don't sleep with lesbians."

"Barbie, tell me again what rock you've been under for the past thirty years," Chris laughed.

CHAPTER 21

"Thank you for bringing me along instead of Barbie," Kat said.

"I know you don't like me fraternizing with Déjà," Java grinned. "I don't know why you're jealous of her. She can't hold a candle to you."

"I am not jealous of her," Kat declared. "I'm afraid she might put you under a spell."

"The only one who has me under a spell is you," Java chuckled. "Surely you know that by now."

"Umm," Kat hummed as she turned her head to look out her side window.

"I'm worried about Kally," Java changed the subject. "I'm afraid her father will beat her to death and feed her body to the gators. No corpus delicti means no case."

"What are you going to do?" Kat asked.

"Try to convince her to let us put her in the witness protection program until this mess is settled."

"That is the safest thing to do," Kat agreed.

"It looks like Déjà is here," Java motioned toward the priest's Cadillac parked between two other expensive vehicles.

"Oh goody," Kat grumped.

"Do be nice to Déjà," Java chuckled. "Believe me she is no match for you."

"Even with those hooters that go into the next county?" Kat asked.

"I promise I've never looked at her as anything but a good CI asset," Java replied. "You know how I feel. Any more than a handful is wasted."

Two Ways to Die
A Java Jarvis Thriller
by Erin Wade

Kat laughed out loud. "How do you always manage to make me laugh?"

Java grinned pleased that she had brought a smile to Kat's beautiful lips. She fought the desire to lean across the console and kiss her.

"We . . . um, should go in," Kat whispered.

##

Déjà's store was cool, a welcome respite from the humid New Orleans air. The jingle of the bell over the door brought Kally from the back. She paused in the beaded doorway and stared at Java.

"Mistress Déjà vu is with a client," she mumbled.

"I'm here to see you, Kally," Java smiled sweetly.

"I'm sorry Miss Java," Kally blurted. "I had to change my story. You know they're going to release him."

"It's okay, Kally," Java comforted the girl.

"He'd kill me," Kally cried as tears ran down her cheeks. "I'm scared what he will do to me anyway. He can be so cruel."

"It's okay," Java took the girl's hand and pulled her into the room. "May we talk with you?"

Kally nodded her head. "I want to help you. I really do."

"I want to help you," Java assured her. "I have an idea. Will you listen to me?"

"Yes ma'am." Kally edged toward the kitchen. "I'll fix coffee for you and your lady."

"Oh, she's not . . ." Java stopped midsentence. "This is Kat Lace. She sings at the club."

"I know who she is," Kally ducked her head and looked at Kat through long lashes. "Everyone knows who she is. Would you prefer tea, Miss Lace?"

"Yes," Kat smiled, "tea would be wonderful." She liked the girl and understood why Java wanted to help her.

Two Ways to Die
A Java Jarvis Thriller
by Erin Wade

The three sat around the small kitchen table and Java spoke reassuringly to Kally. "Kally, I've spoken with the people who arrange things and they will put you into the witness protection program."

"What's that mean?" Kally asked suspiciously.

"It means they can get you out of Orleans and move you to anywhere you want to go. They'll give you a new name and identity and pay you every month until you get on your feet and they'll help you find a job."

"You can do that for me?" Kally gasped.

"If you'll stand by your original testimony about your father." Java replied.

"What about my brother? Can he go with me? He's younger and Pa does awful things to him too. It ain't natural."

"Of course," Java promised. "But both of you will have to stand by your original testimony. I can get you out of here as soon as you give the word for me to get the paperwork started."

"Let me talk to Raymond," Kally beamed. "I'm sure he wants to get out of here too."

"Kally, someone murdered a family in San Antonio," Kat said. "Did your father have anyone working with him?"

Kally closed her eyes and furrowed her forehead. "He always hangs with two guys at the shipyard. He gives Raymond and me to them for favors."

Kat closed her eyes and looked away. Java knew her partner was feeling the same revulsion she was. "Do you know their names?"

"No," Kally gazed into her coffee cup. "You might ask Ma. They came to our house a couple of times when she was there."

Java could feel her case against Latour coming back together. If she could tie the two men to the murders all three would get the death penalty."

Two Ways to Die
A Java Jarvis Thriller
by Erin Wade

Voices from the parlor indicated Déjà's client was leaving. They waited until the closing door signaled the woman was alone.

Déjà poked her head through the beaded entrance. "I thought I heard you talking to someone, Kally. What brings you two to my hallowed halls?"

"Just visiting with Kally," Java stood. "May I speak with you in private? Kat would you continue our conversation with Kally?"

"What's going on?" Déjà asked as she led Java to a small sofa in her private office.

"I'm trying to salvage my case against Budro Latour," Java scowled. "I'm sure you've heard about the murders in San Antonio and that two men have come forward providing alibis for Latour on the Valentine's murders.

"I know Kally and her brother recanted their testimony," Déjà shrugged. "What are you going to do?"

"If I can prove the men are lying and that they are somehow involved with Latour in the murders, I'll have an open and closed case."

"That's a big if," Déjà wrinkled her nose. "Have you questioned the two men yourself?"

"No, you know I keep a low profile in New Orleans." Java answered. "But I'll be in the observation room talking to Beau through the earbud. We should be able to trip them up."

"Who are they?" Déjà asked.

"I don't know if the two men providing Latour's alibi are the same men Kally told me about or not." Java told her. "If they are, I think I'm on to something."

"Good luck my friend," Déjà said.

Java looked around the room. "You've got some new merchandise," she commented. "That's a different looking doll. Um and miniature skulls. Uh, these aren't plastic, Déjà."

"Of course, they are sweet cheeks," Déjà laughed. "We both know that real human skulls are illegal."

##

"Don't be nervous," Kat reassured a fidgeting Kally. "Java will take care of you."

"You don't know my Pa, Miss Lace."

"Please, call me Kat," she patted Kally's arm. "He isn't getting out of jail. I promise."

Kat stood, picked up the coffee cups and saucers she and Java had used and carried them to the sink.

"Please, Miss . . . uh Kat, let me clean up. Déjà won't like it if I don't?"

Kat nodded and walked back into the parlor. Déjà had everything any self-respecting voodoo priestess would have on display in the storefront. She wandered past small animal skulls decorated with feathers and fur, an assortment of voodoo dolls and charms.

A "do it yourself voodoo doll kit" caught her eye. The kit contained several squares of burlap, dark brown thread, a large needle, pins and button eyes. Bowls beside the kit offered extra pins, thread and button eyes.

Kat dipped her hand into the bowl of buttons and examined them closer. They were identical to the two buttons found at the scene of the last two crimes.

"Kally do you sell a lot of these?" Kat held out a handful of buttons.

"Oh yes ma'am. They're one of our best sellers," the girl exclaimed. "Lots of people make their own voodoo dolls. You know jilted lovers, angry wives, mad employees."

"Hum, I might just make a voodoo doll of my own." Kat picked up one of the kits, several strands of thread and placed them on the counter along with the handful of buttons she'd picked up."

Two Ways to Die
A Java Jarvis Thriller
by Erin Wade

"May I pay you for these?" Kat asked opening her purse.

"Yes ma'am," Kally beamed. "Miss Déjà lets me run the cash register." Kally scanned the price tags on the items and carefully placed them into a bag designed to look like a large voodoo doll. "Madam Déjà vu" was scrolled across the top and "High Priestess" was in large letters on front of the bag.

Kat hated to admit it but Déjà did have good taste and a gift for eye-catching advertising.

CHAPTER 22

"What did you buy?" Java asked as she and Kat fastened their seatbelts.

"A do it yourself voodoo doll kit," Kat grinned impishly. "If you'll just give me a lock of your hair, I think I can have complete control over you."

"As if you don't already," Java chuckled. "Seriously babe, why did you buy that?"

"Take me to a nice quiet place for lunch and I'll show you." Kat answered. "Let's try that new Chinese place in the strip center."

Java caught Kat's hand and pulled it onto her lap. "If we ever close this case, I will insist on two weeks' vacation for the team. We've been hitting it pretty hard."

"Mm-hmm, we both know what you've been hitting hard," Kat giggled. "Where do you get your energy?"

Java blushed profusely as she pulled the car into the parking space in front of the restaurant.

"Kat, I know this isn't the ideal situation but if you—"

"Let's not discuss it today," Kat insisted. "I'm having such a good time with you."

"Okay, bring your doll and let's see what you have up your sleeve."

##

They selected a circular booth that allowed them to sit next to each other. Java pressed her thigh against Kat and opened the menu.

After they placed their order Kat pulled the items from her shopping bag. "Do these look familiar?" She held out the buttons.

Two Ways to Die
A Java Jarvis Thriller
by Erin Wade

"Yes, they look like the two buttons we found at the last two crime scenes," Java picked up two of the buttons and examined them. "They're identical."

"Um-hum and this thread," Kat held up a couple of strands of the string from Déjà's, "also identical: same length and same coarseness."

"You think our voodoo doll killer is connected to . . . surely you don't suspect Déjà?"

"You must admit your girlfriend has some peculiar ways," Kat smirked.

"Kat, I don't think—"

"I'm just jerking your chain baby," Kat laughed her deep throaty laugh. "I am saying that it is possible that Budro Latour could have obtained the buttons from Déjà's shop."

"He certainly had opportunity," Java frowned. "If he took Kally to work or picked her up. I'll ask her about that."

"Let's see if we can run down the two fellows that alibied Latour," Kat suggested. "Right now, I'm going to wash my hands."

"I'll call Beau and get all the info I can on Latour's two buddies." Java said.

##

When Kat returned, Java gave her the rundown on Budro's friends. "We already knew they work together at the shipyard, but Beau gave me the name of a bar they hang out in and mugshots of them. Beau's people have been tailing them to see if they show up at anyone's house with an ax."

"Why don't we pay the bar a visit and see if they show up," Kat suggested. "Maybe chat them up and see if we can learn anything."

"That's not a great part of town," Java pointed out.

"We'll be fine," Kat grinned.

Two Ways to Die
A Java Jarvis Thriller
by Erin Wade

"I'll call Barbie and Chris to meet us there," Java said. "You know they'll be furious if we don't let them in on the action."

"Yes, you're right," Kat laughed.

Java called their teammates and gave them the address of the bar.

##

Java and Kat waited in their car until Barbie and Chris parked beside them. "It's only five in the afternoon and this place is already crowded," Chris noted. "Must serve good beer."

"Everyone put in your earbuds. Kat and I will go in," Java instructed. "If it sounds like we're in trouble, come in."

"You got it, boss," Barbie chirped.

"Just for the record," Java added, "do not kill anyone. We're just here to gather information."

Kat and Java entered the bar looking around as if they were confused. They sat down at the bar and ordered wine.

"You ladies lost?" The bartender asked.

"I think so," Kat murmured looking around the room that was filled with single men and a few couples. "I've never been here before."

"I think we have the wrong address," Java worried her bottom lip. "We should finish our drinks and leave."

"Eh, stay," the bartender placed another glass of wine on the bar. "This ones on the house. Sort of a welcome gift."

"Why?" Java snapped.

"Pretty women always help my business," the man shrugged. "You want the wine or not?"

"Don't be such a stick in the mud," Kat slapped Java's arm. "Put some money in the jukebox. I want to dance."

Java sauntered across the room and fed money into the machine and selected five songs. When she turned around

Two Ways to Die
A Java Jarvis Thriller
by Erin Wade

Kat was already dancing in the middle of the floor. She joined her moving to the music and dancing without touching.

As they danced Java spotted the two men they were looking for. She smiled at them and continued her gyrations.

As the song ended, one of the men walked toward them. "My buddy and I'd like to buy you two beautiful ladies a drink," he invited.

"Sure, why not?" Kat sashayed to their table. "Wine for me."

Java followed wondering how Kat could flirt with men so easily. It was difficult for her to feign interest in them.

"I've never seen you two here before," the one named Albert slurred. Obviously, he'd been at the bar for a while.

"That's because we've never been here before," Kat's eyes flashed as if she found Albert amusing and interesting.

"You come here often?" Java asked the man she'd been paired with.

"Every night," he grinned exposing yellowed teeth.

A smoker, Java thought. "Every night? Don't tell me you two are single."

"Yep both of us are," Albert chimed in.

"Handsome fellows like you," Kat flirted, "I can't believe you don't have ladies waiting for you at home."

"Nope," yellow teeth shook his head, drained his beer and ordered another round.

"How about you ladies?" Yellow teeth who turned out to be named Lonnie, asked.

"Nah, I had a fellow," Kat grinned, "but he didn't bring me anything for Valentine's Day, so I kicked him out."

Kat fell against Albert as if she were reeling from the wine. "Can you believe he didn't even bring me candy?"

Two Ways to Die
A Java Jarvis Thriller
by Erin Wade

Java was mesmerized by Kat's performance. *Damn she's good*, she thought.

"What'd you take your girl for Valentine's Day?" Kat demanded. "I bet you took her out to dinner, huh?"

"Yeah," Albert bragged. "And I got lucky afterwards."

Everyone laughed gleefully at Albert's admission.

"You mean she let you spend the night?" Kat giggled.

"Yeah and the next day too," Albert boasted.

"You must be something," Kat egged him on.

"My girl let me spend the night too," Lonnie blustered. "I got her a Valentine's box of chocolates."

"Yeah, that's what I mean," Kat crowed. "Any decent man would give his girl something for Valentine's Day. Where'd you take her?"

"That Bayou Burger with its balcony dining," Albert gloated. "You know the one that has the best burgers in Orleans."

"The one with the dancefloor and jukebox?" Kat asked.

"Yeah that one. You like that place?" Albert said.

"I do," Kat glanced at her watch. "Oh, look at the time. We're going to be late."

Kat stood but Albert caught her wrist and yanked her back into the booth. "We bought you wine," he grinned. "We expect a little show of appreciation."

"Like what?" Kat demanded.

Albert had the decency to bend down and whisper his expectations in Kat's ear.

"Not here in front of everyone," Kat scolded. "Is there an ally out back?"

"Yeah," Albert beamed as they left the table.

"How about you and me going to my place?" Lonnie suggested to Java.

"How about you and me staying right here," Java huffed crossing her arms.

Two Ways to Die
A Java Jarvis Thriller
by Erin Wade

Lonnie leaned against her. "You're not as friendly as your friend, are you?"

"Lonnie, do you feel something sticking you in the side?"

"Damn, hell yes," Lonnie tried to scoot away but Java had him pinned to the wall.

She pushed the point of her knife into his side. "It's a knife," she informed him. "It's between your ribs. All I have to do is give it a shove and it will pierce your liver. You'll bleed out in less than five minutes."

"What do you want?" Lonnie growled.

"I want you to sit here quietly until my friend returns." Java whispered.

"She may not return," Lonnie muttered. "Albert is pretty rough with women. You should go see about her."

"She's fine," Java grinned. "Let's just finish our drinks. Why don't you tell me the name of the lucky lady you took chocolates to on Valentine's Day?"

Lonnie gave her all the information she needed including an address.

Kat entered the room as if she were a runway model. She strode to Java. "Ready to go?"

Java stood. "See ya' around, Lonnie."

##

Chris and Barbie were laughing in their car. "God Kat you almost killed that poor devil."

"He was pawing me," Kat defended. "A hard knee in the crotch always gets their attention."

"Did you get the name of Albert's girlfriend?" Java inquired.

"Of course," Kat slid into the car. "We should call Beau and have them picked up immediately before our Romeos get to them."

"Were you able to record our conversations?" Kat asked Barbie.

Two Ways to Die
A Java Jarvis Thriller
by Erin Wade

"Every word," Barbie beamed.

CHAPTER 23

Lucille Denoise and Becky Cathaway were in the interrogation room by the time Java and her team arrived at the police station. They were in separate rooms. Both women swore they couldn't recall what they did Valentine's Day.

Beau left Lucille's room and joined Java's team in the observation room. "Obviously, they've been schooled on how to answer us," he reported.

"Yeah," Java huffed. "Beau let's run the other girlfriend routine. Kat, you're up."

Kat messed up her long black locks and applied extra lipstick. "How do I look?"

"Like you just got out of bed," Java grinned.

Kat shot her a sultry look, "As if you'd know," she scolded.

"Yeah," Java chortled, "In my dreams."

"Let's do this," Beau stepped out of the room and gave the officer guarding the interrogation room instructions.

"Lucille," Beau tossed a folder on the table, "Lonnie tells us he spent the night at your place Valentine's. Is that true?"

"Like I told you, sir," Lucille drawled, "I don't remember."

"How much longer you gonna' be?" The officer opened the door and poked in his head. "I got this other wild cat out here and all the rooms are full."

Kat was raising a ruckus in the hall. "I told you I only been dating Lonnie a couple of months. I want a lawyer.

Two Ways to Die
A Java Jarvis Thriller
by Erin Wade

You've got to provide me a lawyer. I ain't talkin' to you freaks without a lawyer."

Beau walked to the door and opened it. Kat burst into the room in all her glory. She tossed back her wild hair and glared at Beau. "Either arrest me or let me go."

"Ma'am, I don't want to arrest you," Beau assured her. "I just want to talk to you. Um, please wait just a minute. I'll be right back."

"I can't have both these women in the same room," Beau mumbled to the officer before he closed the door.

"Stupid cops," Kat raged. "Jesus, they haul me in just because my boyfriend's done something wrong."

"Yeah, me too," Lucille said cautiously. "Who's your boyfriend?"

"Lonnie, Lonnie Raine." Kat paced the floor. "He's a fricken' loser anyway." She studied Lucille. "What are you in for?"

"My boyfriend."

"Yeah, men are worthless," Kat spit on the floor. "Classy women like you and me, how do we end up with such losers. Who's your man?"

"Lonnie Raine," Lucille sighed. "Same as yours?"

"You're kidding me!" Kat snorted. "He's gotten both of us in trouble. You ain't knocked up, are you?"

"Hell no!" Lucille bellowed.

"What's he done that they're all hot about?" Kat asked. "He steal a car or rob a store or something? . . . That's it the son-of-a-bitch robbed a jewelry store. I should've known when he gave me this ring." Kat held out her hand so Lucille could admire the wedding ring Kat always wore.

"Lonnie gave you that?" Lucille gasped.

"Yep, and its real," Kat preened. "I had it appraised. Genuine diamonds and gold. Hey, don't tell the cops. They'll take it away from me."

"When did he give it to you? Lucille scowled.

"Um . . . the day before Valentine's Day," Kat answered. "What'd he give you?"

"Chocolates. A crappy box of cheap chocolates," Lucille fumed.

"Well, at least they weren't stolen," Kat declared. "He told me he had to go out of town Valentine's night." Kat narrowed her eyes and glared at Lucille. "Did that slimy little piece of crap spend the night with you?"

"Yep," Lucille beamed as if she'd won the lottery, "and all next day too."

"He was with you Valentine's Day and all that night and the next day too?"

"Sure was," Lucille declared.

"I don't believe you," Kat declared. "You're just saying that to make me jealous."

Lucille pulled out her cellphone and jabbed at the screen. "What's your phone number, honey?"

Kat said the numbers slowly and jumped when her phone dinged the arrival of a message. It was a picture of Lucile and Lonnie holding a box of chocolates. Kat almost squealed when she saw the time and date stamp on the photo.

Beau swept into the room and grabbed Kat's arm. "Come on I've found a room for you."

"Get your hands off me," Kat yelled yanking her arm from Beau's grip and slipping out the door.

"Damn woman, you're good," Beau exclaimed when they joined the team in the observation room.

"And you thought she was just another pretty face," Java quipped. "There's much more to Kat than meets the eye."

"I don't know," Beau smiled. "There's an awful lot that meets the eye that's really nice."

"Kat made it to first base," Java threw down the gauntlet, "let's see you bring in the winning run, Beau."

Two Ways to Die
A Java Jarvis Thriller
by Erin Wade

Beau bowed ceremoniously, "Send Lucille's picture to my phone. Then follow me."

The team moved to the observation room connected to the room holding Becky Cathaway. "Prepare to be amazed," Beau laughed. He left the observation area and joined Becky.

"Now Becky, I'm going to give you one last chance to tell me the truth," Beau smiled. "But before you say anything, I want to remind you it is against the law to lie to me. So, you decide if Albert is worth doing time in prison.

"I thought you might like to know that Lucille not only admitted she spent the night and next day with Lonnie, she provided a date and time stamped photo to prove it." Beau held up the picture so Becky could study it.

"Yes, Albert was with me," Becky blew air through her lips. "We live together. He was with me all week. I fixed him breakfast in bed Valentine's Day and he took me out to dinner that night."

"So, Albert was with you all night Valentine's Eve?" Beau reiterated.

"Yes," Becky deflated.

Beau pushed a legal pad and pen to Becky. "Please write down exactly what you've just told me, and I'll let you go."

"Albert can't find out," Becky pleaded. "He'll beat the hell out of me."

"We'll have him in custody before you leave here," Beau promised.

Beau showed Lucille the statement from Becky and Lucille caved giving him all the information he needed to prove Lonnie was lying.

"We need to get to the club," Java informed Beau. "Please join us when you finish and let us know where we stand."

"I will," Beau nodded. "Is it okay if I bring Penny along. She needs to be brought up to speed on this case."

"Of course," Java agreed.

CHAPTER 24

"Everyone, the server will take your order then let's go to the balcony dining," Java instructed. "I don't know about you, but I'm starving."

"I am so proud to be a part of this team," Barbie beamed as they gathered around the table. "I mean, Kat . . . Wow! Just wow! I had no idea you had that in you. You had everyone eating out of your hand: the men and their girlfriends. I'm so impressed."

"Thank you," Kat blushed. "I've no doubt you could pull off the same thing."

"I don't know," Barbie shook her head, "but I'd sure like to try. Can I Java? Next time can I be the bitchy floozy?"

All eyes turned to Kat to see her reaction to Barbie's statement.

"Bitchy floozy!" Kat yelped. "I prefer to think of it as convincing seductress."

"That too," Java laughed as everyone joined in, relieved that Kat hadn't taken offense to Barbie's remark.

Penny and Beau joined them as drinks were being served and gave the server their orders.

"I talked to Karen on the way here," Java informed them. "As far as she's concerned, we can consider Latour The Basher."

"I spoke with the ADA," Beau added. "She's getting skittish about the case. After all we had Latour locked up tight when the San Antonio murders happened. She's also concerned about the recanted, then reversal of the statements from his children. She said any good prosecutor will make them look like liars on the stand."

"And honestly," Penny jumped in, "They screwed up the San Antonio scene so badly I can't say for sure if it's our basher or not. The MO is awfully close but the prints on the window screen definitely are not Latour's."

"This case is beginning to give me nightmares," Chris said. "We know Lonnie and Albert didn't commit the murders. They were with those two women all night.

"We do have blood and semen from Latour and bloody clothes also covered with his fluids and the victims' blood. I say he is our killer. I don't know what to say about the SA murders. Maybe a copycat."

"I'd feel good about sticking a needle in Latour," Penny said.

Beau's phone rang and he listened closely to the person on the other end. "Thanks, we needed that."

"That was my partner. He's interrogated Lonnie and Albert. Both have admitted that Latour promised them money and time with his daughter and son in exchange for their alibis."

"Geeze, what an ass," Barbie mumbled. "Trading his kid's bodies for favors. Even if he is innocent, I'd still like to see the sorry S.O.B. get the needle."

"This strengthens our case," Java noted. "He has no alibi and was so desperate to get one he was bartering his kids. The clothes we confiscated at his home are definitely his. All the clothes we dug up in the back yard belong to Latour and are covered with his semen and blood from previous victims. There's no doubt in my mind Budro Latour is The Basher."

"What about our bodiless ladies?" Java asked. "Is Jody Schooley showing your surveillance guys anything?"

"Nothing yet," Beau frowned. "He has an office on St Peters but doesn't stay there much. He seems to troll the streets. He met with a real-estate lady last week but other than that, he hangs out in your place or Rochelle's. Takes and makes a lot of short phone calls. We're having trouble identifying his girls.

"You know he took over Pender's girls," Beau informed them. "They've been slowly disappearing ever since. He says he sent them back home. I know he dropped the underaged ones off at Covenant Place."

"That's strange behavior for a pimp," Java noted.

"I thought so too." Beau agreed. "I know he's up to something. I can feel it in my bones."

"He knows we have a strict policy against prostitutes in Java's Place," Java said. "We have no private rooms or strippers. Rochelle's has both. If he's running prostitutes it'd have to be Rochelle's place."

"I don't know," Beau shrugged, "Since the sweeping raids last year by the NOLA Office of Alcohol & Tobacco Control most of the clubs now have cameras in their private rooms. Strippers can entertain private customers any way they wish except having intercourse with them."

"Like that slows down sex trafficking," Kat groused. "Walk down the street, on any night, Beau. Scantily clad women are standing in the doorways of clubs and dingy bars hawking their wares."

"A&TC doesn't have the funding to arrest the hooker who is on her own," Beau noted. "They go after the pimps running multiple women—some against their will. Pimps feed on stupid young girls who run away from home and think they can make a living in Orleans. Once a pimp gets his hooks into a girl, she doesn't stand a chance. It's the pimps like Pender we don't want in Orleans."

"Apparently someone else didn't want Pender in Orleans either," Java pointed out. "I know that Lindy's security system was on the blink, but I don't see how someone could walk into Rochelle's, stab the guy and steal his cellphone without anyone seeing it. You know all his women and clients were on that phone."

"Yeah, I'm certain they instantly downloaded the info then destroyed the sims card." Beau noted.

"Maybe we should pull Jody in for questioning?" Chris said. "He was the last one to speak with Pender before he was murdered."

"I have a better idea," Java said. "Barbie, why don't you see if he'll hire you. We'll have a big fight in front of him and I'll fire you. Then later you can ask him if he has a job you can do."

"I don't know Java," Barbie replied. "Everyone knows he has the hots for Kat."

Java's back stiffened as she considered sending Kat into Jody Schooley's operation. "I don't know—"

"Barbie's right," Kat said. "But you don't have to fire me. I'll just tell Jody I need to make some extra money. He'll jump at the chance."

"I'm sure he will," Java mumbled. "He'll probably pay you himself. I don't like it. Let's continue the surveillance and put this idea on hold for right now. Beau, do you know the name of the real-estate agent he was talking to?"

"I can find out," Beau dialed a number and spoke with someone in his office. "Thanks, I appreciate the info." He hung up and wrote the number on a napkin. "Sandy Cray, here's her number."

CHAPTER 25

The next morning Java visited Sandy Cray right after her agency opened.

"I'm Java Jarvis," she introduced herself.

"I know who you are," Sandy smiled. "You own Java's Place. Nice supper club."

"Thank you," Java faked a blush. "I'm thinking about expanding and wondered what's on the market."

Sandy's long nails clicked against her keyboard as she scrolled through her listings. "Are you going to sell your location on Bourbon Street?" She asked.

"No, I'll probably lease it to some other club owner," Java answered. "It's been in my family for over sixty years."

"You looking to expand your services?" Sandy asked.

"Possibly," Java nodded. "I need something in the ten to twelve thousand square feet range. Several bedrooms with baths.

"We just sold a property like that," Sandy bragged. "You know that two-story mansion on Esplanade Ave. Eleven bedrooms, Twelve baths and thirteen-thousand square feet."

"Is it under contract or has the deal been closed?" Java asked.

"Oh yes, the buyer paid cash, closed last week." Sandy informed her.

"I guess I'll have even more competition," Java feigned concern.

"Just between you and me, Java I don't think you have anything to worry about." Sandy patted her hand. "I don't think it's going to be a restaurant/club like your place. I think it's going to be a gentleman's club."

"Seriously," Java exclaimed. "Are they calling it a gentleman's club?"

"They filed for a license for a private club." Sandy added. "So, I think they can call it anything they want."

"That place didn't go cheap," Java noted. "It's one of the nicest places in Orleans. Must be a group of investors."

"Could be," Sandy agreed. "Jody Schooley is the front man on it."

"Schooley?" Java gasped. "How'd Schooley pull together that much money?

"You'd have to ask him," Sandy shrugged suddenly aware that she had given out more information than she should about another client.

"If anything happens and it comes back on the market please let me know," Java slid her business card to Sandy. "And next time you dine at Java's Place ask for me, I'll buy you dinner."

"I may just do that," Sandy winked.

##

The DA's office threw the book at Budro Latour although they couldn't explain the San Antonio massacre. The San Antonio authorities declared the slaughter the work of a copycat killer. The case was dragging its way through the criminal process. It was almost November and there hadn't been a massacre since the San Antonio slaughter. Everyone was breathing easier and thankful the senseless killings had stopped.

Java kept a close watch on the progress of the remodeling going on at the Esplanade Avenue mansion. She kept a closer watch on Lindy Rochelle who was now a regular at Kat's performances. The woman was obviously enamored of the brunette singer.

123

"Your girlfriend is here," Java nudged Kat as Lindy entered Java's Place.

"She's not my girlfriend," Kat hissed. "She's always sweet and respectful. Unlike some women I know."

"I'm always respectful," Java defended. "I just have a hard time hiding my feelings for you."

"And an even harder time keeping your hands off me," Kat pointed out.

"You know you love it," Java made a salacious face.

Kat laughed out loud. "You really are incorrigible."

"Hopeless," Java grinned. "Heads up. Girlfriend headed your way."

"Lindy," Java greeted her competitor, "How's business?"

"Good," Lindy shrugged. "I'm sure it would be better if I could find a singer like Kat for my showroom."

"Um, I'm not sure a woman with Kat's talent would want to share a stage with strippers," Java pointed out.

"Oh, I'd get rid of the strippers for Kat," Lindy blurted. "Err. . . um, for someone of Kat's caliber."

"You're in for a treat tonight," Java grinned. "Kat is introducing her new routine."

"Perhaps we could celebrate afterwards," Lindy turned to Kat, "I could take you to dinner."

Java caught Kat's hand and held up her wedding ring. "Married lady here, Lindy. You do know that, right?"

"Of course," Lindy mumbled. "I have respected that in every way. Kat if you think I've stepped out of line . . ."

"Ignore her, Lindy," Kat giggled. "She's just giving you a hard time."

"I'd like to give you a—"

"Stop it, Java," Kat stomped her foot. "You're being childish."

Java rolled her eyes and walked into her office slamming the door behind her. She pulled out her file on the bodiless prostitutes. In their usual compassionate way, the news media had dubbed the killings the Decap Murders. Beau had hauled in Jody Schooley and questioned him about the death of the bleached blonde.

Jody swore he knew nothing about her death. He gave Beau the number of the man who had requested Lilly, but it was a burner phone. The Decap Murders had also ceased. Java wanted to tie the Decap Murders to The Basher but could find no connection. She closed the files when someone knocked on her door. "Come in."

"Java," Chris entered, "Déjà vu is on the phone. She is insisting that she has reservations for Thanksgiving, but she doesn't. She does this every year. She waits until the day before and—"

"I know," Java chuckled. "Give her the table next to Jody Schooley. That should be a hoot."

"Seriously?" Chris smirked. "You know how Jody is around big boobs."

"Yeah, I figure Déjà will break his arms." Java laughed.

"Kat's right," Chris giggled, "you really are evil."

"We're maxed out," Chris examined her seating chart. "I couldn't squeeze in a two-year old tomorrow, but I'll find Deja a table somewhere."

CHAPTER 26

"Boss," Barbie charged into Java's office. "Penny's on the phone—"

"I can't do it," Chris interrupted. "I can't seat another single soul—"

"Chris, she doesn't want a seat," Barbie frowned. "There's been another massacre in Lafayette."

"Damn," Java cursed.

"Penny wants all of us there," Barbie continued. "Lafayette learned from the fiasco they caused last time. They've roped everything off and have officers stationed all around the house until we get there to secure the scene."

"Let's move it," Java put her files into her lap drawer and pulled on her jacket. "My car's out back."

"What about Kat?" Barbie asked. "She's running through her Thanksgiving show for the first time tonight."

"Yeah," Java hesitated. "Barbie get her. I don't want to leave her alone."

##

"What's so important you have to drag me away—"

The look on Java's face told Kat something was terribly wrong.

"Oh no," she whispered. "Don't tell me he's back."

"Someone is back," Java hissed. "At least this time we've got a clean crime scene. We'll be the first to go over it."

"How many?" Kat asked.

"We don't know," Barbie replied. "No one went inside the house. They just roped it off until we arrive. Penny is on her way too."

"It's a two-hour drive," Java accelerated. "Hold on we're going to break some records getting there."

##

Penny and her team were unloading their forensic paraphernalia when Java parked in front of the house.

"From the looks of all the blood," Penny said, "this is going to be one gory crime scene. Look at that sidewalk."

The sidewalk looked as if someone had hosed it down with blood. Every inch of it was covered in the coagulated sticky stuff. Java pulled on her gloves and picked up a five-gallon plastic bucket that had been used to douse the sidewalk with the sanguine fluid. She held it up for the videographer to film. "It has Tractor Supply Company written on the side," Java turned the bucket so he could film it. She wondered if the killer had brought his own bucket or had found it on the premises.

"Bag that," Penny ordered as one of her people held out a large clear bag for Java to put the bucket into.

"Just look at the footprints," Penny crowed. "They're everywhere but they're only from one person. Measure and video every inch of this. Then take stills of the footprints."

Java couldn't tear her eyes away from the pattern of the footprints in the blood. "Kat you're the musician," she said. "but this pattern looks as if—"

"The killer danced in the blood," Kat mumbled.

"Yeah, a waltz," Java pointed out the steps.

"Sick bastard," Penny growled. "Poured his victims' blood all over the sidewalk then danced in it."

"Java have your agents pair with mine," Penny instructed. "Two sets of eyes are better than one. My people will collect the evidence, bag and tag it. Your people need to keep their eyes open for anything my people might overlook. Let's go in through the carport. There's no blood trail there. Everyone have on their booties and scrub caps?"

Two Ways to Die
A Java Jarvis Thriller
by Erin Wade

The stench and sight in the house made even the most seasoned investigator gag. Java was pleased that her teammates weren't with those who bolted and ran outside to throw up in a plastic bag to keep from contaminating the crime scene.

Unlike the other crime scenes, the black man and white woman had been shot in the head. The woman's skull was also cracked open while the man's head was intact. Four children under the age of nine were bludgeoned to death.

The signature voodoo doll was placed on each victim. For the first time each doll had a pin through its head. The mattress on the bed was soaked with blood from the six victims stacked on it.

Penny's team carefully spread out clear sheets of plastic and began the arduous job of separating the bodies.

Each body was carefully wrapped in clear plastic, loaded onto the gurney and wheeled to the waiting coroner's box truck. Penny had learned a single coroner's van wouldn't hold the depravity from The Basher's kills.

The teams worked until the last ray of sunlight disappeared from the sky then flooded the inside of the house with halogen flood lights. Sometime around midnight Penny declared the scene cleared for release.

"Java, we've got to find something in all this carnage." Penny's tired face showed the ravages of the horrible scene she had torn apart piece by piece.

"Get some sleep tonight Penny," Java put her arm around her friend's shoulder and walked her to her truck. "Join us for Thanksgiving tomorrow then you can tackle this puzzle with a fresh eye Friday."

"I think you're right, Java," Penny agreed.

##

It was after two in the morning Thanksgiving Day when Java dropped Barbie and Chris off at their cars. "I'll drive you home," she told Kat who nodded numbly.

128

Two Ways to Die
A Java Jarvis Thriller
by Erin Wade

As they pulled from the parking lot Kat caught Java's hand and pulled it into her stomach. "I don't want to be alone, Java."

"I know, honey." Java murmured. "Neither do I."

CHAPTER 27

Thanksgiving Day arrived enveloped in clouds and drizzling rain. *A typical rainy November day in Orleans,* Java thought as she lay on her back gazing at the sky through her window. The warm woman beside her drew her attention to more pleasant thoughts.

"Thank you," Kat whispered sliding her arm across Java's torso. "I just couldn't sleep alone last night. The thought of someone creating all that carnage and then gleefully dancing in it was more than I could comprehend."

"I felt the same way," Java murmured. "Holding you drove the vile images from my mind.

"I'm sorry you didn't get to run through your new routine yesterday," Java turned on her side to face Kat. "I know how you hate to do a show cold turkey."

"It'll be fine," Kat cooed. "We're professionals, the band will cover for me if I mess up."

"I don't recall you ever missing a note," Java chuckled.

"See how good they cover for me," Kat giggled.

"Umm, Kat I—"

Kat's soft fingertips on her lips stopped Java's sentence. "We must shower and get to the club. It's already late afternoon."

##

The smell of cornbread dressing and turkey that greeted Java when she ushered Kat through the back door of the supper club made her mouth water. The fragrance that floated from the brunette's hair teased all her senses.

Two Ways to Die
A Java Jarvis Thriller
by Erin Wade

"About time you two got here," Barbie barked. "Two waitresses have reported out ill and one of the ovens is on the blink."

"No rest for the wicked," Java laughed. "Chris is there anyone we can call in to waitress?"

"Already on their way, boss," Chris grinned. "Barbie just panicked."

"You're darn right I panicked," Barbie scowled, "I still have mental scars from Valentine's Day and I think tonight's crowd is going to be worse."

"Has there been anything on the news about yesterday?" Java asked.

"No, somehow Penny and Beau are keeping a lid on it," Chris replied. "If we can just deal with one thing at a time, we'll be okay."

"Which oven is on the blink?" Java asked following Chris into the kitchen.

"This one," Chris opened the large oven door. "The top heating element isn't working."

Java jiggled the heating element and discovered it was loose. She caught hold of the heat unit and pushed it hard into the socket and smiled when it clicked into place. She turned on the oven and the top and bottom elements glowed red.

"Why didn't I think of that?" Chris mumbled.

"I think we're all still shell shocked from yesterday's experience," Java soothed her. "I'm glad today will be crazy busy. It will keep our minds off other things."

##

The staff of Java's Place stood silently looking over the supper club one last time before opening the door and allowing the crowd that had gathered to enter.

"I'd like to say a little blessing, if no one minds," Kat smiled.

Two Ways to Die
A Java Jarvis Thriller
by Erin Wade

Everyone nodded and Kat prayed out loud. As everyone echoed her amen, Java opened the door and Java's Place took on a life of its own.

Java greeted the town's elite and several politicians as they were led to their tables and treated like royalty. She glanced at Jody Schooley when he entered with a very attractive brunette that bore an uncanny resemblance to Kat.

"I trust I'm sitting at your table," a throaty, sexy voice hummed in Java's ear.

"Déjà, of course," Java laughed. "Follow me." Java knew Chris would want to kill her for upsetting her seating chart, but thought it was a good idea to get upstairs and away from others who would expect the same treatment Déjà was getting.

"I've heard rumors," Déjà said as she sat down. "Not good rumors."

"Um," Java nodded for her to continue.

"Lafayette, yesterday." Déjà raised an eyebrow.

"How do you know about it?" Java asked.

"You forget I reign over the voodoo realm, darling," Déjà smirked. "I am very aware of what my followers are doing."

"I hope you're aware of whoever slaughtered the Claymore family in Lafayette," Java scowled. "I also hope it wasn't one of your followers."

"You insult me, Java Jarvis," Déjà's throaty response shocked Java.

"Tell me what you know!" Java demanded.

"Six people murdered. Black man, white woman," Déjà said. "Four children. I have no idea who did it."

"A name, Déjà, I need a name. Who told you about the murders?"

Déjà pulled her purse onto her lap and rummaged through it withdrawing a folded piece of paper. She shoved it toward Java. "This was under my door this morning. Why would someone feel it necessary to give me this information?"

Java unfolded the paper and read the facts of the murder that were written in blood on the paper. She slipped the sheet into her pocket cognizant that both she and Déjà had compromised the evidence by handling it. *Penny can pull a blood sample from it and see if it matches our crime scene*, she thought.

The balcony began to fill as customers climbed the stairs to join Java and Déjà in celebrating the holiday. The laughter and frivolity of the diners seemed incongruous with the turmoil roiling in Java's mind.

The band began to play, and Lindy Rochelle led Kat to the dancefloor.

"Someone's courting your woman," Déjà pointed out.

"She's not my woman," Java said through gritted teeth.

"You want to dance?" Déjà tilted her head toward the dancefloor.

"I get to lead," Java grinned knowing the ebony beauty would be the one leading.

##

Jody Schooley stood and took the hand of the woman with him leading her to the dancefloor. Java was surprised by how well Jody danced.

"Even Jody gets to lead," Java pretended to pout as Déjà moved them around the dancefloor.

"He's the taller of the two, sweetness," Déjà chuckled. "Like me."

Jody tapped Java on the shoulder, "Change partners," he grinned passing Java his brunette partner and pulling Déjà into his arms.

"This should get interesting," Java snickered as Déjà struggled to follow Jody.

"You're an excellent dancer," the brunette said to Java.

"Thank you," Java responded. "We haven't been introduced. I'm Java Jarvis."

"Java Jarvis," the brunette repeated the name as if trying it out on her tongue.

"Do you have a name?" Java teased.

"Amanda," the woman replied. "My name is Amanda."

"Do you like women, Java Jarvis?" Amanda asked.

"Um, that's a strange question," Java responded. "Do you like women?"

"I like men and women," Amanda declared. "I especially like you."

"Thank you," Java wished the dance would end so she could return Amanda to Jody.

"I'd like to take you to bed," Amanda whispered in Java's ear.

"No, I . . . um . . . I'm not—" The music stopped, and Java grabbed Amanda's arm leading her back to Jody.

Déjà slipped her arm through Java's and dragged her toward the elevator to return to their table in the balcony. "Don't ever let him dance with me again," Déjà's throaty growl filled the elevator. "He's all hands."

"Did he grab you?" Java laughed at Déjà's indignation knowing that she could have decked Jody at will.

"He stopped short of grabbing," Déjà fumed. "All he could do was stare at my breasts and rub against me."

"Um, they're a pair," Java stammered. "I . . . I mean Jody and Amanda are a pair not your, uh . . ."

"I know what you mean, sugar," Déjà laughed.

##

The band began Kat's introduction and the brunette made her way to the stage, touching outstretched hands and speaking to those who were vying for her attention. She stepped onto the stage and leaned into the microphone. Java couldn't pull her eyes away from Kat's beautiful face. She

Two Ways to Die
A Java Jarvis Thriller
by Erin Wade

loved everything about Kat Lace, the way she moved, the
way she smiled, the way she glanced in Java's direction
and the way she sang.

As Kat's set ended Beau and Penny joined Java and
Déjà at their table. Java watched as Lindy walked to Kat
and led the singer back to her table.

"I'll be right back," Java strode to the elevator. She
intended to share Thanksgiving dinner with Kat she didn't
give a damn what others thought.

Kat watched as Java made her way to their table. She
wondered if this was going to be a sparring match or if Java
would be cordial to Lindy.

"Lindy," Java started, "I'm having a private
Thanksgiving dinner for the folks I'm thankful for all year
long. I hope you won't mind if I steal Kat for a little
while."

"I won't be long," Kat patted Lindy's hand and stood.
"It's tradition."

Lindy watched them walk away wondering what had
just happened. She shrugged and ordered another drink. Kat
would return that was all that mattered.

##

"I do believe you are mellowing in your old age," Kat
kissed Java on the cheek as the elevator ascended to the
balcony. "At least more diplomatic."

"Mmhmm," Java grinned. "I really wanted to flip her
chair over backwards and step on her face."

"Oh my, you truly did exercise self-control." Kat
smirked.

CHAPTER 28

The shrill of her cell phone pulled Java from dreams of Kat. She noted it was still dark outside as she reached for the offending device. "Jarvis," she groaned.

"Java," Penny's voice was unusually shrill. "I'm on my way to get you. I'll be there in fifteen minutes."

"What's going on?" Java squinted her eyes trying to get them to focus in the dark. "It's five in the morning."

"I'll tell you when I get there," Penny insisted. "Now, get dressed."

Java pulled a sweater from her closet and a pair of jeans. She pushed a pod into her Keurig and let it start brewing as she pulled on her socks and boots. She combed her long blonde hair into a ponytail and brushed her teeth. The machine delivered a full cup of coffee and cut off as Penny squealed to a stop in Java's circular drive.

For the first time in a long time, Java slipped on her shoulder holster, racked her Glock and holstered it. She hoped she wouldn't need it today but had a strong feeling she would. She pulled on her favorite black leather jacket to cover the firearm.

Penny leaned over the truck's console and shoved open the door on the passenger's side. "Get in."

"And good morning to you too," Java frowned. "What's got you in such a state?"

"Guess!" Penny barked.

"Oh, hell no," Java gasped. "Please don't tell me The Basher struck again last night? That's two days in a row."

"You called it," Penny sipped her coffee. "Crowley, Louisiana, a white woman and three children."

Java checked her watch, "About two-and-a-half hours away. Same driving time as Lafayette."

"Yeah," Penny confirmed. "This is the first time no man is involved. The sheriff said the woman is a local prostitute with illegitimate bi-racial children."

"The killer could leave Orleans at nine-thirty and arrive at the crime scene by midnight," Java figured. "Go on their killing spree then get back to New Orleans around five in the morning. Damn Penny, if I had a suspect, I could pin down their alibi or lack of one. My only suspect is standing trial as we speak while a killer is continuing his rampage."

"If this scene is similar to the others, we may have an innocent man on trial." Penny pointed out.

"No way," Java declared. "I'm certain Budro Latour is guilty. Too much evidence points to him. But I'm equally certain he has a partner."

"I've never had a case like this," Penny seethed. "All the chaos and not a single usable clue. Thirty-two people have been slaughtered since January first. Thirty-two, Java."

"Did you notify the others?" Java asked. "Is the rest of my team meeting us there?"

"No," Penny answered. "I want to go over every inch of this scene myself. We must be missing something."

"Just the two of us?" Java rasped.

"I will leave no stone unturned," Penny raised her voice.

"What's the address?" Java asked an uneasy feeling settled over her.

"It's in the GPS," Penny motioned toward the dashboard. "I want to get there by sunrise."

"Just the two of us?" Java questioned again.

"Yeah," Penny huffed. "You are the only one I trust to be as thorough as I."

Two Ways to Die
A Java Jarvis Thriller
by Erin Wade

Java sipped her coffee and looked out the window at fence posts flying by. *Penny must be driving a hundred*, she thought.

CHAPTER 29

"Your destination is ahead on the right," The GPS announced as Penny slowed the truck. "You have arrived at your destination."

Penny turned off the engine and surveyed the house and its surroundings. It was silhouetted by the gray dawn. The yard was immaculate. The house was neat and freshly painted. It didn't look like home to a prostitute trying to make ends meet with three children.

"Where's the crime scene tape and officers securing the place?" Java quizzed. "There's no blood on the sidewalk. Are you certain we have the correct address?"

"Let's take a look," Penny said reaching for the door handle.

"No," Java grabbed her wrist. "Something's not right. Who called this in? Who did you speak with?"

"The sergeant on duty," Penny mumbled. She pulled out her notebook and flipped the pages. "A Sergeant Renfro. 131 Harper Lane. This is the address he gave me."

As they talked, they watched a light move around inside the house as if someone carrying a flashlight were moving from room to room.

"I don't like this, Penny," Java cautioned. "Hopefully we're at the wrong address. Are you carrying a gun?"

"Yes," Penny nodded. "And I'm very good with it."

"Let's hope you won't have to show me," Java uttered. "Call into the sheriff's office and double check the address."

Two Ways to Die
A Java Jarvis Thriller
by Erin Wade

Java listened as Penny verified the address. "They said they didn't call me," Penny frowned hanging up. "They have no crime scene."

"Someone is setting us up," Java surmised. "You cover the front door. I'll go around back. And Penny, don't hesitate to shoot if you feel in danger. Here, put in this earbud so we can maintain contact."

Penny flipped the switch that would keep the truck's interior lights from coming on when they opened the doors. They slipped out of the truck and ran to the side of the house.

Java watched as Penny made her way to the front door then moved quickly to the back door. She couldn't see the light in the house. Whoever was inside had turned off the flashlight.

"Ready, Penny," Java whispered.

"Yes,"

"On three—" Shots rang out stopping Java's countdown.

"I'm hit," Penny gasped. "He's running around the house."

Java flattened against the house and readied her Glock. The man ran around the corner and stopped in panic when he saw Java.

"FBI," Java yelled, "Drop your gun."

The man raised his gun and fired at Java, missing. One shot from Java's Glock tore off his right shoulder. He fell to the ground scratching at the dirt for his gun. As Java approached, he grabbed the gun with his left hand, pointed it at her and fired. Java's next shot took off the side of the man's face throwing him backwards onto the ground.

Java kicked away the gun and ascertained the man was dead then sprinted to the front door to check on Penny.

Two Ways to Die
A Java Jarvis Thriller
by Erin Wade

Penny was on her feet, leaning against the house. Blood dripped from her elbow. "It's a clean through shot," a twisted grin played on her lips, "but it hurts like hell."

Java called for an ambulance and notified the sheriff's department of the incident.

"There's a first aid kit in the truck," Penny informed her. "You need to stop the bleeding."

Java helped her to the truck, opened the back and located the kit. Penny was right, it was a clean shot. Java stuffed gauze into the holes and secured it with an ace bandage. "That should hold you until a real doctor can stitch it up," she reassured Penny. "I'm going to see if I can find any identification on our shooter."

"Go ahead," Penny agreed. "I'll be fine, and you need to find out as much as you can before the locals get here."

Java entered the house through the front door. The early morning sun was casting shadows everywhere, but it was easy to tell the house was empty. No one lived in it.

She checked all the rooms just in case someone was hiding in them. After clearing the house, she walked to the body in the backyard. The man was lying on his back. There wasn't enough of his face left to identify him.

Java pulled back his jacket with the barrel of her gun. A wallet and cellphone were in his inside pockets. She holstered her gun and pulled on gloves.

She pocketed the man's cellphone and rifled through his wallet. A driver's license identified the man as Raymond Latour.

"Damn," Java hissed. "What the hell is going on?"

She slipped Raymond's wallet back into his jacket pocket. *I'll let the locals figure this one out,* she thought.

##

The sheriff wasted no time declaring Raymond Latour's death a justifiable shooting in self-defense. The local crime lab ran the usual tests on Java's gun then returned it to her.

Penny spent a couple of hours in the emergency room as they attended to her bullet wound. Java called Karen and reported to her. "It looks like Raymond was his father's accomplice. I'm certain Budro will try to get off by swearing Raymond is the only killer."

"No doubt it is a battle we'll have to fight," Karen agreed.

Java paced the hospital waiting room putting off her call to Kat. She knew the brunette would be furious that she had left Orleans without letting her know.

Her phone rang and Kat's face on the screen made Java's heart skip a beat. She took a deep breath and answered the phone.

"I just received a phone call from Beau," Kat's voice wavered. "Are you okay?"

"Yes," Java answered. "I'm fine."

"Then I'm going to kill you when you get back," Kat threatened. "What is wrong with you, Java Jarvis?"

"Kat cut me some slack," Java begged. "I've had the day from hell."

"When will you be home?" Kat asked.

"Hopefully tomorrow morning," Java answered. "The doctor wants to keep Penny overnight and I must drive her van back. The bullet was a clean through shot, but she's going to be in a sling for a few weeks."

"I still don't understand why you didn't notify the rest of the team," Kat cajoled. "That's not like you."

"I thought Penny had notified everyone," Java mumbled. "Can we discuss this when I get back?"

"Of course," Kat's tone softened. "I . . . I just worry about you, baby."

"That's good to know," Java replied. "I think about you all the time."

Two Ways to Die
A Java Jarvis Thriller
by Erin Wade

"Call me as soon as you hit the Orleans city limits tomorrow," Kat sighed. "We'll hold down the fort until you return."

CHAPTER 30

The next morning Java rushed to the hospital anxious to get Penny and return home. Penny was dressed and pacing the floor waiting for the doctor to sign her release forms.

"You don't act like someone who's been used for target practice," Java grinned.

"If you mean I'm rearing to go," Penny snapped. "You've got that right. Where's that doctor?"

"Right here, Ms. Short," the doctor entered the room. "I've signed the release forms. You're free to go."

"But you must ride to your vehicle in this chair," a nurse pushed a wheelchair toward Penny.

"I don't think so," Penny snorted.

"Just do it Penny," Java advised. "We'll get out of here quicker."

Penny plopped down into the chair and glared at her blonde friend.

Loud talking in the hallway caused everyone to look toward the door as the Crowley Sheriff and a couple of deputies entered the room.

"Dr. Short," the sheriff addressed Penny, "You need to come with us."

"Are you arresting her?" Java asked stepping between Penny and the sheriff.

"Lord no," the sheriff blurted. "We've found the crime scene you were looking for last night. It's one block down from the address you had."

"Holy . . ." Penny bit her lip. "Have you secured it? Who found it? Java let's get moving!"

Two Ways to Die
A Java Jarvis Thriller
by Erin Wade

Penny ignored the doctor and nurse with the wheelchair as she led the entourage from the room.

"Be sure she takes these," the nurse pressed a couple of prescription containers into Java's hand. "The instructions are on the bottles."

##

Java pulled the van to the curb in front of a house that was a cookie cutter copy of the one they had entered the night before.

Blood covered the sidewalk and was smeared down the front door. Crime scene tape encircled the perimeter of the yard. The sheriff and his deputies joined Penny and Java as they stepped from the coroner's van.

"When we saw the bloody sidewalk and door, we immediately threw up the crime scene tape," the sheriff explained proudly. "No one has entered the house. We took every precaution to preserve the scene for you."

"I appreciate that," Penny smiled weakly.

"I'll call in our team," Java pulled her phone from her pocket.

"We can work it ourselves," Penny frowned handing Java the requisite blue shoe covers. "It will take them two to three hours to get here. Let's go room by room. You video and I'll take photos. Let's look at everything we see."

Java nodded and mentally prepared herself for the odor they would encounter when she opened the door. They entered the living room that was undisturbed. It was clean and neat. The kitchen adjoined the living room on the left and two doors centered on the living room wall led to the rest of the house.

"I'll take door number three," Penny mimicked a gameshow contestant.

Java filmed the living room and kitchen area then videoed Penny as she opened the door leading into a long hallway. Penny froze at the sight in front of her, bowed her head then stepped aside so Java could film the blood bath in the hall.

"Oh my God!" Java croaked.

"Yes, but look at the perfect footprints," Penny gushed, "and surely we can pull some decent prints from the writing on the wall."

Java slowly panned down each wall and the hall coming to rest on the wall with the bloody writing.

"What does it say?" Penny asked.

"It's a Bible verse," Java exhaled and began to read. "Hosea 2:5: For their mother has played the whore; she who conceived them has acted shamefully. . ."

"Dear God," Penny groaned. "Please don't let this be a sanctimonious Bible thumper."

"It's the first motive we've found for all this carnage," Java snorted trying to get the stench of blood out of her nose.

"Java, if I had a dollar for every crime committed in the name of religion, I'd be a wealthy woman," Penny declared. "Religious fanatics are damn hard to catch because they are so certain they are doing God's will they don't act like the common criminal."

"Chris may be right," Java worried, "this may have something to do with the Christ's Sanctity Church."

Penny slid her arm from the sling and gasped at the pain as she grasped her camera with both hands.

"Give me that," Java commanded. "You record your findings on audio, and I'll take the photos and videos."

Penny began recording her impressions of the hall and the handwriting on the wall. Java took photos and measurements on the footprints.

"I'm ready to view the bodies now," Penny shivered as she opened the door covered in the most blood.

Java videoed her every move. "Four bodies," Penny noted. "One Caucasian woman and three black children."

Two Ways to Die
A Java Jarvis Thriller
by Erin Wade

Each body was stretched across the bed and placed side by side. Their arms were crossed across the usual voodoo doll placed on their chest and their skulls were crushed.

"Same MO as all the other murders, except for the bible verse," Penny noted.

Java carefully videoed each body then stepped back so Penny could go to work while Java videoed.

"Time of death between midnight and two this morning," Penny rattled off the specifics required of every evidentiary investigation. "Victims defaced beyond recognition. I'll have to verify identity with fingerprints and DNA. The most damage is inflicted on the adult female. The killer has almost pulverized her head."

Java zoomed in on each detail as Penny recorded her descriptions and collected fluid samples.

"I need a break," Java scowled after three hours of videoing. "I need to call the team and let them know we're still here."

"Go on," Penny smiled. "Call Kat. She'll be worried about you."

##

Java followed Penny from the house and wished she had some habit like smoking to take her mind off the scene behind her. *Yeah, I'd light up, take a drag then blow the smoke into the air, and for two seconds I'd forget about what we're dealing with,* she thought. Instead she turned to her other addiction and dialed Kat's number.

"Java, thank God," Kat sighed. "Where are you?"

"Still in Crowley," Java said. "We're working a crime scene. We were at the wrong address last night. Today we're in nightmare land."

"Why didn't you call me?" Kat demanded.

"Penny wanted to jump right on it. She insisted that we do it ourselves and not call in the team." Java explained.

"And honestly this has been the most thorough crime scene investigation I've been involved in. Penny's a slave driver.

"We've completed our examination of the bodies and will dismantle the sinks, showers and commodes to see if we can find any DNA from the killer."

"All hell has broken loose here," Kat advised her. "Apparently the Crowley sheriff felt compelled to report the death of Raymond Latour on the local news station and Budro's attorney is calling for a hiatus in the trial saying that Raymond, not Budro, is The Basher."

"I expected that," Java groaned.

"Java!"

"Humm?"

"Please hurry home," Kat pleaded. "I . . . I miss you."

"I miss you too, honey." Java murmured.

##

It was almost sundown when Java closed and locked the back doors of the van. Her growling stomach reminded her she hadn't eaten all day. *Penny must be dying*, she thought as her hand closed around the prescription bottles in her jacket pocket.

"First things first," Java said fastening her seatbelt. "We're going to find a place to get a good meal and you're going to take the meds the doctor prescribed for you."

"We're close to Fezzo's Seafood and Steakhouse," Penny groaned. "Is that okay with you?"

"Right now, I could eat anything," Java grumbled shifting the van into drive. "I can't believe we didn't stop long enough to feed you and give you your meds."

"That's as close to a decent meal as we'll get," Penny gestured toward a flat roofed, rambling building featuring a huge sign trumpeting, "FEZZO'S." A square, lighted marque sign hawked the "Trucker's Special of the Day."

They parked the van and Java steadied Penny as they entered the restaurant. Both ordered coffee and Java pushed

148

the large basket of hushpuppies toward Penny. "Eat three or four of these," she instructed. "It says not to take the meds on an empty stomach."

"I hope one of them is for pain," Penny groaned.

"Yeah, it is," Java nodded shaking two of the pain pills into her hand along with an antibiotic and handing them to Penny.

Penny's pale, haggard face reflected the pain she was beginning to experience since the adrenaline rush of the murder scene had drained away.

Java waited until the pills started to take affect then broached the subject that had been driving her crazy since yesterday.

"Penny what's going on?" Java asked. "Raymond Latour didn't have a speck of blood on him last night. He couldn't possible butcher four people and be so spotless."

"I know," Penny sighed. "This case has me chasing my own tail. Nothing about it makes sense."

They finished their meal in silence and ordered coffee to go.

Java settled Penny into the passenger's seat and fastened her seatbelt. The ME was asleep by the time Java fastened her own seatbelt.

Java called Kat to let her know when they'd arrive in New Orleans. "I need to take Penny home with me tonight," she informed the brunette. "She's in no shape to be alone. She really overdid it today."

Kat moaned into the phone. "I was hoping . . ."

"I know, baby," Java grimaced. "So was I."

Java couldn't get her mind off the recent events. The death of Raymond Latour haunted her. She was surprised that Penny hadn't questioned the circumstances surrounding the man's demise.

The glow from The Big Easy lit up the night miles before Java reached New Orleans. She vaguely recalled

Two Ways to Die
A Java Jarvis Thriller
by Erin Wade

how the town had gotten its nickname. Some gossip columnist in the sixties had compared New York with its frantic pace and bustling atmosphere to New Orleans's easy going, laid back tempo writing that if New York was The Big Apple then New Orleans had to be The Big Easy. The moniker had been embraced by the citizens of Orleans and became the city's descriptive name.

Java pulled the ME's van under her house, rolled down her window and listened to the waves of Lake Pontchartrain wash against the shore.

Her home was an eighteen-hundred-square feet stilt house. Raised on pilings over the water, the front of the house hung over the lot while the back of the home with its wrap-around veranda jutted out over the waters of the lake. Java loved her home. Situated on an acre, it was private and peaceful.

She considered the problem of getting Penny up the stairs then decided the doctor could walk. *She's a tiny little thing*, Java thought. *If nothing else, I'll carry her up.*

She rolled up the van window, walked around to the passenger's side of the vehicle, and opened the door. Penny stirred and looked around confused about her surroundings.

"It's best you stay at my place tonight," Java insisted. "You're in no condition to stay alone."

Penny didn't argue. She didn't have the strength. All she wanted to do was undress and crawl into bed.

Leaning heavily on Java, Penny managed to climb the stairs to the house. Java led her to the guest bedroom pointing out the bathroom and fresh linens.

"I'll be right outside," Java said. "Just call if you need help and I'll come running."

Java walked to the refrigerator and pulled out a cold beer. She twisted the cap off the bottle of Shiner Bock and took a long drink of the cool liquid. She walked to the expansive windows overlooking the lake and realized she hadn't thought about the murder case since her arrival home.

My happy place, she thought. *The only thing missing is Kat.*

The guestroom door opened. "I'm going to bed now," Penny informed her as Java pulled a bottle of water from the fridge and the prescription bottles from her pocket.

"You must take another round of these," Java advised as she shook the pills from the bottles, handed them to Penny and held out the water.

Penny downed the pain pills and antibiotics then stumbled back into the guestroom. Java followed with her water. "I'll leave this on the night table in case you get thirsty," she smiled.

Penny climbed into bed and mumbled, "Good night."

Java silently closed the door to Penny's room, retrieved her Shiner from the kitchen table and headed for the dock.

Java pulled her jacket tighter around her as she inhaled the crisp cool November air. Fish arched out of the water then splashed back into the river. She sat down on the edge of the dock dangling her feet over the water. Her thoughts went to Kat.

She loved working for the FBI but had been giving serious thought to leaving the agency. The rule forbidding affairs between coworkers was constantly niggling in the back of her mind. She knew she and Kat would be fired if anyone ever found out they were together.

Java sensed it before she felt it. The scent wafted to her on a gentle breeze. She tensed in anticipation of the touch that always accompanied the fragrance. A soft hand rested on her shoulder. "It's me," Kat said softly.

"I know," Java reached for her hand and pulled Kat to sit down beside her.

Two Ways to Die
A Java Jarvis Thriller
by Erin Wade

Kat dangled her long legs over the water and leaned against Java's shoulder. "Did you sense me or smell my perfume?" she giggled taking a drink of Java's Shiner.

"Both," Java put her arm around the brunette and pulled her into her side. "I was hoping you'd come. Penny's dead to the world."

"Then why are we wasting time sitting on this dock?" Kat turned up her face for a kiss. "I'd much rather be in your bed."

CHAPTER 31

A slit of sunlight fell across Java's closed eyes as she reached for the woman who had filled her night with fireworks, but Kat was gone. *Maybe I dreamed it*, Java thought.

The sounds from the kitchen and the smell of coffee made her smile. Kat was cooking breakfast. Java hurriedly showered and dressed in jeans and a Henley. Again, she thought about leaving the FBI. She wanted to wake up next to Kat every morning for the rest of her life. She decided she'd broach the subject with Kat when this case was over.

Penny was sitting at the kitchen island drinking coffee when Java entered. Kat poured a cup of the dark liquid into an oversized cup and placed it on the counter. Java fought the urge to pull Kat into her arms and kiss her soundly. Instead she picked up the cup and grinned at the brunette over the rim of the cup as she inhaled the coffee.

"Penny, did you take your meds this morning?" Java asked.

"As soon as I eat something," Penny shifted on the stool and moaned. "Believe me, I'm ready for a pain pill."

Java took a gulp of her coffee then moved to the counter to put bread into the toaster as Kat began plating their eggs and bacon.

##

"I'll clean up the kitchen," Java said, "while you two get ready to face the day."

Suddenly the phones of the three women started ringing.

"Damn," Penny cursed. "Please don't let this be what I think it is."

Java answered her phone. "Java put me on speaker," Beau ordered. "Are you with Penny and Kat?"

"Yes," Java replied as she pushed the button to allow everyone to hear Beau's voice.

"We've got another bashing," Beau informed them. "Lake Charles. Five bodies were found around nine this morning. I'm on my way with Chris and Barbie. We'll meet you there."

"Beau, that's three massacres in three days," Java gasped. "This guy is on a feeding frenzy. We've got to stop him."

"I'm very aware of that, Java," Beau barked. "I've had my butt chewed on by so many people this morning I feel like a free buffet at Mardi Gras. I'm sure you'll receive a call from Karen as soon as I release your line."

Penny moved stiffly as she headed for the guest room.

"Penny that's a three-hour trip," Java said handing Penny her meds. "Are you sure you can make it?"

"You'd have to knock me out to leave me behind," Penny declared.

##

Kat piled pillows into the back seat of the van making Penny as comfortable as possible then covered her with a light blanket.

"You should get as much rest as you can," Kat advised. "Sooner or later that gunshot wound is going to stop you."

Penny was sleeping by the time they pulled onto the interstate. Kat took the opportunity to grill Java.

"Tell me about the last two days?" Kat said. "All hell broke loose here. Karen called us in and read us the riot act for our failure to catch The Basher.

Two Ways to Die
A Java Jarvis Thriller
by Erin Wade

"Your shooting Raymond Latour sent Budro's attorney into a media storm. He's been on every news show imaginable declaring Budro's innocence. He's saying Penny manipulated the DNA evidence to implicate Budro when all along it was his son with similar DNA."

"Yeah, similar being the key word," Java scowled. "He knows Penny didn't screw up."

"It's a good thing she had an independent lab run tests on Budro's clothes," Kat noted.

"Penny's a sharp cookie," Java added. "She knew this would turn into a crap shoot, so she covered her butt and ours too."

Kat was studying a map on her iPad.

"Java don't you think it unusual that we found no tire tracks at any of the murder scenes?" Kat asked. "There is a geographical pattern to the killings. All the murders have occurred along the Union Pacific Railroad Line and have been perpetrated on victims within walking distance of the railroad stations. I know this sounds crazy, but could our killer be riding the train from New Orleans to the crime scene?"

"It's possible," Java agreed, "but how do they conceal the ax. The overall weapon is about thirty inches long. More importantly, the killer would be drenched in blood. You know the blood splatter from one person would cover the killer. Four or five victims would turn his clothes scarlet."

"What if they were naked and wore only coveralls?" Kat persisted. "We've found evidence that the killer showers after each kill. What if they wear something that covers them from head to toe, stripped that off and bagged it in a trash bag then showered and put on clean clothes. That is doable. They could dispose of the trash bag anywhere along the way back to the train station."

155

Two Ways to Die
A Java Jarvis Thriller
by Erin Wade

"You are on to something," Java enthused. "That would explain why no one has seen any vehicles at the crime scenes. We have assumed the killer is driving a car. Call the Lake Charles police and see if they will search all the dumpsters at the railroad station and anything between the station and the crime scene"

"This should make me popular," Kat huffed dialing the phone number of the sergeant they had spoken with earlier.

Java listened as Kat's sultry voice purred into the phone. "Yes, I appreciate that you will meet us at the crime scene," she concluded her call.

"Sergeant Adams will personally manage the search team," Kat reported.

"Um-hum and wants to meet you at the crime scene, right?" Java added.

Kat shrugged.

"Do you have any idea how tired I get of others hitting on my woman?" Java asked.

"Who's your woman?" Kat teased.

"You!" Java growled.

"Yes, I am," Kat giggled, "and you have nothing to worry about." She caught Java's hand and pulled in onto her lap. "I love you Java Jarvis," she whispered.

CHAPTER 32

Penny roused as Java slowed the van in front of the house surrounded by yellow crime scene tape. She groaned as she sat up and tried to move her arm

"Good, you're awake," Java noted handing Penny a bottle of water. "Take your meds right now or you'll forget them."

Penny swallowed the pills and listened as Kat related their theory that the killer was a train rider.

"Could be," Penny agreed. "It certainly explains why all the massacres are within walking distance of the train stations. Perhaps we can forecast where he'll strike next."

"Kat has the Lake Charles police searching every dumpster between the crime scene and the train station," Java informed her. "If we can find the clothes he wore, we can pull DNA from inside them."

"Let's pray they find them" Penny nodded. "I'm not sure I can work many more of these macabre scenes."

"I'm with you, Pen," Kat chimed in. "I'm beginning to have nightmares about the slaughter."

"Is that what you were screaming about last night?" The gleam in Penny's eyes told Kat the ME hadn't been as sound asleep as Java had promised.

Java cleared her throat. "You go ahead Penny. We'll unload the equipment."

"You said she was knocked out with pain killers," Kat elbowed Java's side.

"I didn't say she was dead," Java chuckled. "You do tend to get loud."

"Umm," Kat shrugged.

Two Ways to Die
A Java Jarvis Thriller
by Erin Wade

##

The three joined Beau, Barbie and Chris in the carport of the house. "It looks like the killer broke in through this." Chris gestured toward the broken glass of the back door.

"Java, another thing all these murders have in common," Kat pointed out. "The victims had no dog or anything to provide warning of an intruder."

"So, the killer did some research to make certain his presence wouldn't be announced until he'd struck his deadly blow."

Penny nodded. "From what we've gathered at all the scenes, I'd say the male was murdered first then quickly followed by the woman and children. The killer was very strong. The man was murdered with one blow. I suspect the woman was too, but he continued to pulverize her face after killing the children. I found DNA from all the victims in the remains of the mother's skull."

Kat shivered. "Such evil," she mumbled.

They worked their way through the house room by room, collecting hair, threads, buttons, dirt clods, anything that wasn't nailed down went into an evidence bag.

The three children shared one bedroom with two twin-sized beds. It was easy to track the path of the killer. He almost decapitated the boy closest to the door, then the girl in the bed next to his and finally the toddler in a baby bed.

They worked the room collecting blood samples, brain matter, hair matted with blood and saliva in hopes of lucking onto the killer's DNA.

They followed The Basher's bloody footprints down the hall and into the master bedroom where all five bodies were lined up across the bed beginning with the man then from the tallest to the shortest.

Everyone glanced away from the carnage giving their brain a chance to protect them from the horror of the sight before them. The stench of blood filled their nostrils as they moved into the room and methodically began filming and photographing the scene.

"Be sure you get good clear photos and film footage of that Bible verse," Penny nodded toward a wall that was almost completely covered in the bloody message. "The more I work this case the more confusing it becomes. Is it racially motivated or religiously driven?"

Kat read the bible verse out loud. "Deuteronomy 7:1-26 . . . You shall not intermarry with them, giving your daughters to their sons or taking their daughters for your sons, for they would turn away your sons from following me, to serve other gods. . .

"I'm guessing both," Kat shook her head. "A religious fanatic using the Bible as an excuse to kill those they find offensive."

It was late in the afternoon when Penny's team bagged the last body and rolled it to the van. Java looked away from the hollow stare in the eyes of her team members.

Beau joined them closing his note pad. "Thoughts, anyone?"

"I think we need to get Penny home and in bed," Java grimaced. "Her assistant changed her bandage and gave her pain killers, but she's pretty exhausted. This is her second crime scene in two days. Both have been brutal."

"Penny's assistant is going to drive the van to the morgue and take care of unloading so Penny can ride with us," Beau informed them. "Let's all ride in my Suburban. We can kick around theories on the way home."

Kat pulled the pillows from Penny's van and made the woman comfortable in the front seat of Beau's SUV.

Beau turned on the voice amplification system in his vehicle as he pulled away from the crime scene. "Can you

159

hear us?" He asked Chris and Barbie who were sitting in the far back seat.

"Clear as a bell," Barbie chirped. "Great system, Beau."

Kat shared her suspicion that the killer was using the railroad to reach his victims and added that he had to observe his prey in advance to ascertain there were no animals to raise an alarm.

"This isn't a spur of the moment thing," Penny surmised, "like we first thought. It is carefully planned and scoped out for the kill."

"He is killing in a blood-lust frenzy," Java added. "Only he has planned it. He planned to butcher three families in three days."

"He's toying with us," Beau growled.

"I think so," Java agreed.

"What about Budro?" Barbie asked. "Do you still believe he committed the first murders?"

"Yes, I do," Java barked. "We have too much incriminating evidence against him."

"The latest bloodbath wasn't Budro's son Raymond," Beau pointed out. "It happened after you shot him."

"Yeah," Java huffed. "I don't know how he's connected or why he shot Penny. We weren't threatening him. He wasn't even at a crime scene."

"But he was in the vicinity for some reason," Penny added. "It was no coincidence that he was on the same street as the murders."

"Going on the assumption that Raymond was somehow involved in his father's dirty work," Chris chimed in, "there must have been three of them."

"The footprints only showed one," Penny insisted.

"Obviously our killer or killers are smarter than we give them credit for," Kat frowned. "It wouldn't take a phi beta kapa to have three or four people wearing the same size shoe just to throw us off the multi-killer theory."

"They have always left many shoe prints," Penny agreed. "Too many for someone trying to get away with murder. I'll see if Raymond's shoes match Budro's."

##

They helped Penny into her home and waited until she was safely in bed then headed for the club where the women's cars were parked.

Java scowled when she saw Jody Schooley's Corvette parked in the lot behind the supper club. "What's he doing here?" She growled.

"Probably showing off his latest girl," Barbie offered. "He brings her in and parades her around the place, buys her a drink, dances with her then walks out with her fawning over him."

"He is a handsome fellow," Kat commented. "Too bad he's a pimp."

"Am I the only one that's hungry?" Barbie exclaimed.

"I could eat something," Kat said. "None of us have eaten all day."

"I don't have much of an appetite," Java scowled, "but a cup of coffee would hit the spot."

CHAPTER 33

The next morning Java left Kat sleeping and drove to the office before sunup. She started her coffee, flipped on her computer and the television.

The Basher case was now making the national news headlines. Java cringed as she listened to the morning news hawks discuss the Lake Charles murders. The banner beneath the newscaster read "Police clueless."

Java was furious, but knew the newscaster was right. They were clueless. She searched her mind for any thing they had missed. *I'm grasping at straws*, she thought as she tried to find a trail to follow, a suspect they hadn't thoroughly vetted or a motive they'd missed. She recalled Déjà's veiled hint that the killings weren't original, but someone copying other murderers.

"Serial killers," Java mumbled out loud as she searched the internet for Louisiana serial killers. "Oh my God," she gasped as she pulled up an old news article titled *Mulatto Ax Murders 1911-1912.*

The ax murders had happened over a hundred years ago, but they followed the same MO as The Basher's bloody rampage. She printed out the article and made a chronological list of the towns the killer had targeted a hundred years ago. The Basher's murders followed the same pattern.

Java dialed Beau's phone. "Beau here," the deep baritone sang across the line.

"Beau, I'm emailing you a link right now," Java said as she pushed the button sending the *Mulatto Ax Murders* article to him. "I'll hold on while you read it."

Two Ways to Die
A Java Jarvis Thriller
by Erin Wade

"Jesus," Beau whistled. "How'd you figure this out?"

"Déjà put me on to it," Java answered. "If The Basher is using this as his game plan, we should be able to anticipate his next move. I'll run this by my team," Java said. "You see what your people think."

Java disconnected the call pleased with her morning's work. Now to run her theory by Chris, Barbie and Kat. If anyone could punch holes in it, they could.

When Java heard voices in the restaurant, she leaned over the balcony to see who was in so early. To her surprise the other members of her team were present.

"I have coffee," she called to them. "Come up and let's talk."

The three popped out of the elevator in less than sixty seconds. "What are you doing here so early," Kat scowled. She didn't share her displeasure at waking in an empty bed.

"This case is driving me crazy," Java said as the others poured their coffee.

A text message from Beau popped in. "I'm at the back door. Let me in."

"Barbie, Beau is at the back door, please let him in," Java instructed.

They waited for Beau to fix his coffee then gathered around a dining table.

"In less than a year The Basher has mutilated seven families and murdered thirty-one people," Java sipped her coffee. "It's almost Christmas and we're no closer to catching him than we were in January."

"Do we have a paper map?" Kat asked. "One we can spread out on the table."

"I have one in my office," Java pushed her chair back and strode to her office returning with a map of the United States.

They spread it on the table and Kat began to trace the path of destruction on the map. "The first was in Crowley.

Two Ways to Die
A Java Jarvis Thriller
by Erin Wade

The second was Rayne, then Lafayette and San Antonio. The fifth slaughter was back to Lafayette then Crowley again and Lake Charles was number seven and our last."

She shook her head. "I was hoping there'd be some rhyme or reason to his killings, but I don't see one."

"He killed a second time in Lafayette," Chris noted. "Then hit Crowley the next day and Lake Charles last. I'm thinking he was familiar with Lafayette and Crowley and just threw in Lake Charles because it was in the vicinity.

"If we could make an educated guess at where he will strike next, maybe we could be waiting for him?

"I'd hate to guess," Java shook her head. "There's no pattern. Maybe he's killed enough in Louisiana and will move toward Texas towns along the line. We could stake out all the train stations and watch for anything out of the ordinary."

"My men checked with the railroad line," Beau informed them, "and no one purchased tickets to the same place twice in the past eleven months."

"Train tickets can be used by anyone," Kat pointed out. "Even though certain tickets will have the name of the traveler or person who booked the tickets printed on them anyone can use them."

"Yes," Beau agreed. "That's what makes it impossible to track down anyone purchasing tickets to our crime scenes."

"He seems to be revisiting the sites of his former crimes," Kat ran her finger along the map. "Maybe we should concentrate on Rayne, Lake Charles and San Antonio."

Beau studied the map. "I think you may be on to something," he mused. "We need to pinpoint one station. We don't have enough manpower to cover every station along the line. Has Java shared her discovery with you?"

Two Ways to Die
A Java Jarvis Thriller
by Erin Wade

All eyes turned toward the blonde as she explained her discovery about the hundred-year old serial killer case.

"What made you think of that?" Kat inquired. "That's brilliant."

"Not really," Java blushed. "It was Déjà vu's idea."

"Was she here this morning?" Kat puffed.

"No, no!" Java defended. "It was something she mentioned to me a while back. I had no idea what she was talking about and didn't follow up on it. I should have. Our killer is following in the tracks of the killer from a century ago."

"So, the next crime should be committed in San Antonio," Beau added.

"If he continues to emulate the original ax murderer," Java nodded.

"We'll visit the priest that leads the Christ's Sanctity Church," Java said. "Since this has taken a religious turn maybe he can shed some light on it."

"Take Déjà vu with you," Beau advised. "He might be more cooperative with her. You know he's pretty radical."

Java nodded as Kat scowled.

"I'll go with you," Kat volunteered.

"Works for me," Java took Kat's elbow. And steered her toward the elevator as the others followed.

Kat elbowed Java hard in the ribs and walked onto the elevator as Java gasped for breath. "I don't need you holding my elbow," she snarled at the blonde. "You may drive me to our destination, but you may not touch me."

Java bent over trying to catch her breath as the others snickered.

##

Java and Kat sat in the car watching Beau leave the parking lot. "I've wanted to do this from the moment you walked in this morning," Java whispered as she leaned over and kissed Kat.

165

Two Ways to Die
A Java Jarvis Thriller
by Erin Wade

Kat pushed her away and slapped her hard snapping Java's head back. Blood oozed from Java's cut lip. "I take it we have watcher's," Java mumbled, wiping the back of her hand across her injured mouth.

Kat motioned to the driver's side window where Barbie was peering into the car. Java rolled down the window.

"Java, I just wanted to tell you I'll close tonight if you want to leave early," Barbie smirked.

"Thanks Barbie," Java dabbed at her lip with a napkin. "I may take you up on that."

CHAPTER 34

Kat wrapped her arms around Java's waist and pulled the blonde on top of her. "Ouch, I think you cracked my ribs today," Java whined. "That really hurts."

"I could move from your arms and sleep on my side of the bed, as far away from you as possible."

"Hum," Java hummed. "A little hurt sleeping with you in my arms or sleeping without touching you? You know me, I like a little hurt."

"I thought so," Kat giggled as she tightened her arms around Java.

"God, Kat, you're killing me."

"Let me do something that will take your mind off the pain," Kat purred.

"What do you want from me, Kat?" Java looked into dark eyes that ruled her world.

"Everything you've got to give," Kat mumbled just before she bit Java's lip. She sucked on Java's full lower lip. "I love the taste of copper."

Java pulled back from her and let a drop of blood fall from her lip to Kat's. "Sometimes I think you enjoy hurting me," she mumbled.

"You know I do," Kat kissed her hard, sucking the soul from her. "Because I know how much you like it. You drive me wild. You're the other half of my soul, Java."

"I've thought about this all day," Java breathed in Kat's ear. She slid her hand up to caress Kat's breast.

"Do you know what I'm going to do to you?" she whispered as both her hands paid homage to Kat's ample breasts.

Two Ways to Die
A Java Jarvis Thriller
by Erin Wade

"Surprise me," Kat challenged.

Java rolled Kat onto her side and wrapped around her back. She pulled Kat's back against her and the brunette moaned loudly as Java rubbed her bare breasts against Kat's back. "You like this, hum?" Java cooed.

"You know I do." Kat gasped. "I love the feel of you touching me anywhere. I want you all over me."

Java splayed her hands down Kat's torso to her abdomen stopping just above the area that was her intended target. She buried her face in soft fragrant hair and nibbled at Kat's shoulder. She hoped she was arousing Kat because she was driving herself insane.

"Oh God, Java," Kat cried out. "Do something, anything. You're killing me."

Java pushed Kat into the bed face down and slipped between her legs. Supporting herself so she was barely touching Kat she slowly rubbed her breasts from Kat's soft buttocks up her silky back until her body covered the brunette's. She kissed and nipped Kat's neck as she let her weight press Kat into the mattress.

"Please, Java, don't make me beg."

Java trailed long fingers down Kat's side and slipped her hand between Kat's legs. "Yesss," Kat hissed. "A thousand times yes!"

##

Much later they lay wrapped in each other's arms. "That was incredible," Kat gasped for air. "After all these years you still turn me into a simpering, begging wench."

"And I'm still your slave," Java laughed softly. "You are bewitching and addictive. I still can't get enough of you."

"Good," Kat snuggled in closer. "Because I'm not through with you yet." She rolled Java onto her back. "Prepare to beg, darling."

Two Ways to Die
A Java Jarvis Thriller
by Erin Wade

"I'll get into the club around four," Kat handed Java a cup of coffee and sat down on the bed beside her. "I want to run through a couple of new songs with the band."

"Umm, I wish I could stay with you until then," Java looked longingly at the brunette, "but I need to be there before the others to make sure things get off to a smooth start."

"I know, baby." Kat cooed. "It's best we arrive at different times anyway. If the agency knew we were involved with one another, they wouldn't let us work together and we'd probably be fired. I'm surprised they assign me with you as often as they do."

"I always request you," Java grinned. "I tell them you're hard as hell to work with, but the best agent I've ever met. They're all about results so they don't care. The way you treat me convinces them you hate me."

"Oh, but they don't know how phenomenal the makeup sex is," Kat laughed.

CHAPTER 35

Java carried her coffee cup into her office and turned on the morning news. Beau was bearing the brunt of the public's outrage over The Basher's three-day butchering spree.

She wished her team didn't have to remain undercover. Poor Beau needed some backup and wasn't getting any from his superiors.

"We've heard the church is involved in this," one of the news reporters screamed as she shoved her microphone in front of Beau's face.

Beau's, "No comment." Enraged her.

"The public has a right to know," the reporter persisted. "Is this some religions heretic killing African Americans and mixed-race people?" She demanded.

Great, Java thought, *just what we need, inciting panic in the black community.*

"Is it true that voodoo dolls are left on each body?" The reporter yelled.

Beau ignored her question and Java wondered who had leaked that information to the reporter.

"Why aren't you calling in the FBI on this case? Is it because the victims are black or of mixed race?" The reporter demanded. "They're not important enough to engage the services of the FBI?"

Java grimaced sympathizing with Beau as he clenched his teeth. He backed away from the reporters and entered the police station.

The reporter turned to face her news camera with the police station in the background. "African Americans and mixed-race people are arming themselves," she spewed. "Realizing they can't count on the police to protect them; they're hiring guards to guard their houses and neighborhoods."

Barbie entered with two cups of coffee. "I thought you might be ready for a fresh cup," she smiled at Java.

"Thanks Barbie. You thought right." Java grinned.

"The Basher is all over the news this morning," Barbie noted. "I'm glad Beau's fielding their questions. I'd hate to be in his shoes."

"If the news media continues to fuel the flames everyone with an ounce of African blood will be armed and dangerous." Java fretted. "All we need is some vigilante group hunting The Basher and shooting at each other."

Java's phone rang and Director Karen Pierce's face appeared on the screen. "Java," she answered putting the call on the speaker so Barbie could hear.

"Java, I want you and your entire team in the headquarters briefing room in an hour. I'll call Beau. We've got to get ahead of this killer. He's making law enforcement the laughingstock of Louisiana."

"We'll be there," Java assured her raising her eyebrows at Barbie.

"I'll inform everyone," Barbie headed for the doorway. "Oh, um Kat's the only one not here."

"I'll call her and have her meet us there," Java said, pushing the button on her phone. "I'll meet you in the parking lot. We can ride to headquarters together."

##

Kat and Beau's cars were already parked behind the FBI field office when the rest of the team arrived. Penny pulled up behind them. They were silent as they filed into the meeting room.

Two Ways to Die
A Java Jarvis Thriller
by Erin Wade

"Good, you're all here," Karen breezed into the room and sat down at the end of the oval table hosting her task force. "Talk to me Java," Karen barked.

Java took a deep breath and exhaled slowly. "Karen, I wish I had something for you. Beau's department has interrogated every criminal who used an ax but there are no solid suspects."

"I've handled so many blood samples, I'm beginning to feel like a vampire," Penny added, "and I've found nothing but the blood of our victims. I can say for certain our killer is left-handed."

"Well that narrows our search down to eight percent of the population. What about you Kat?" Karen demanded. "Profile."

Kat thought for a moment then shared her thoughts. "He's strong. He easily lifts a grown man onto a bed. He's smart. He never leaves a shred of evidence. He has no remorse. He kills, showers and leaves the house with no blood on him.

"He is beginning to taunt us with his Bible verses, so he believes he's smarter than anyone in law enforcement."

"And so far, he's been correct," Barbie blurted.

Kat glared at Barbie and continued. "The more he kills, the more he wants to kill. He loves killing. He uses his abhorrence of mixed race as a justification for the carnage.

"We believe his mode of transportation to the murder scenes is the railroad. All the murders have occurred within two miles of the train stations.

"He's a narcissist who believes he is doing God's work and that God will protect him. We need to be looking for someone who is uber religious."

"So, who fits your profile?" Karen asked.

"No one we've encountered," Kat responded.

"You killed Raymond Latour," Karen swung her gaze toward Java. "How did that go down?"

Two Ways to Die
A Java Jarvis Thriller
by Erin Wade

"I believe Raymond intended to kill Penny," Java reasoned. "He didn't count on me being there. He called Penny in the early hours of the morning pretending to be with the Crowley Police Department. He encouraged her to hurry so she would get to the crime scene before looky-loos discovered it.

"The look of disbelief on his face when he turned the corner and saw me was almost laughable. He hesitated only seconds before firing at me. I think he believed he could kill Penny and then Beau and the authorities would drop the manhunt. I believe he is the perpetrator of the crimes that have been committed while his father has been in jail."

"But there was another massacre after you killed him." Karen noted.

"I know," Java huffed. "Which means we have at least three killers involved."

Java moved to the electronic white board. There was no teasing or cajoling of one another as the agents silently watched their leader write on the board.

"I've done this a dozen times," she said, "but let's list anyone we might remotely consider a suspect."

"That spikey-haired preacher at Sanctity Church," Barbie suggested, "Driscol Ames."

"Budro's buddies," Chris offered. "Lonnie and Albert."

"Déjà vu LaBlanc," Kat hissed.

"Déjà?" Java gasped. "Why would you suspect Déjà? She's a woman and the best CI we have on the streets."

"A six-foot-tall woman," Kat shrugged. "She's certainly capable of lifting a grown man. She has voodoo dolls and the buttons on the dolls at the murder scene came from her place. Just because she's your criminal informant doesn't mean she's not a criminal."

"Kally also fits that description," Java barked.

Two Ways to Die
A Java Jarvis Thriller
by Erin Wade

"Kally's crippled," Kat pointed out. "Déjà vu is able bodied. I'm putting my money on the witch doctor."

"No!" Java argued. "No way Déjà is a killer and every tourist trap in Orleans carries that same doll and the buttons. We all know they're made in China."

"You're just swayed by her big ti—"

"Kat's right," Karen interrupted. "Déjà vu would be physically able to commit the crimes."

"I think we should put Lindy Rochelle on our list," Java countered.

"Lindy!" Kat snorted. "She's a pussycat. She wouldn't hurt a fly."

"She has the physique to commit the crimes," Java insisted. "She's as butch as they come, stout, and muscled up and we should add your admirer Jody Schooley."

"Humph," Kat huffed. "Schooley is certainly a suspect on my list."

"Ladies," Karen snapped. "Is this a pissing contest? If so, you need to take it outside."

Java shrugged and wrote the three names on the list."

"Pierre and Tiny Roche are up to something," Chris added.

"The Roach Brothers," Java smirked. "They're up to no good for sure, but slaughter seems a little excessive even for them.

"Anyone else?" Java began to read down the list of names.

Reverend Driscol Ames
Lonnie Raine
Albert Tremont
Déjà vu LaBlanc
Lindy Rochelle
Jody Schooley
Tiny Roche
Pierre Roche

Two Ways to Die
A Java Jarvis Thriller
by Erin Wade

"Eight suspects," Karen frowned. "As always I want you working in pairs. Each pair take four suspects and concentrate on them this week. We'll meet back here Friday and see what you've shaken loose."

"Chris you and Barbie work together," Java directed. "Find out everything you can about Albert Tremont, Lonnie Raine, Tiny Roche and Pierre Roche. Obviously, we can discount anyone that is right-handed.

"Kat and I will concentrate on Déjà, Reverend Driscol Ames, Lindy Rochelle and Jody Schooley. Beau, please provide us all the background information your department has on the eight suspects?"

"Bring me something by Friday," Karen reiterated. "We need a viable suspect."

Java cleared the white board and looked around for Kat but the brunette had left.

CHAPTER 36

Java groaned when she saw Kat's Benz parked next to Déjà's black Cadillac on the restaurant parking lot. She steeled herself for the inevitable confrontation between the two women.

"Here's the love of my life now," Déjà gushed as Java entered the restaurant.

Java's eyes darted around the area looking for Kat.

"Don't worry sweet cheeks," Déjà laughed. "She's in her dressing room. It's okay to flirt with me."

"Join me for lunch?" Java invited.

"Delighted," Déjà grinned. "You do know that will piss off your woman?"

"She's not my woman!" Java declared. "She's someone's wife."

"She wants to be yours," Déjà taunted.

Java walked into the kitchen, plated their food and nodded toward the elevator for Déjà to push the up button.

"I missed you yesterday," Déjà said as they took their seats at Java's usual table.

"I didn't know you were looking for me," Java shrugged. "What do you need?"

"My community needs this basher case closed," Déjà grumped. "Tell me what I can do to help make that happen. Folks are getting nervous and jumpy. It's just a matter of time before innocents begin to die at the hands of vigilantes."

"I know," Java agreed. "Déjà do you keep a record of who purchases items like the buttons for the voodoo dolls' eyes?"

Two Ways to Die
A Java Jarvis Thriller
by Erin Wade

"No," Déjà shook her head. "Some people buy two and others will buy twenty at a time. Unless they pay with a credit card, we have no record of who made the purchase. For inventory purposes our register only keeps track of how many of each item is sold."

"I hate to ask you this," Java grimaced, "but could you pull all button purchases of twenty or more then see who paid by credit card?"

Déjà leaned back, a twisted smile played on her lips. "That would require a lot of my time."

"I know," Java agreed, "but—"

Déjà trailed her long fingers down Java's arm and let her hand rest on top of Java's hand. "If you'd help me after the shop closes, I could do it faster."

Kat shoved a chair across the floor as she stepped from the shadows of the stairway. She approached their table much like a lioness stalking her prey. "You're needed downstairs, Java," she growled.

As the elevator doors closed on Java, Déjà folded her napkin and prepared to rise. Kat's firm hand on her shoulder forced Déjà to stay seated.

"I should go," Deja pushed Kat's hand from her shoulder and stood.

"I saw the way you were touching Java," Kat accused.

"What's it to you?" Déjà sneered. "Surely she's getting tired of the way you treat her. I'd treat her right. Get her blood to pumping. Show her what it's like with a real woman."

Kat's eyes narrowed as she caught Déjà by her blouse lapels and pulled her down to look into her eyes.

"Déjà I don't care how often you pump up the tires," Kat snarled. "I'll always be the one riding that bike. Put that in your voodoo pipe and smoke it." She pushed the priestess backwards and walked to the elevator.

Two Ways to Die
A Java Jarvis Thriller
by Erin Wade

Déjà watched the singer enter the elevator and turn to face her. They glared at each other as the elevator doors slid shut. Déjà's smirk disappeared. She knew Kat was right. Java only had eyes for Kat Lace. The only way Déjà would have a chance with Java would be if something happened to Kat.

The elevator doors opened, and Kat pushed past Java. Java caught her by the arm and turned Kat to face her. "Kat what's going on?"

"I saw the way she was touching you," Kat snapped yanking her arm from Java's grip.

"Kat," Java groaned as the brunette sashayed away from her. Java fought the urge to run after Kat and shake her.

Java bowed her head and walked into the elevator. Déjà was still standing watching the elevator. She smiled when the opening doors revealed Java.

"What did you say to Kat?" Java asked

"Chère, I told her she should step aside and give a real woman a chance to make you happy," Déjà shrugged.

Déjà picked up her purse and hung the strap over her shoulder. "Tomorrow night at six," she instructed. "I'll have dinner ready then we can go over the receipts together."

Java nodded as the ebony beauty pushed the button to ride the elevator to the ground floor.

##

Java carried her cup to the serving counter and refilled it with strong hot coffee. Kat began to sing into the microphone as Java sat down at the table.

Java sipped her coffee trying to tamp down her desire for the brunette whose sultry voice was caressing her senses. As she'd done a thousand times before Java tried to figure out what it was about Kat Lace that drove her crazy.

Two Ways to Die
A Java Jarvis Thriller
by Erin Wade

"Everything," she mumbled out loud. *Everything about Kat makes my brain short circuit,* Java thought. *Her mane of glorious black hair. Eyes that steal my soul and full soft lips I can't kiss enough. Damn she's a good kisser.* A shiver ran through Java's body as she recalled kissing Kat.

CHAPTER 37

The next morning Java jerked awake as her phone blared Beau's ringtone. "Jarvis," she mumbled.

"Java get to the police station in Gonzales," Beau barked. "All hell is breaking loose there."

"On my way," Java rubbed the sleep from her eyes as soft hands slipped around her and Kat snuggled into her.

"What's going on?" Kat murmured.

"I don't know. Beau just said for us to get to Gonzales on the double."

"Do we have time for a shower?" Kat snuggled in closer.

"Humm, if we shower together," Java hummed.

"I was hoping you'd say that," Kat giggled throwing the covers off her and heading for the shower.

##

An hour later Kat and Java arrived at the Gonzales police station. It looked like a convention of news stations. A half dozen news vans were parked in front of the station and cameramen were everywhere filming anyone that even looked as if they were a law enforcement officer.

Java was glad she and Kat were dressed in faded jeans and Kat's were even worn with holes. Intending to be inconspicuous, they looked more like indigents than FBI agents. No one paid them any attention as they strolled through the front door of the Gonzales police station.

Beau motioned for them to follow him to an empty room closing the door behind them.

"What's going on?" Java asked.

Two Ways to Die
A Java Jarvis Thriller
by Erin Wade

"Seven people last night," Beau choked. "Man and woman with five kids under the age of 12. Every news station in the state is here. Penny hasn't arrived yet and the locals are screaming for blood. It appears The Basher is retracing his steps—Crowley, Lafayette and now Gonzales.

"If we're right and he's copycatting the 1912 murders, he should strike in San Antonio next."

Java pinched the bridge of her nose trying to stave off the caffeine-withdrawal headache she had. "Is there a Starbucks close by?" She grumbled.

"Yeah, couple of blocks over," Beau shrugged.

"Ride with us," Java pleaded. "You can fill us in while I feed my addiction."

Beau laughed at his friend. "I'm surprised you didn't get coffee on the way."

"You sounded frantic," Java smirked. "We got here as fast as we could."

"I appreciate that," Beau nodded.

##

"We should stake out the San Antonio railway station," Java commented as they found a table and sat down. "If you're right we should be able to catch The Basher before he kills anyone else."

"We need to coordinate with the San Antonio authorities," Kat pointed out. "It will need to be their boots on the ground. We don't have the manpower."

"I'll coordinate that," Beau agreed. "My biggest fear right now is hot heads taking matters into their own hands. People are already buying guns to protect themselves.

"Should we alert the citizens of San Antonio of our suspicions or just keep them to ourselves?"

"Forewarned is forearmed," Java exhaled.

"My point exactly," Beau cautioned.

"Let's not make any public announcements," Java worried. "It would only cause mass hysteria and God knows we have enough of that already."

The three agreed to keep their theory to themselves for the time being.

Beau's phone played Penny's ringtone. "Where are you," Beau answered.

"At the crime scene," Penny barked. "It's a circus over here. The locals are stomping all over my crime scene. Why didn't you secure it?"

"I tried," Beau groaned. "The Chief of Police informed me he was quite capable of handling his own crime scene."

"We'll work it and get the bodies," Penny informed him. "Why don't you come over and give me a hand. Where's Java and her team?

"Java and Kat are with me," Beau informed her. "I didn't call in Barbie and Chris after the chief refused to cooperate. They're interviewing the Roach brothers today."

"Roche," Kat corrected. "You're as bad as Java."

"We're grabbing coffee," Beau told Penny. "You want a Starbucks?"

"Always," Penny chuckled.

Java couldn't believe the chaos of Penny's crime scene. Not only had the local authorities stomped through the blood, brains and gore, the police chief was giving interviews standing on the blood covered sidewalk.

Fighting the urge to choke the showboating chief in front of the cameras, Java threw her long blonde hair up into a ponytail, pulled on a Saints ball cap and her sunshades. Stepping in front of the news cameras, she prayed no one would recognize her on the evening news. As she approached the sheriff, she pulled open her jacket showing him her badge. She walked him away from the news people, showed him her FBI ID and threatened to file charges against him for the obstruction of a federal investigation.

"Get these clowns out of here now," she growled, "or I will embarrass you beyond belief."

"You wouldn't dare," the sheriff snarled.

"Just watch me," Java promised. "If they aren't gone by my three count, I will make you the laughingstock of Louisiana. One, two—"

"Everyone out," the chief screamed herding the reporters away from the house.

"You promised us a look inside the house," a pretty blonde reminded the chief.

"As soon as we clear the scene," the chief replied. "Right now, all of you need to move your vans and staff down to the end of the street where we'll wait for the ME to give us the go head on entering the crime scene."

As soon as the area was cleared Penny's team began loading the bodies into the coroner's truck. Java noticed they had stacked two smaller bodies onto one gurney.

"Where were you when I needed you," Penny grumbled as she emerged from the house. "It's pretty gory in there but take a look around and see if you notice anything I might have missed."

Java nodded waving for Kat and Beau to follow her.

The scene was much like all the others they'd worked. The murder weapon was lodged in the wall and an iced-tea pitcher filled with blood was sitting on the cabinet. The Bible verse was missing, but the killer had carefully tallied the score of his kills in segments of five. Eight groups of five—four straight marks connected by a diagonal line for the fifth mark—plus four more marks. The Basher's kills now totaled 44. He was throwing it in their face.

Penny had bagged the voodoo dolls with the body they were placed on. Java took photos of the body count carefully tallied on the wall. "Sick bastard," she muttered.

Two Ways to Die
A Java Jarvis Thriller
by Erin Wade

##

Kat held Java's hand as they drove back to Orleans. "This is the worst case I've ever worked," she confided. "It makes me know that the monsters among us are human."

"I know baby," Java tightened her grip on Kat's hand.

"Mark my word," Kat continued. "This is going to be some bible thumping fanatic doing God's work."

"Yeah and hell couldn't even begin to get hot enough to make him pay for his debauchery," Java concluded.

"Are you having dinner with Déjà vu tonight?" Kat almost whispered.

"Yes, it's the only way I could get her to go over her credit card receipts looking for people who purchased twenty or more of the buttons."

Kat nodded and said nothing.

Java shifted uneasily in her seat. "Honey you know it's strictly business."

"If you ever cheat on me, it will be the end of us," Kat warned.

"You think I don't know that," Java gasped. "There's no way in hell I'd take a chance on losing you. Surely you know that."

"I know," Kat confessed. "I also know how women throw themselves at you."

"Oh, and look who's talking," Java chided, "I have to fight suitors off you with a stick."

"I wish we could be open about us," Kat said. "I want everyone to know that you belong to me and I belong to you."

"Have you thought any more about what we discussed?" Java asked.

"Leaving the FBI?" Kat huffed. "You love being an FBI agent. Honestly Java, I think you'd be miserable outside the agency."

Two Ways to Die
A Java Jarvis Thriller
by Erin Wade

"We can't live like this for the rest of our lives," Java pointed out. "I hate being away from you Kat. You're on my mind every minute of the day. When you're not with me I'm like a cat on a hot tin roof until you are back beside me."

"I feel the same," Kat agreed. "Maybe if we talk to Karen. Explain our situation."

"After we solve this case," Java said. "Let's get away for a few days—just the two of us and weigh the pros and cons. All I know is that I want to fall asleep with you every night and wake up beside you every morning."

Kat nodded. "I want that more than anything."

They arrived at Java's home with just enough time for her to shower and dress. "I'll be back as soon as I can," she promised as she kissed Kat goodbye.

"Just remember what will be waiting for you when you return," Kat smiled salaciously.

Java moaned loudly as the brunette pulled from her arms and pushed her toward the door. "That's all I'll think about," Java promised.

Two Ways to Die
A Java Jarvis Thriller
by Erin Wade

CHAPTER 38

Java pulled her car into the circular drive in front of Déjà's two-story southern mansion featuring antebellum architecture with its Georgian columns. Java knew the plantation had been home to five generations of LeBlanc's. Two generations of slaves from Africa's western slave coast and the next three generations as servants. Déjà had managed to pull together enough funds to pay cash for the place when it went into foreclosure. Java wasn't certain where the money came from and she really didn't want to know.

Rumor was that Déjà's great-grandmother was Marie Laveau, New Orleans famous voodoo practitioner. Laveau's knowledge and skills had been passed down to Déjà.

Java was a little nervous about her first visit to the priestess' home and sat in the car observing the house and immaculate grounds. Shaking off her feeling of apprehension, she stepped from her car and walked to the front door.

Déjà opened the door and beamed at Java. "You're right on time," she said. "I just took the blackened chicken breast off the stove."

Déjà held out her hand for Java's jacket and hung it in the foyer closet. "I gave my staff the night off," she said as she led Java toward the kitchen. "I thought it best since we will be discussing The Basher case."

Java nodded and followed her hostess noting the many Catholic crosses and voodoo rosaries used to decorate the mansion. "That's quite an eclectic collection of religious items," Java commented.

"Umm," Déjà hummed. "In Orleans, Voodoo became intertwined with the Catholic teachings centuries ago. It's an eclectic religion.

"Something smells incredible," Java sniffed the air.

"I hope you like blackened chicken," Déjà replied. "It's my own special recipe of herbs and spices."

"It's mouthwatering," Java grinned. "What can I do to help?"

"Pour the wine and we'll be ready to dine," Déjà laughed.

"The voodoo dolls are all we have to go on," Java admitted as they discussed the various aspects of the case. "If I can narrow our search to anyone purchasing twenty or more buttons at a time, we may be able to locate the killer."

"I brought home the cash register receipts covering the period since the murders began," Déjà said helping Java clear the table. "Why don't you refill our wine glasses and I'll go get them?"

"Whoa, that's a lot of receipts," Java exclaimed as Déjà carried in two large banker's boxes.

"Yes, this could take all night," Déjà grinned. She didn't miss the look of anguish that crossed Java's face.

##

It was after midnight when they finished going through the register receipts. They had two-hundred purchases of twenty or more buttons.

"Who is this that buys them a hundred at a time?" Java showed the receipt to Déjà. "They buy them once a month."

"Reverend Ames of the Sanctity Church," Déjà frowned. "That's a fundraiser for them. The ladies club meets once a month and makes voodoo dolls to sell to tourists."

Two Ways to Die
A Java Jarvis Thriller
by Erin Wade

"Still we should look into it," Java bit her lip. "Make sure all the buttons go onto church dolls."

"Be careful," Déjà cautioned. "The last thing you want is the local newsies tying these slaughters to the church. I feel confident they sell fifty dolls a month."

"Yeah, you're right," Java agreed.

"All the receipts have the buyer's name," Déjà pointed out reaching to refill Java's wine glass. "You should be able to track them down."

Java placed her hand over her goblet. "No more for me. I've got to drive home and I've already had too much to drink."

"You could spend the night," Déjà appraised the blonde. "All work and no play makes Java a dull girl."

Java stood, swaying a little as she collected the receipts. "I really need to go," she insisted.

"Just remember my door is always open for you," Déjà murmured.

CHAPTER 39

As soon as she pulled from Déjà's driveway she instructed her car phone to dial Kat's cellphone. The phone rang several times then went into voice mail. Java hung up. She prayed Kat was asleep in her bed, but she knew the spitfire. More than likely Kat had gone home.

Java's fears were confirmed when she drove up the drive to her lake house. Kat's car wasn't there.

Just as well, Java thought. *I'm too tired to argue with Kat tonight anyway. She'll be furious but at least I'll have my wits about me tomorrow.*

##

Java awoke with a splitting headache. *I know I shouldn't drink wine,* she thought as she stumbled to the bathroom. *A good strong cup of coffee is what I need.*

She tried to call Kat as the coffee pot dripped the much-needed brown liquid into its carafe, but the brunette wasn't answering her phone.

Java carried her cup out to the veranda overlooking the lake and inhaled the crisp morning air. Her head cleared after the second cup of coffee and she poured a third cup to take with her. By the time she reached the restaurant she was ready to face the world. She picked up the large envelope containing Déjà's receipts, took a deep breath and marched into her place of business.

The bustling activity in the restaurant soothed her nerves as she greeted Barbie and Chris. "Where's Kat?" She inquired.

"In her dressing room," Barbie shrugged. "Do you want me to get her?"

Two Ways to Die
A Java Jarvis Thriller
by Erin Wade

"No, I didn't see her car on the parking lot," Java responded. "I thought maybe she'd had car trouble."

"The dealership brought her to work," Chris volunteered. "She took her car in for service this morning."

Java informed Chris and Barbie of her search through Déjà's receipts. "I'll be in my office locating addresses," she finished refilling her coffee cup. *It's going to be a long day, she thought.*

Java separated the credit card receipts by type of card. Each credit card company had different quantities of information. Some had the customer's full name. Those would go to Chris who could locate the owner's address. American Express printed only the last four digits of the card and no customer name. There was no problem if the customer's signature was legible but most of them weren't. It was like trying to decipher hieroglyphics. Those cards were placed in the stack that would require Java's computer skills. Basically, she would hack the card companies' data bases and extract the card owners name and address.

##

"Sir, we're not open for business yet," Chris informed a handsome man in his early forties. "We won't open for another hour."

"I need to speak with Kat Lace," the man insisted. "Please tell her I'm here. I'm certain she will want to see me."

"I need your name," Chris said.

"Marcus Lace." He smiled as he handed Chris his business card.

Chris studied the card then looked up at the balcony. "She's in her dressing room," Chris said.

"I'm afraid I don't know where that is," he smiled his easy smile again. "Would you please show me where to go?"

Two Ways to Die
A Java Jarvis Thriller
by Erin Wade

Chris glanced up again then nodded. "Please follow me."

Marcus Lace was handsome by anyone's standards and carried himself with the ease of a man who always got what he wanted.

"Kat," Chris knocked on the dressing room door, "you have a visitor."

Kat opened the door and looked around Chris. "Marcus," she beamed catching the man's hand and dragging him into her dressing room.

Chris heard the door lock after Kat closed it. She still had the man's card in her hand. *I probably should let Java know what's going on*, she thought.

Java looked up from her computer as Chris entered her office. "Chris, I need you to take this stack with names clearly imprinted on them and find the address for the card owner. I'll—"

"Java," Chris cut her off, "Kat's husband is in her dressing room."

"Oh!" Java exclaimed. "That's good to know. Now about these receipts—"

Chris interrupted her boss again. "Aren't you upset?"

"Umm, no," Java frowned. "I'm more concerned about catching The Basher than meeting Kat's husband."

Chris held out Marcus Lace's business card. "He's an airline pilot. That explains why he's rarely around."

"Mm-hum," Java nodded.

"We were beginning to think she wasn't really married," Chris blurted.

"She's definitely married," Java squinted her eyes. "I've got a killer headache. Do you have any aspirin?"

"Downstairs. I'll get the bottle for you." Chris reached for Java's cup. "You want a refill? I just made a fresh pot."

"That would be great," Java nodded, "and Chris, thanks for the heads up."

Two Ways to Die
A Java Jarvis Thriller
by Erin Wade

"I thought you'd want to know." Chris shrugged as she left the room.

##

Marcus Lace stayed with Kat for over two hours then she escorted him to the front of the restaurant where she hugged him goodbye and watched him walk to his car.

"Nice," Barbie whistled. "Does this mean Java is a free agent?"

Kat glared at the blonde. "Sometimes I worry about you Barbie," she hissed. "You say the dumbest things."

"I'll take that as a no," Barbie mumbled as Kat entered the elevator.

Java looked up as Kat entered her office, "I think I may have a couple of viable suspects," she said trying to avoid the tongue lashing she knew was inevitable because of her late night with Déjà.

Kat closed the door and locked it. She held Java's gaze as she slowly walked toward her. She stopped beside Java and perched on her desk leaning down to whisper in the blonde's ear. "First I need you to bend me over this desk and—."

Java needed no further invitation, she pulled Kat onto her lap and nibbled at her lips before kissing her breathless.

"You're not angry with me?" Java whispered as she eased her hand up Kat's skirt.

"I didn't say that," Kat purred. "You'll pay for that later. Right now, I need you to take care of me."

##

Later Java stroked Kats hair as she leaned her head against Java's chest. "I love hearing your heart hammer like this," Kat admitted. "I'm glad to know I excite you the same way you excite me."

"You drive me crazy," Java whispered.

"Umm," Kat hummed reluctant to leave the warmth of Java's arms.

Java kissed the top of her head and continued to stroke her hair. "Marcus okay?"

"Yes. He came by to tell me he will be flying intercontinental flights, so he won't be home much. His home base will be New York until further notice."

"He was with you for a long time," Java muttered.

"I know," Kat said flatly.

"We should make ourselves presentable," Java sighed. "I'm pretty sure I have makeup smeared all over my face just like you do."

"Your hair's a mess," Kat agreed. "We do look like we just got out of bed."

CHAPTER 40

While Kat finished reapplying her makeup Java called Chris and Barbie to join them. By the time the other two agents arrived Kat had struck a lady-like pose in an office chair, her long legs crossed at the knees.

"We need to find out if the ladies at The Sanctity Church sell fifty dolls a month," Kat studied the church's sales receipt provided by Déjà.

"I've narrowed it down to a hundred possibilities," Java explained as she handed each woman a stack of receipts. "Look through your stack and start with the ones you deem the most suspicious."

"Kat and I are going to visit Reverend Driscol Ames today and give him a personal invitation to have Christmas Eve dinner here as our guest. That'll give us an excuse for being in his church.

"I gave Déjà a pretty good once over last night--."

"I bet you did," Kat interrupted.

"I don't suspect her," Java continued.

"We visited with the Roach brothers," Chris added. "They're up to something, but it's not slaughtering entire families."

"They're almost too stupid to exist," Barbie said. "They act like old-time mobsters speaking Pidgin. But I think that is an act. They only lapse into Pidgin when they don't want to answer questions."

"Lindy said they tried to sell her protection," Kat chuckled. "She kicked them out."

Two Ways to Die
A Java Jarvis Thriller
by Erin Wade

"Jody Schooley has reservations for two around one today," Chris informed Java. "You might want to talk to him then."

"I wonder what big-breasted woman he'll bring with him today," Barbie chimed in.

"He's certainly been showing off his girls around Bourbon Street," Chris agreed.

"Are you getting any chatter about his place?" Kat asked. "I've heard nothing."

"Not a peep," Chris answered. "It's strange. We usually hear all the sordid jokes and uncouth comments imaginable when a new whore house opens."

"I know he received his license to operate," Barbie informed them. "And there's been no complaints from his girls. I haven't heard a word about them being disenchanted or wanting out of their job."

"Beau's already contacted the San Antonio Sheriff's department to set up around the clock surveillance on the train station," Java shared her information. "He called this morning. Everyone should be in place in a couple of days. We've got to catch The Basher."

"Kat and I are off to visit with Driscol Ames," Java stood. "Chris you get addresses on your receipts and I'll finish getting information on the ones I have tonight."

##

Kat scanned through the photos of the last crime scene as they drove to the Sanctity Church. They were disappointed to find Reverend Ames was out of town but delighted to find out the ladies' club was hard at work constructing voodoo dolls.

The church secretary fawned over Kat. "I've heard you sing," she gushed. "My husband took me to Java's Place for our anniversary and you sang our request."

"Yes, I remember you," Kat lied. "The two of you danced as I sang your song."

"Yes," the woman beamed. Delighted that Kat remembered her.

"I'm thinking about getting my family authentic voodoo dolls for their birthdays this year," Kat said. "I heard your ladies' club makes them. Is there any chance I might see them in action?"

"Oh, yes," the secretary agreed pointing to a closed door. "Just go down that hallway and take the third door on the left. The ladies are in there now working on the dolls."

Java followed Kat to the production room and was pleased to see half-a-dozen women busily stitching and gluing voodoo dolls together. There was a huge bowl of buttons in the center of the worktable.

The women were happy to show the two beautiful visitors how a voodoo doll was constructed.

"How much do you sell the dolls for?" Kat asked.

"Twenty-Five dollars each," the president of the club answered. "We meet once a month and make the dolls."

"That's very reasonable," Kat smiled. "How many do you make a month?"

"Fifty," the woman answered. "Our goal is to sell enough dolls every month to cover the salary of the daycare worker."

"And do you?" Kat picked up one of the dolls and began inspecting it.

"Oh yes. We make just enough to pay the worker," the president said. "Rev. Ames wants us to meet twice a month and make a hundred dolls so the church can hire a second day-care worker. Our kindergarten program is booming."

"Does any one person purchase a large number of the dolls," Java asked. "Say, five or six at a time."

"Miss Déjà vu LaBlanc has a standing order for twenty-five dolls," the woman beamed. "Six months ago, she placed a special order for one hundred dolls."

Kat smirked at Java then thanked the ladies for their information as they left.

"So, your high priestess is buying voodoo dolls in bulk," Kat chided. "She probably has one with your name on it."

"More likely it's your name," Java stated the obvious.

"Yes, she'd like to get me out of the way," Kat agreed. "I think we should make Miss LeBlanc's day and pay her a visit."

"Are you going to play nice with her?" Java asked.

"I'm not going to play with her at all," Kat smirked. "That's your bailiwick."

"Kat, I've never—"

"I know," Kat interrupted. "I just like to watch the look on your face when I tease you about her. Honestly, if I weren't around wouldn't you court Déjà vu? She is very beautiful."

"No," Java shook her head. "If you weren't around, I'd be too miserable to function with others. I'd become a recluse coming out only when Karen gave me a case with a license to kill."

"Oh my," Kat feigned shock. "I suppose I'd better stay around just to keep you happy."

"You do make me happy," Java smiled.

CHAPTER 41

Déjà was with a customer in her private office when they arrived at her shop. Kally greeted them coolly and Java wondered why the girl was so subdued then she remembered that she'd just killed her brother.

"Kally," Java touched her arm, "I wanted to personally tell you how sorry I am about Raymond. I had to defend myself."

"I know, Miss Java," Kally sulked.

"Is there anything I can do to help you and your mother?"

"No, Mother moved on," Kally shrugged. "She's already living with another man."

"Where are you living?" Java asked.

"Same place. Mother's new beau owns his own home, so she let me have ours. It's in my father's name so I guess I can stay there as long as he's in prison. There's no chance of him getting out, is there?"

"No chance at all," Java reassured her.

"Kally," Kat smiled at the girl, "can you think of anyone who would be involved in these horrible crimes with your father and brother?"

Kally cocked her head to one side and limped across the room to join them. "I was shocked that my brother was involved," she whispered. "Are you certain he committed any of the murders?"

"We're certain," Kat scowled. "I'm sorry."

"But another family was killed after you shot Raymond," Kally sobbed.

Two Ways to Die
A Java Jarvis Thriller
by Erin Wade

"Do you know where Déjà was when the last murder occurred?" Kat asked.

"Kat," Java blurted.

"No, it's okay, Miss Java," Kally half smiled. "She was here. We did inventory that night. There's no way Miss Déjà vu would commit those crimes."

Beads rattling behind her made Kat jump. She turned to find herself face-to-face with the high priestess decked out in all her voodoo regalia.

"Now you're accusing me," Déjà snarled at Kat. "I must be making you nervous?"

"Déjà, Kat didn't mean anything by her question," Java assured the ebony beauty. "We're just going over everything. We're at our wits end."

"I understand," Déjà shrugged. "Everyone is on pins and needles." She laughed as she picked up a voodoo doll that looked very much like Kat and stabbed a long pin into its stomach.

Kat gasped, clutched her stomach and doubled over. An eerie silence fell on the room as the other three gaped at Kat.

Kat's laughter filled the room. "I wish you could see the expression on your faces." She straightened. "That was just too good to pass up."

The look of hatred on Déjà vu's face told Java that her lover had gone too far. The priestess was furious.

"You dare to mock me," Déjà, railed. "Leave my establishment right now."

"Déjà she didn't mean anything by that," Java tried to smooth things over. "She was just having a bit of fun."

"At my expense," Déjà roared. "You're always welcome here, Java. But you," she pointed her finger at Kat, "never darken my doorway again."

Two Ways to Die
A Java Jarvis Thriller
by Erin Wade

Java caught Kat's elbow and pushed her toward the door. "I'll call you later," she tossed over her shoulder as she left Déjà.

Java kept a firm grip on Kat's arm until they reached the car. "What was that all about?" She demanded.

"That was for her intentionally keeping you out late last night," Kat smirked.

"Kat you can't go around alienating people just because—"

Kat caught Java's face between her hands and kissed her soundly. "She's in love with you," Kat said as she pulled her lips from Java's. "And she's behind these murders. I don't know how or why, but I know she is."

Two Ways to Die
A Java Jarvis Thriller
by Erin Wade

CHAPTER 42

Friday wasn't a happy meeting for Java. Her team knew no more than it had the previous Friday. All their suspects had iron-clad alibis except for Driscoll Ames, and he was still out of town so neither she nor Kat had been able to talk with him.

The best thing Java had to report was that no murders had occurred in the past week. She was beginning to be thankful for the tiniest blessings and considered a week without The Basher claiming more victims a win.

The Gonzales Police Chief had tried to lodge a formal complaint against the FBI's, "blonde bitch of an agent." But after Karen finished rattling off the charges she would file on him for the desecration of the crime scene, he quietly went away.

San Antonio had their officers in place waiting for The Basher to show his face.

"Now we are playing a waiting game," Java concluded her pathetic report.

Director Karen Pierce took Java's place in front of the white board. She had been watching her team that was made up of the FBI's finest agents. To say their morale was low was the understatement of the year. She knew they had left no stone unturned and had come up empty handed while The Basher or bashers continued their bloody rampage. She too counted each week without a massacre a win.

"I know all of you have been pounding the pavement and looking into every nook and cranny for a lead," Karen began. "This is the most frustrating case of my career and I know you feel the same. Be constantly vigilant and take in the most minute details. We're grasping at straws, but maybe one of those straws will pull up a lead."

"We'll visit Ames as soon as he's back in town," Java added.

"I've never worked so many crime scenes with so little results," Penny noted. "It's as if a ghost committed those crimes."

"Oh, Lord," Karen chortled, "Don't give the press any ideas. God only knows what they'd make of that statement."

"Penny's right," Beau jumped in. "I can't believe there is such carnage and so little evidence of the perpetrator. Whoever he is, he's brilliant."

"Is your undercover still intact?" Karen asked Java.

"Obviously Déjà vu and Kally know I'm FBI," Java admitted, "but I don't think anyone else knows. And I'm certain they have no idea Kat, is an agent."

"I want to go on the record as saying, I believe Déjà is a prime suspect," Kat said.

Java glared at her lover but didn't respond. She had gone through Déjà's receipts searching for sales to account for the hundred dolls the priestess had purchased from the church. They were unaccounted for. She wanted to check Déjà's inventory before she shared her discovery.

CHAPTER 43

A good night's sleep with Kat beside her started Java's day off on the best note possible. She sat at her desk and scrutinized her list of suspects one more time. *What am I missing?* she thought. *Or more appropriately, who am I missing?*

She turned on her TV and watched the morning news as she sipped her third cup of coffee. She was shocked to see the San Antonio Police Chief holding a press conference.

"Why haven't you notified citizens about your suspicions?" A reporter screamed from the crowd.

"We feared public reaction would result in unnecessary deaths," the chief responded. "You know how the public can panic over cases like this."

The station cut from the press conference to a single anchorwoman facing the camera. "I broke this story late last night," the woman reported. "I discovered a strong police presence at the San Antonio railway station.

"Authorities believe The Basher will strike in San Antonio next."

"Dammit," Java cursed. "Obviously not now, you stupid cow. Now that you've informed the world."

She fought the urge to throw her paperweight at the TV screen. How could the news media be so obtuse? They had just destroyed the only opportunity law enforcement had of catching The Basher wasting thousands of dollars and man hours devoted to stopping the insane murderer.

The TV coverage shifted back to the press conference. "Obviously, you have destroyed all hope of our plan working," the chief kept his voice even. "You've informed The Basher of our plan to capture him."

"But chief—"

"This press conference is over," the chief switched off the microphone and walked away from the podium.

Java was in the middle of a mumbled rant when Kat entered her office. "My, what happened to the happy woman I woke up with this morning?"

"Have you seen the news?" Java blurted.

Kat shook her head no and turned to watch the anchor woman. Her mouth dropped open as she realized what a fool the news reporter was.

"Java," Kat gasped, "she's just negated the only chance we had of capturing The Basher."

"I know," Java huffed.

"Beau's on his way here," Kat informed her. "I wondered what he was so excited about. I guess this is it."

The elevator dinged announcing the arrival of a guest to Java's floor. "That's probably him, now," Kat surmised.

Beau strolled into Java's office and headed for the coffee bar. "Help yourself," Java encouraged.

"Have you seen the news?" Beau frowned as he stirred cream into his coffee.

"Yeah," Java shrugged. "I figured that's what you were here about."

"No, thinking about that will only give me indigestion," Beau settled into the chair across from Java. "There's something hinky going on at Jody Schooley's house of ill repute."

"Why do you say that?" Java scowled ignoring the sinking feeling in her stomach.

"All the ladies that used to work for him have disappeared and no one knows where they've gone," Beau replied. "They've just vanished."

"And you want—"

Two Ways to Die
A Java Jarvis Thriller
by Erin Wade

"Kat to go undercover at his place." Beau finished Java's sentence.

"Not no, but hell no!" Java growled. "You know he has the hots for Kat and there's no way she's going to work in a whore house."

As soon as the words left her mouth Java regretted them. The worst thing one could do was tell Kat there was no way she could do something.

"Maybe he needs a receptionist," Kat smirked. "I'm quite capable of answering the telephone."

Java bit her tongue. She wasn't having a conversation in front of everyone, but she also wasn't about to sign off on Kat working in Jody's cat house.

"Folks," Java said calmly, "I believe all of us need to be concentrating on The Basher. Jody's bordello isn't going anywhere. We can deal with him when we catch the person or persons slaughtering their way across the state."

Kat nodded in agreement. *Thank God reason always works with Kat,* Java thought.

"Am I the only one starving?" Java grinned rising from her desk. "Everyone, lunch on the house."

They moved to their regular round table overlooking the main floor of the restaurant. To Java's surprise, Jody Schooley and one of his bimbos were already seated below.

"He's here with one of his girls now," Beau whispered. "She must be new. I haven't seen her around."

"Pretty," Barbie commented.

"They all are," Beau replied. "Look at the size of those hooters."

"Uh, Beau, ladies present," Java's sweeping gesture included all the members of her team.

"I'm sorry," Beau blushed. "I didn't mean to be lewd. I'm just amazed that she can sit up without help. Seriously, look at her Java."

Java studied the woman for several minutes. "She is well endowed," she muttered.

"They all are," Beau noted. "It's like Schooley's replaced all the skanks he had with every man's wet dream."

"Why don't you have Alcohol & Tobacco Control make an unannounced visit to his place? You know, to make certain nothing illegal is going on."

"They are allowed by law to do that," Beau agreed. "I'll go that route first, but if they turn up empty handed, I need Kat to help me. Something's not right with Jody Schooley."

"We'll cross that bridge when we come to it," Java promised.

##

As the dinner crowd filled the restaurant, Java moved among her customers thanking them for dining at Java's Place and introducing herself to the new faces she saw.

"When does your blues singer come on?" A dark man with sunken black eyes asked. "I came just to see her."

"Soon," Java answered trying to overcome her instant aversion to the man. "Are you from around here?"

"No, on vacation," the man chirped.

"Alone?" Java surveyed the empty booth the man was occupying.

"I'm meeting a date." Thin lips tightened across crooked teeth as the man smiled.

"Humph," Java snorted.

"Here she is now." The man stood and waved to a gorgeous brunette who beamed back at him and quickly made her way to his table.

"Melody," the man half bowed, "I'd like to introduce you to . . . I'm sorry, I don't know your name."

"Java Jarvis," Java held out her hand to the woman.

Two Ways to Die
A Java Jarvis Thriller
by Erin Wade

"Java Jarvis," Melody repeated the name as if cataloging it. "You're the owner." She held Java's hand tighter.

"Yes," Java nodded trying to pull her hand from Melody's grip.

"Oh, I apologize," Melody said releasing Java's hand. She smiled exposing perfect white teeth. "I didn't mean to cling to you."

"No problem," Java motioned for her to sit down. "I hope you enjoy your dinner."

The band began playing and the diners quieted waiting for Kat Lace to appear on stage. Kat's rich, sultry voice floated over the crowd as she walked from the back of the room to the stage. *God, she knows how to make an entrance,* Java thought licking her lips to restore the moisture to them.

When the song ended Java realized that she had stood in the center of the dining room mesmerized by the woman who always took away her breath. Kat held Java's gaze as she began singing her next song.

The vibration of her phone broke Java's trance and she walked to the elevator trying to calm the ache in the pit of her stomach. *I wonder if Kat will always affect me like this,* Java thought.

A quick glance at her phone revealed Penny's face. Java answered her phone as the elevator doors closed. "Hey Penny, what's up?"

"Turn on the TV, channel 5," Penny quavered. "This is the damnedest thing I've ever seen."

Java closed her office door and turned on her TV. The channel five news crew was live on the scene of a shooting. They were filming the silhouette of a man who was running and screaming, "It's The Basher! The Basher is here!"

A loud bang filled the night, the man flew off his feet and landed on the ground with a loud thud. As the cameraman zoomed in on him a dark red stain spread across the front of his wifebeater.

"It's him!" Someone yelled. "We got The Basher."

Pandemonium broke loose as residents pulled their cars around to light up the scene with their headlights. People approached from every direction. Suddenly an ear-splitting scream filled the night as a woman dressed in her night clothes fell over the body of the dying man.

"Phillip, oh dear God," she screamed. "You've killed Phillip. He was going to help."

Awkward silence fell over the bystanders as the wail of an ambulance grew louder as the vehicle approached followed by a police car.

"Stupid bastards," Penny railed over the phone. "I knew this would happen. Their shooting at anyone who moves. They're scared to death and killing each other."

"Where are you?" Java asked.

"I just pulled into your employee parking lot," Penny answered. "I'll be with you in a minute. Beau is right behind me."

By the time Kat had finished her performance and joined Java and Penny, the police and news media had sorted out the details of the shootings and the bodies of two men were being loaded into the coroner's van.

Java called Barbie and Chris into her office and closed the door behind them.

Java pinched the bridge of her nose between her thumb and forefinger as she spoke with San Antonio Detective Trilton Joe White. "Thanks, Trilton Joe. Please keep me informed of any new incidents."

"What's happened?" Barbie asked.

"After that newscast this morning this was inevitable," Java sighed. "From what the authorities have been able to piece together a man named Elroy Smoot was guarding his home when a friend stopped by to check on him and his family to make certain they were okay.

"Without knocking the friend turned the doorknob to open the door and Smoot opened fire with a shotgun killing his friend instantly.

"Smoot's neighbor Phillip Walker ran over to check on the Smoots, but fearing he'd stumbled onto The Basher, he ran back to his home to get his gun shouting, "There goes The Basher." Another neighbor gunned down Walker thinking he was The Basher.

"Detective White said it was unbelievable how many of the bystanders were armed."

"Jesus, I knew this would happen," Beau declared. "Java, we've got to shake this case loose before Louisiana and Texas are covered in the blood of innocent bystanders."

A knock on Java's door caused them all to turn and look at the intruder. "Miss Lace," the manager stuck his head around the door. "It's time for your next performance."

"The show must go on." Kat frowned as she left the room.

"Order drinks or dinner and relax," Java told her team. "I'm going down on the floor. There's a creepy fellow I want to keep an eye on."

CHAPTER 44

Java leaned against the wall and scrutinized Melody and her date. The man was all over the woman. At one point, Java decided to ask them to leave but the man seemed to come to his senses and began acting civilized.

Melody didn't seem to mind that he was pawing her in public. She kept giggling and whispering in the man's ear. He slipped his hand inside her dress and began fondling her breast. Java wondered how a woman could tolerate such contemptable behavior in public.

As Kat's set ended and the lights came up, the man pulled his hand from Melody's dress and clapped for Kat.

"Who's waiting on table twelve?" Java asked Chris. "I need the check for them."

Chris returned quickly with the man's check. Java walked to the table. "I hope you've enjoyed yourselves tonight," she scowled. "Here's your check."

"We're not leaving yet," the man snickered.

"Yes, you are," Java hissed. "This is not a make-out place. We have teenagers dining with their parents in here."

"Java Jarvis," Melody caught Java's hand and squeezed it. "I could make you very happy Java Jarvis."

"I'll be happy when your friend pays his bill and the two of you leave," Java scoffed. "Your credit card please?"

The man handed Java his card and she passed the check and card to Chris staying at the table while the bill was cleared.

"You should come visit me, Java Jarvis," Melody insisted.

Two Ways to Die
A Java Jarvis Thriller
by Erin Wade

"Umm, and where would I find you Miss Melody," Java cooed realizing that the brunette looked like a Jody Schooley protégé. If she could convert Melody to an informant, she wouldn't have to worry about sending in Kat.

Melody opened her purse and took out a business card. "You may call me anytime, day or night," she winked.

Chris returned with the couple's receipt and card. Java waited for the man to sign then escorted them from the restaurant.

As they stumbled down the sidewalk Java read the business card Melody had given her. "Every Request Granted" was written across the top of the card with a phone number underneath. There was no address or business name. Java wondered if this was Jody's operation. She slipped the card in her pocket and returned to the restaurant.

Java joined her team upstairs and showed them Melody's card. "It's a cellphone number," she noted. "Give me a minute and I'll see if there is an address associated with it."

Java frowned as she ran the phone number. "It's one of those month-by-month phones," she informed her team. "It's a Google number and we'll need a court order to force Straight Talk to give us the credit card used to pay for the service."

"Why don't you call her and tell her you want to meet her," Beau suggested. "She'll have to give you an address."

"Or come to your place," Kat pointed out. "She probably makes house calls."

"Let's call it a night," Penny said. "God only knows what tomorrow will bring. It seems that there are only two ways for women to die in Louisiana right now. Either The Basher butchers them, or some psycho decapitates them."

"Thanks for that Penny," Barbie scowled. "That's a thought I want to take home to an empty apartment."

"Barbie, I didn't mean to be so morbid," Penny shrugged. "I'm . . . this case is so frustrating."

"Do you want me to drive you home?" Chris asked Barbie.

"Maybe," Barbie flirted.

Java flinched. *Just what we need, another couple*, she thought herding the group from her office.

"Kat, it looks like your butch is here," Barbie gestured toward Lindy Rochelle who had just entered the restaurant.

Kat groaned. "I'm not up to dealing with her tonight,"

"I'll handle it," Java smirked as she pushed the elevator button. "Why don't you wait in my office until she leaves?"

##

Lindy was questioning one of the waitresses about Kat's whereabouts when Java stepped off the elevator. "Lindy," Java chatted. "What brings you to my place at closing time?"

Lindy looked around. "I was hoping to catch Kat," she responded. "I thought she might like a nightcap."

"I believe she's already gone," Java quipped. "I'll tell her tomorrow that you came by."

"Don't bother," Lindy scowled. "I'll call her."

CHAPTER 45

"Barbie you and Chris go," Java insisted. "Kat and I'll close tonight. And do let Chris take you home. We're all a little on edge."

The restaurant staff finished cleaning the dining room and kitchen as Java ran the daily sales report and Kat placed cups and saucers on each table getting them ready for the next day.

Java waited until everyone was gone then checked to make certain all the doors were locked. "Everything's secure," she announced. "Are you going home with me tonight?'

"You couldn't stop me if you tried," Kat smiled. "I've been waiting all day to be alone with you."

Java slipped her arms around the brunette and pulled her in soft and slow, enjoying the feel of Kat's softness against her. She inhaled deeply as the fragrance from Kat's dark hair filled her senses. "You smell so damned good," she muttered as her lips found Kat's.

"Let's go," Kat kissed her one more time then pulled away.

##

While Kat showered Java pulled a cold Shiner from the fridge and strolled onto the porch overhanging Lake Pontchartrain. The cool air felt good against her face as she listened to the music of the night played by bullfrogs and Devil's Horses—the large, black crickets—that invaded Louisiana every year.

Two Ways to Die
A Java Jarvis Thriller
by Erin Wade

A splash off to her left made her jerk her head around but not fast enough to catch sight of the fish that had made the sound.

Java sensed Kat before she touched her. The brunette's soft fragrance floated on the night air and a tremor ran through Java's body as Kat wrapped her arms around Java's waist pushing her body hard against Java's.

Kat nestled her face between Java's shoulder blades and hummed her satisfaction at making contact with the blonde.

"You feel so good against me," Java sighed.

Kat eased her hands under Java's shirt and inched her way to Java's breasts, caressing them as she hugged Java.

"You're killing me," Java hissed turning around to embrace Kat. "Let me shower and we'll talk."

"Talk?" Kat raised a quizzical brow.

"Or not," Java grinned mischievously.

##

Java awoke the next morning with Kat draped over her. The side of Kat's head rested on Java's heart and her arm was thrown across her lover's chest. One leg rested on Java's lower abdomen. Without opening her eyes Kat's lips found Java's nipple.

Kat ran her tongue around Java's nipple. The blonde shuddered and moaned. "A good rule of thumb is to never put anything in your mouth that is too big to swallow," Java teased.

"So, I shouldn't pull this into my mouth?" Kat caressed Java's breasts.

"Oh, you definitely should," Java gasped.

They made love then fell asleep in each other's arms.

##

Much later Java slid her hand to Kat's side of the bed and was disappointed to find the woman of her dreams wasn't beside her.

214

Two Ways to Die
A Java Jarvis Thriller
by Erin Wade

The smell of bacon frying in the kitchen made Java smile as she pulled on her jeans and a soft sweatshirt.

"I'm glad you're awake," Kat greeted her with a kiss and a cup of freshly brewed Cajun coffee. "I almost have breakfast ready."

"Umm, you, breakfast, coffee, I'm definitely living the dream," Java brushed Kat's lips with hers. "How can I help?"

"You can butter the toast when it pops up," Kat smiled.

They ate breakfast basking in the sheer joy of being together without inquiring minds observing their every move.

As Java placed the last of the dishes into the dishwasher Kat opened the door and stepped outside. She was leaning on the porch railing when Java joined her.

"It's still a little nippy," Kat shivered and Java wrapped her arm around Kat's shoulders.

They stood quietly watching the current carry leaves and small tree limbs past the lake house. Out of the corner of her eye Kat noticed something bobbing under the surface of the water and wondered why it wasn't being carried downstream like everything else.

"Java, what is that?"

"I don't know," Java sat down her coffee cup. "I was just wondering the same thing."

"It seems to be anchored to that spot like it's weighted down," Kat observed.

"I heard a loud splash in that vicinity last night," Java said. "I thought it was a big fish, but I think someone has thrown something into the lake."

They continued to watch the object as it bobbed up and down in the water. "I should check to see what it is," Java concluded, reluctant to move away from the warmth of Kat.

"I'll go with you," Kat offered.

Two Ways to Die
A Java Jarvis Thriller
by Erin Wade

Java found her gaff hook and carried it to the water's edge. "I'm going to put on my waders. That water is cold, and I'd rather not get wet."

Kat watched as Java waded into the lake and snagged the bobbing object. It was wrapped in burlap like the kind of material used for voodoo dolls.

"What is it baby?" Kat called.

"I'm not sure," Java firmly hooked the object with the gaff and pulled it toward the shore. She was surprised to find it was weighted with a cinderblock. A bungee cord was just long enough to let the thing float under the surface without being carried away by the current.

Java carried the burlap wrapped item underneath her house and placed it on a picnic table. Kat caught hold of Java's arm as the blonde unwrapped the object.

"Oh my God!" Kat screamed as the material fell away and she found herself staring into the vacant eyes of a woman's head.

"Jesus," Java choked. "What the hell is that?"

She tried to tamp down the sick feeling that the head had been intentionally tossed into the lake in front of her home as a threat. *They know where I live*, she thought. *They know Kat spends the night with me. This is intentional. Someone is stalking us.*

Kat was already calling Penny. "Penny come to Java's home. We've found a bodiless head. Hurry Penny, please."

Java looked around to see if anyone was watching them. She saw nothing. "Let's put it on the porch," she said. "I don't want to leave it unattended until Penny gets here. There were some footprints leading to the lake. Penny should be able to get casts of them."

She carefully picked up the burlap bag and eased the head back into it. There was no doubt in her mind that it was a threat aimed specifically at Kat and her.

##

Two Ways to Die
A Java Jarvis Thriller
by Erin Wade

Penny arrived in record time and Java jogged down the stairs to meet her. "It looks like the work of The Decapitator," Java informed her. She showed Penny the footprints and the cinderblock with the bungee cord still attached.

Penny directed her team to comb the area around Java's house and look for tire tracks. She greeted Kat when she entered the kitchen and pointed toward the coffee pot. Kat poured her a cup of coffee and followed her and Java onto the porch.

"I touched the bag," Java informed Penny. "But as soon as I realized what it was, I was careful not to get my prints all over it."

"It looks like the madman that has been decapitating women in Louisiana and Texas," Penny declared. "It's the same precise cut. No jagged edges. Almost professional."

"I'll know for sure once I get it back to the lab and compare the striations to the heads I have in cold storage. This is the freshest head I've gotten hold of so far. Maybe I can learn more from it.

"I think this is a direct threat against the two of you," Penny added. "Please be careful. Someone has you in their crosshairs and they know where you live."

CHAPTER 46

"It could be anyone," Java worried as she drove toward the FBI headquarters. "Someone could have followed us from the restaurant to my house. I wonder if they've followed you to your place."

"Who knows?" Kat mumbled.

"You should pack clothes and things to stay at my house until we catch this lunatic," Java suggested. "He scares me more than The Basher. He's after women not entire families."

Kat hated to admit she was afraid for Java and herself. Although they were trained fighters and—if need be—killers, she still worried about someone blindsiding them.

"I'd like that," Kat replied pulling Java's hand onto her lap.

##

The entire team was in the briefing room when Java and Kat entered. Penny was showing pictures on the white board. "As I suspected this was the worker of The Decapitator," Penny said as her laptop flashed two photos on the screen. "As you can see the striations on the bone are the same. The object used to severe the head Java found is the same one used on all our other heads.

"The Decapitator has thrown down the gauntlet to Java," Kat exclaimed.

Penny nodded her agreement.

"So, this is someone who is targeting our team," Java added.

"Or you," Penny added.

Two Ways to Die
A Java Jarvis Thriller
by Erin Wade

"Regardless, I want you two to team up for everything," Java addressed Barbie and Chris. "Don't even take trash to the dumpster alone. Understood? I want everyone armed. I want to see blazers over holstered Glocks."

"Do we have anything new on The Basher?" Karen asked. "I'm getting hammered from all sides after the citizens had their little version of gunfight at O. K. Corral."

"We haven't been able to talk to Ames," Java informed the group. "We'll make another visit to his church when we leave here."

"Chris and I are heading to the restaurant from here," Barbie said.

"We'll be there as soon as we visit the Sanctity Church," Java added.

##

Kat took Java's hand as they pulled from the FBI parking lot. "Baby," Kat said softly, "I truly think you should take a closer look at Déjà vu in The Basher killings."

"I know," Java inhaled deeply. "She has the height and strength."

"We need to find out what she did with the hundred voodoo dolls she ordered," Kat added as Java headed the car toward Déjà's store.

"Déjà isn't here," Kat noted as they parked in front of the priestess' store. "I'm going in with you."

"Okay, but if she comes in you need to go to the car," Java agreed. "I don't want to referee a fight between the two of you."

Kally was in the back when they arrived but limped to greet them. "Miss Java," she beamed, "It is so good to see you."

"Good to see you too," Java smiled. "You look great. Being on your own seems to agree with you."

Two Ways to Die
A Java Jarvis Thriller
by Erin Wade

"It is a blessing from the gods," Kally giggled. "It is so nice to have my own home. You should visit me. It's so clean and neat. No one to mess it up or bother me. I've never been happier."

"Where's Déjà?" Kat asked.

"She's gone to the buyers' market," Kally replied. "We're out of burlap squares and a few other things. The tourists really spent their money over the weekend."

"I'm doing inventory," Kally volunteered. "But I can stop and make you a cup of coffee."

"Oh no," Java smiled. "You're busy but I do need a couple of those voodoo dolls you sell."

"I think that is one of the things Miss Déjà vu is buying at the market but let me see if we have any in the back."

After Kally left the room, Java thumbed through a ledger lying on top of the counter. She caught her breath when she saw the tally marks on the pages. Four straight lines then a diagonal line to count in groups of five. The bloody tally on the wall of the last crime scene flashed through her mind. She flipped toward the front of the book to last year and tore out a page stuffing it into her jacket pocket. She closed the book before Kally returned.

"No ma'am, were plum out of dolls right now," Kally informed her, "but Miss Déjà vu should be back around four this afternoon."

Java picked up the ledger as if seeing if for the first time. "Don't tell me Déjà keeps a handwritten ledger," she laughed. "I thought the store was computerized."

Java let the ledger fall open. "You use the old-fashioned tally method to take inventory?" She asked casually. "This is your handwriting, isn't it?"

"Oh, no ma'am," Kally exclaimed, "I didn't realize that was lying around. That's Miss Déjà vu's personal way of tracking things. She doesn't trust computers."

Two Ways to Die
A Java Jarvis Thriller
by Erin Wade

"I understand that," Java placed the ledger back on the counter. "Sometimes ours go down and it's chaos."

Kat's cell phone dinged as a message arrived. "We'd better go," she said. "We have an appointment in half an hour."

They bid Kally goodbye and strolled to their car.

"What was that all about?" Kat asked buckling her seatbelt.

Java drove the car down the block then pulled the ledger sheet from her jacket pocket. "Does this look familiar?"

"The wall," Kat gasped. "That's the way The Basher tallied his kills at the last crime scene."

"You're right," Java scowled, "Our killer is Déjà vu."

"We've got to build a case against her," Kat thought out loud. "We can't use this ledger sheet. You did obtain it illegally."

"Oh, yeah, I guess I did," Java grinned sheepishly.

"Let's pull her in for questioning," Kat suggested. "If she has no alibi for the last murder then she's our killer. We should get a search warrant and search her premises—both home and shop."

"We have to handle this with kid gloves," Java mused. "If we stir up her followers and we're wrong there will be hell to pay."

"You need to drop me at my place so I can pick up my things and my car," Kat said. "Everyone will begin talking if I continue to arrive and leave everyday with you."

"As much as I hate to let you out of my sight, I know you're right," Java grinned.

##

Java walked into Kat's home checking all the rooms and closets. "All clear," she called as she entered Kat's bedroom. "What can I do to help you pack?"

Two Ways to Die
A Java Jarvis Thriller
by Erin Wade

"Why don't you go to the restaurant?" Kat suggested. "It will be good for you to arrive a little ahead of me."

Java pulled Kat into her arms and kissed her sweetly. "Hurry, I hate being away from you."

"I will," Kat promised.

CHAPTER 47

The dinner crowd was already filling the restaurant when Java walked through the back door.

"Where's Kat?" Barbie asked.

"I dropped her off at her home," Java replied. "Is there a problem?"

"No, Lindy Rochelle has been demanding to speak with her," Barbie said. "She says Kat was supposed to have dinner with her."

"Where is Lindy?" Java grumbled. "I'll talk to her."

"At her usual table," Barbie gestured toward the table closest to the bandstand.

Java walked to Lindy's table and welcomed her to the restaurant. "Is the staff taking good care of you?" Java asked.

"Oh, yes," Lindy stood and held out her hand to Java. "I'm just missing Kat. She is supposed to dine with me tonight."

"I think she had car trouble," Java mumbled, "but she'll be along later. How about an appetizer on the house while you wait?"

"That'd be nice," Lindy smiled sitting back down. "So, you're okay with me dating Kat?"

"Dating?" Java raised an eyebrow. "Surely you don't consider her having dinner with you here, dating?"

"I'd take her other places," Lindy groused, "if you ever gave her a day off."

"She works seven days a week because she needs the money," Java blurted.

"Really?" Lindy narrowed her eyes, "I thought you paid her well."

"She's supporting a sick mother," Java lied. "Her mother's doctor bills are horrendous. She's also married."

"I like dating married women," Lindy smirked. "They don't make demands on you."

"I'll send someone to take your appetizer order," Java turned and walked away before she planted her fist in Lindy's face.

##

Java strolled into the kitchen sniffing the air. "Umm, something smells incredible," she complimented the chef.

"Miss Kat requested it tonight," the chef grinned. "It's her favorite."

"Have you seen Kat," she asked Chris.

"I don't think she's here yet," Chris replied, "which is very unusual. She goes on in thirty minutes."

"I'll check the parking lot," Java frowned trying to ignore the uneasy feeling in the pit of her stomach.

A search of the parking lots surrounding the restaurant verified Java's suspicions that Kat wasn't on the premises.

Java pulled her cellphone from her pocket and tapped the number that would connect her to Kat. The call went into voicemail. "Honey, I'm getting worried about you," Java recorded. "Please call me immediately."

Java returned to the hostess stand where Chris and Barbie were talking. "She's not here and I can't get her on the cellphone," Java reported.

Jody Schooley pushed his way through the customers waiting to be seated. He pulled Melody behind him. "I have reservations," Jody barked.

The maître d' turned to Java.

"As do all the people you just shoved past," Java glowered. "If you'll return to the end of the line, we'll seat you in less than five minutes."

Two Ways to Die
A Java Jarvis Thriller
by Erin Wade

The hostess continued seating those in line.

Melody slipped her arm through Java's. "Surely you can take care of us now," she smiled lowering her voice to a whisper. "I could certainly take care of you right now."

Java pulled her arm from Melody's. "The hostess will seat you shortly, but you must get back in line."

Java took the elevator upstairs and set down at the table overlooking the diners in the main room. She called Kat's phone again and left another message.

"God, please let her be okay," Java prayed as she walked into her office, holstered her Glock and headed back downstairs.

Java's mind was going in a hundred different directions. *What if The Decapitator has gotten her? What if—*

When the elevator doors opened, Kat walked out.

"Oh, thank God," Java gasped. "Kat I was so worried about you. Where have you been? I've been calling you."

"The battery's dead on my phone," Kat explained. "I fell asleep after you left and didn't set an alarm. I didn't realize I was so tired."

Java pushed Kat back into the elevator and wrapped her arms around her. "I was so scared you'd been kidnapped or worse."

"I'm fine baby," Kat said. "I can take care of myself Java."

"I know you can," Java breathed. "I still worry about you. I'd die if anything happened to you."

Kat lightly brushed her lips against Java's. "You can tell me how much you'd miss me tonight," she giggled. "Right now, I must sing for your guests."

Java's arms tightened around the brunette. "No," Kat murmured. "You'll destroy my lipstick and I don't have time to reapply it."

Two Ways to Die
A Java Jarvis Thriller
by Erin Wade

She shoved Java from the elevator and pushed the button that would take her to the main floor.

Java watched as Kat sang her first set then joined Lindy at her table. Lindy had downed several straight scotch drinks and was in a playful mood.

"Let's blow this joint," Lindy murmured in Kat's ear.

"You know I can't do that," Kat frowned. "I have to sing again in an hour."

"What I have in mind shouldn't take an hour," Lindy grinned salaciously and slid her hand up Kat's leg under her dress.

"I don't think so," Kat pushed Lindy's hand off her leg. "You're drunk."

Lindy slid her arm across the back of Kat's chair. "Don't you think you've toyed with me long enough?"

"I'm not toying with you, Lindy," Kat insisted. "I'm married and I don't fool around." Kat slid back her chair and stood to leave but Lindy yanked her back into her seat.

Java considered going downstairs and throwing Lindy out of her restaurant but was mesmerized by the look on Kat's face.

Like a choreographed dance Kat stood. Sliding her hand behind Lindy's neck she slammed the woman's face into the tabletop rendering her unconscious.

"Ouch," Java mumbled "That's what I've wanted to do to the pig all night."

Java sprinted down the stairs and directed two of her bouncers to quietly remove Lindy.

"I think you broke her nose," Java informed Kat as she handed the bouncer a handful of cloth napkins. "Try to contain the blood, please." The man nodded and the two bouncers carried Lindy out the back door.

"Seems you've lost your dinner partner," Java chuckled. "Want to join me upstairs?"

"I'd like that," Kat laughed.

CHAPTER 48

The next morning Kat and Java made another attempt to see Reverend Driscoll Ames, but he was still out of town.

"Do you have a number where I can reach him?" Java asked.

"No ma'am," the secretary answered. "He was supposed to be back two days ago."

They thanked the secretary and walked to their car. "Let's visit the buyers' market," Kat suggested. "Maybe we can learn more about Déjà. I don't know much about her."

"Neither do I really," Java grimaced. "I do know she comes from a long line of witches. Her great grandmother was Marie Laveau."

"Seriously," Kat raised a perfectly arched brow. "I didn't realize that. We should be more careful."

"Don't tell me you take that voodoo stuff seriously," Java teased.

"I never underestimate any religion or its followers," Kat said seriously. "More atrocities have been committed in the name of religion than for any other reason."

"For instance?" Java encouraged Kat to back up her statement.

"The Catholic Church's massacre of the Protestant Huguenots in France," Kat quipped. "Um, the St. Bartholomew's Day Massacre where Catholics murdered some three thousand Huguenots gathered for a royal wedding. The carnage spread throughout the countryside where rampaging soldiers wiped out entire Huguenot villages. Some 10,000 protestant Huguenots were slaughtered before it was all over.

"They didn't just butcher them, Java, they drove sticks into the eardrums of children killing them. How can one human do that to another, especially a child?"

A shiver ran through Java as Kat described the fiendish acts committed in the name of the Catholic religion.

"Do you believe The Basher is acting out of some twisted religious conviction?" Java asked.

"I don't know," Kat fretted. "The religious aspect was introduced in the last two murders. I feel like it was just used to confuse us."

"That's my thought too," Java agreed.

Java's car phone blared, and she pushed the speaker phone button to connect them with Chris. "What's up?" She asked.

"Jody Schooley's here," Chris whispered into the phone. "He claims one of his ladies is hiding here."

"On our way," Java replied. "Get him out of the restaurant. I don't want our customers hearing his drivel."

Java disconnected the call then glanced at Kat. "Sounds like your boyfriend has lost one of his moneymakers."

"She's probably wised up and headed home," Kat declared. "I'll never understand why women voluntarily sell themselves."

"Sometimes they're working under duress," Java noted.

"True, but some of them prefer that line of work instead of an eight to five existence." Kat replied. "When it comes to men, I can't even imagine being with several in one night."

"I can't imagine being with anyone but you," Java smiled.

"Aren't you the silver-tongued devil," Kat chided. "You're the only one I ever want to be with," she said seriously.

Chris and Jody were waiting on the employee parking lot when Java stopped the car.

Jody stepped back as the blonde approached him. "I'm not trying to cause trouble," he said. "I just want my girl."

"Which one is missing?" Java asked.

"Melody," Jody barked. "She said she was coming to see you and I haven't seen her since."

"I haven't been here all day," Java frowned. "Chris said she isn't here."

"Maybe she got smart and returned home," Kat suggested.

"She wouldn't do that," Jody assured them. "She actually enjoys her job."

"That's what all pimps say," Kat snapped.

Jody's glare alarmed Kat. She couldn't recall anyone ever looking at her with such animosity.

"Why don't you file a missing person report with the police?" Java asked.

"I'll find her," Jody groused. "I don't want the police involved."

"I bet you don't," Kat smirked.

"Maybe you'd like to take her place," Jody snarled. "I'll bet you'd be good at her job."

"She's not here," Java stepped in. "You need to leave."

Jody kicked at the ground trying to control his temper. "If you have her so help me, I'll—"

"You'll what?" Java moved into Jody's space.

Jody backed away from her remembering how quickly she had decked him a few months earlier.

"Don't mess with my girls," Jody shook his finger in Java's face.

CHAPTER 49

"What a day," Java sighed as she locked the doors to the restaurant. "Let's park your car in the tunnel beneath Harrah's and you ride home with me. I hate being away from you for even a short time."

"I know, baby. It's much more pleasant to ride with you," Kat said touching her car to unlock it. "I'll have to follow you. I don't know anything about a tunnel beneath Harrah's."

Java nodded and hurried to her car.

They parked Kat's car in the underground parking space used by Harrah's clientele. Kat was happy to be with Java. Both the cases they were working were beginning to give her the willies.

Kat watched out the passenger side window as Java guided her vehicle from the dimly lit parking garage. "What is this place? It's huge and gloomy."

"One of the city council's biggest screw ups," Java snickered. "1.3 million tax-payer dollars for a giant coffin."

"Is Harrah's sitting on top of it?" Kat asked.

"Part of Harrah's is built over it. See those huge steel piers," Java motioned toward the beams supported by the piers. "They hold up Harrah's and the casino keeps the tunnel from floating to the surface. Talk about something built on shifting sand."

Kat giggled at her lover's explanation.

"It's true," Java insisted.

"I believe you," Kat smiled. "You're just so damn cute when you talk about things most people never heard of. Not only do I find you sexy as hell, I think you're one of the most interesting people I've ever met."

Java basked in the brunette's approval. "Have I ever told you how good you make me feel both mentally and physically," she murmured. "Just one of the many reasons I love you."

Kat caught Java's hand and pulled it onto her lap. "Thank you."

"Don't let me forget to stop at that little convenience store at our exit," Java said. "We're out of coffee."

"We must have coffee," Kat teased. "The sun won't rise without it."

"I'm glad you understand," Java laughed.

##

Java parked the car in front of the convenience store. "I'll be right back," she informed Kat.

"I'll go in with you," Kat shrugged. "I need to wash my hands."

Java paid for the coffee and waited at the counter for Kat to return from the ladies' room. Three unshaven young men sauntered into the store. "You got beer?" One of them bellowed.

The clerk pointed to the back of the store and all three men swaggered toward the beer cooler. Kat came out of the bathroom to find the isle blocked by the three thugs.

"Whoa," the largest one exclaimed. "Umm um, you are really something, mama."

"Excuse me," Kat mumbled and tried to walk past the men.

"Not so fast," the largest man snickered. "I was talking to you."

"I'm in a hurry," Kat drawled. "Please let me pass."

"We're getting beer," the man announced. "You should go for a ride with us. We'd have some fun and bring you back here."

Two Ways to Die
A Java Jarvis Thriller
by Erin Wade

Kat assessed her situation. She didn't want to destroy the convenience store. She nodded her head and allowed the man to take her elbow. An evil grin crossed his face.

"Don't let them take your friend," the clerk warned Java.

"They won't," Java assured her.

The large man and his friend walked Kat outside while the other man paid for the six pack of beer.

Java watched the large man talk to Kat as they waited for the third man to join them. As the man left the store the clerk ran around the counter. "Coward," she spat at Java, "you're just going to stand here while they take her. Do you have any idea what they'll do to her?"

Java caught the clerk's arm. "Watch!" She commanded.

As the three men crowded around her, Kat took the six pack of beer by the handle and pulled one of the bottles from the carton as if she would drink it.

"I really do need to go," Kat reiterated.

One of the men grabbed her arm and dragged her toward their car. "You can leave when we get through with you," he crowed. "And that will take a while."

Java watched closely. Kat was always so fast Java was never certain what happened when she went into action.

Kat broke the beer bottle over one man's face and shanked the broken bottle neck into the throat of the large man.

As the third man reached for her, she swung the carton of beer against the side of his face knocking him down. A perfectly aimed kick to the groin sent him into the fetal position as he howled in pain.

"Jesus," Exclaimed the clerk. "She's a one-woman wrecking machine."

"Yeah," Java grinned, "and she's being very nice right now. You have any zip ties?"

Two Ways to Die
A Java Jarvis Thriller
by Erin Wade

The clerk went behind the counter and handed Java a handful of zip ties. "There's more if you need them."

"This'll do," Java grinned heading out the door to secure the would-be rapists.

"Nice job, baby," Java beamed at Kat. "Someday, you've got to show me how you do that."

They bound the three criminals as the clerk called the police.

Java opened the car door for Kat then sprinted to the other side of the car. "What should I tell the cops?" The clerk yelled.

"That it happened so fast you didn't get a good look at us, but you're certain we were two redheads," Java grinned.

Kat called Beau and filled him in. "You need to take over the case so we can file charges," she said.

"I love it when I get a collar without leaving my office," Beau laughed.

CHAPTER 50

Waiting for the DNA analysis to complete Penny examined the latest head one more time. The machine began beeping and she walked to the screen to see who the latest victim was.

"Delores Ruiz," she mumbled typing the name into the missing person database.

Ruiz had a long history of arrests for prostitution and had worked for Pender Crane. She had disappeared several months ago, but according to Penny's forensics she had only been dead about a week. Penny called Java and Beau on a conference call to report her findings.

"Beau," Java said, "was she one of Jody Schooley's girls?"

"For a short time," Beau reported, "but Jody said she was one of the girls he sent home. Her boyfriend filed a missing person's report and I investigated it."

"I think it's time we paid Jody a visit," Java declared. "Ruiz isn't a redhead, so this continues to break The Decapitators mode of operation. We must assume he is targeting prostitutes in general and not just redheads."

"You want me to do it as the police or do you want to do it as an interested person?" Beau asked.

"Interested in what?" Penny laughed.

"Not funny, Penny," Java barked. "I'll handle it, Beau."

"I still think you should send in Kat," Beau added. "She can handle herself and she can get close to Jody."

"I'll discuss it with her," Java huffed hanging up the phone.

Two Ways to Die
A Java Jarvis Thriller
by Erin Wade

Java looked up as Kat entered her office, closed the door and locked it.

"I recognize that look," Java blushed.

"Good, then you won't waste time with small talk," Kat smiled as she sat down in Java's lap.

##

"That was unexpected but very welcomed," Java tried to catch her breath as she fastened Kat's bra.

"You know how sometimes you have an overpowering urge?" Kat murmured.

"Umm-hum," Java kissed Kat on the neck. "Please, always feel free to act on those urges."

Kat didn't move from Java's lap. She leaned her head against the blonde's chest as Java cradled her like a child. "What's on the agenda for today?" Kat asked.

"I must visit Jody Schooley's house of ill repute," Java laughed.

"Oh! You *must* visit Jody's," Kat snickered. "You've been dying for an excuse to go there. So, what's your excuse."

"The head thrown into my little piece of heaven belongs to one of Jody's girls," Java replied. "I think that gives me the right to ask Jody about it."

"Who is it?" Kat asked.

"A woman named Delores Ruiz," Java said. "She worked for Pender Crane before Jody took over his operation."

"Did Beau ever arrest anyone for Pender's murder?" Kat moved from Java's lap and straightened her skirt.

"No. They never had a suspect. The trail was cold on that one before Pender was."

"May I tag along?" Kat asked.

"It might be better if I go alone," Java gulped. "I don't want to overwhelm Jody."

"You're probably right," Kat agreed. "I need to mend fences with Lindy anyway. It's difficult to get information from someone you've knocked out."

CHAPTER 51

The antebellum mansion on Esplanade Avenue dominated the neighborhood. Java paused to admire its architecture. *How can anything so beautiful house things so vile*, she thought.

She rang the doorbell and waited. After a respectful amount of time she rang the bell again. The sound of high heels clicking across marble floors preceded the opening of the door.

Melody opened the door. "Java Jarvis," she smiled seductively. "I wondered how long it would be before you came to see me."

"I'm here to see Jody Schooley," Java announced standing on the veranda.

"Come in," Melody opened the door wider and stepped back.

Java was almost intimidated by the size of the great room. Large enough to be a ballroom, the elegant space housed priceless antiques and handwoven rugs. The area was well lighted and pleasant. Tastefully arranged seating areas were sprinkled around the room. Not at all what Java had expected.

The great room rose to the ceiling through three stories of bedrooms and bathrooms. A cupola topped the third floor forming a fourth story.

The house was elegance personified. Everything smelled fresh and clean. The mansion lacked the usual whore house odor.

Two Ways to Die
A Java Jarvis Thriller
by Erin Wade

"Mr. Schooley isn't here right now. He should be back in an hour or so." Melody informed her. "May I offer you a drink?"

"Coffee would be nice," Java smiled.

"I just put on a fresh pot," Melody smiled back. "You can wait here if you like or you're welcome to follow me into the kitchen."

"I'll keep you company," Java said.

"What brings you to our home?" Melody asked as she poured the coffee. "As I recall you like your coffee black."

"Yes," Java nodded. Surprised that the woman knew her preference in coffee.

"Why don't we relax in the sitting room?" Melody placed the coffee, sugar and cream on a tray and led the way to a smaller room. "It's more intimate."

Melody sat on the sofa and patted the seat beside her. "If you'll sit here, I'll serve your coffee."

Java retrieved her coffee and saucer then sat down in a chair across from Melody.

"Do I make you nervous Java Jarvis?" Melody asked

"No, not really," Java replied. "Why do you always call me by my full name?"

"I like the way it feels on my tongue," Melody laughed. "Java Jarvis. Java Jarvis. It tickles the tongue. I have a very sensitive tongue."

Java squirmed in her chair.

"Oh, I've made you uncomfortable," Melody giggled. "Good. I meant to. You didn't answer my question, Java Jarvis. What brings you to our home?"

"I'm looking for a woman named Delores Ruiz," Java shrugged. "She worked for me as a waitress and I need an address for her. IRS W2 forms that sort of thing."

"Humm," Melody shook her head and openly appraised Java from head to toe. "You're a beautiful woman, Java Jarvis."

"As are you, Melody . . . I don't know your last name."

"Rogers," Melody supplied.

"Melody Rogers," Java repeated the name. "It has a nice ring to it."

"Kinda' rolls off your tongue," Melody grinned salaciously. "Silky."

"You didn't answer my question, Melody," Java steered the conversation back on track. "Do you know Delores Ruiz?"

"I think Mr. Schooley got her from Mr. Pender." Melody furrowed her brow as if trying to recall something. "I was Mr. Schooley's first girl then he acquired Mr. Pender's women, but they didn't stay long.

"Mr. Schooley brought in new girls like me. Younger, prettier than the ones he had. He gave all the girls that wanted to leave a thousand dollars and a bus ticket to anywhere in the United States. I took them all to the bus station.

"Delores took the money and the ticket. She hung around for a couple of days then left."

"Do you have a forwarding address for her?" Java sipped her coffee.

"You'll have to ask Mr. Schooley about that."

"Excuse me Ms. Rogers," a man dressed in old-South butler attire entered the room. "You have a gentleman caller."

Java raised her eyebrows. "I'll just wait here for Jody," she said.

"I'll keep you company," Amanda, the brunette Jody often had hanging on his arm joined them.

"Don't let me keep you from your business," Java quipped. "I can entertain myself."

"I'm free," Amanda smiled. "Would you like to go to my room. It's quieter and more private there."

Two Ways to Die
A Java Jarvis Thriller
by Erin Wade

"I think Java Jarvis prefers to wait here," Melody snapped. "I won't be long, Java. Please make yourself at home."

Java waited until Melody left the room then began to question Amanda. She was certain Melody was the smarter of the two women and hoped to glean more information from Amanda.

"Amanda how many women were here when you came to work?"

"Nine, I think," Amanda surmised. "Maybe ten. I'm not sure. Melody has been here the longest. She'll know."

"Where did they go?" Java repeated the question she had asked Melody.

"Mr. Schooley gave all the girls that wanted to leave a thousand dollars and a bus ticket to anywhere in the United States." Amanda repeated the same thing Melody had said.

"Did anyone stay?" Java pushed.

"Four or five hung around for a few days, but they finally left."

"Did this woman stay?" Java showed Amanda a driver's license photo of Delores Ruiz.

"For about a week," Amanda verified. "Why?"

"She waitressed for me in January of this year and I need to mail her a W2 form for her tax return." Java responded. "Does Jody have a list of forwarding addresses for the women?"

"You'll need to talk to Mr. Schooley," Amanda advised.

"When did you go to work here?" Java asked.

"Last October," Amanda said. "We all went through rigorous schooling and testing."

"Why?" Java frowned.

"Mr. Schooley said we had to be perfect. The best in Orleans. He taught us how to talk and walk and how to please a man or a woman." Amanda cocked her head and looked at Java. "You'd be amazed at the things we do and how good we are at our trade."

"I'm sure," Java smiled slightly. "How many work here?"

"There are eleven of us," Amanda replied. "We have our own private bedrooms and baths. It's very nice. We clean constantly and make sure everything is sterile and smells nice."

Java noticed the fading sunlight. "I guess Jody is running late today," she noted. "Would you tell him I came by and need to talk to him?"

Amanda walked Java to the door. "You really should pay me a visit sometime," she whispered closing the door.

CHAPTER 52

Kat was working on a new number with the band when Java entered the restaurant kitchen through the back door. She picked up two glasses and a bottle of wine as she passed through the wine closet and headed for her office.

She stopped to watch Kat sing. She couldn't imagine life without Kat. Kat made her laugh and sing. Sometimes the brunette made her want to scream but only because she wanted to hold her and couldn't. Kat was her world.

Kat looked for Java in the shadows of the balcony and smiled when their gazes met. Java knew the brunette loved her as desperately and completely as Java loved her.

Suddenly nothing in the world was as important as getting home and spending time alone with Kat.

Java held up the two wine glasses and gestured toward the balcony. Kat nodded and continued her rehearsal.

Java turned toward the elevator but stopped when she saw Lindy at the hostess stand. She walked to the woman.

"Can I help you with something Lindy?" Java asked eyeing the splint across Lindy's nose.

"I just need to see Kat," Lindy mumbled looking down at her feet.

"I don't think she wants to see you," Java advised.

"I really need to talk to her," Lindy insisted. "I owe her an apology. I was a bastard last night."

"Um," Java shook her head. "Come back in an hour. We have no reservations open right now. I'll try to smooth things over for you."

"Really," Lindy questioned, "you'd do that for me?"

Two Ways to Die
A Java Jarvis Thriller
by Erin Wade

"Sure." Java shrugged pushing Lindy toward the door. "Come back in an hour."

As Lindy went out the door Jody and Melody entered. "Java," Jody bellowed, "Melody says you want to talk to me."

"Yeah," Java looked around for a table where they could have a private conversation but found none. She grabbed two more wine glasses and motioned for Jody and Melody to follow her into the elevator.

Jody flopped down in the chair that gave him the best view of Kat. Java briefly entertained the idea of throwing him off the balcony but remembered he was there at her request.

"I need to talk to you about a woman named Delores Ruiz," Java started. "I need a mailing address for her."

"Delores Ruiz?" Jody pretended he didn't recognize the name.

"She was in the group of women you inherited from Pender Crane." Java jarred his memory.

"Oh, yeah," Jody drawled. "She didn't work for me long. I sent that entire stable packing. They were either too old or so young they were illegal. I run a clean operation. I don't want any trouble with the law.

"All my employees look like Melody here," he gestured toward the brunette. "All American, beautiful, girl-next-door women."

"Do you have forwarding address for any of the women that left?" Java pushed for information.

"Nah," Jody shook his head. "All my dealings with them were in cash. So, no IRS forms and all that malarkey. Say, you got a john up here?"

"Downstairs," Java said. "Go to your right as you get off the elevator. It says 'Gentlemen' on the door."

"You keep an eye on Melody," Jody frowned. "Don't let anyone bother her."

Two Ways to Die
A Java Jarvis Thriller
by Erin Wade

"There's no one up her but me," Java pointed out.

"Wouldn't you like to bother me?" Melody glanced at Java as Jody got on the elevator.

"No," Java choked as she sipped her wine.

"Liar," Melody grinned. "You'd love to know the things I'd let you do to me." She dropped her voice to a whisper, "And the things I'd do to you."

"No," Java squeaked as Melody trailed her long fingers across Java's cleavage.

"What the hell do you think you're doing?" Kat demanded as she stomped from the stairwell. "What is she doing up here?"

"Kat! Thank heaven," Java piped. "I was just asking Jody about—"

"And yet Jody isn't here," Kat stormed. "Only this . . . this . . . hooker."

Melody stood to face Kat.

"Believe me, you don't want to do that," Java pulled Melody back into her chair.

Melody narrowed her eyes and looked Kat up and down. "What's she to you?" She asked Java.

"She works for me," Java replied hoping Kat wouldn't explode.

"I'll bet she doesn't take care of you like I will." Melody poured gasoline on the fire named Kat.

Kat grabbed Melody by her hair.

"Kat," Java snapped. "The band is playing your introduction."

Kat glared at Java but backed down. "I'll talk to you later," she glowered heading for the stairwell.

"She works for you?" Melody reiterated.

"Yes," Java tamped down her anguish. She hated having words with Kat.

"I can sing," Melody informed her. "Anything she does for you I can do better."

Two Ways to Die
A Java Jarvis Thriller
by Erin Wade

"Are you trying to change jobs?" Java asked.

"No just locations." Melody assured her. "I could show you things that will blow your mind Java Jarvis."

"My mind is pretty blown most of the time," Java laughed trying to change the subject.

"Why don't you take me seriously?" Melody asked.

"I do," Java retorted. "The truth is I have a woman and she more than takes care of me in every way."

"It's her isn't it?" Melody tossed her head toward Kat.

"Can we dine up here?" Jody bellowed as he charged off the elevator.

"No," Java said. "You'll need to be on the main floor where someone can take your order. I appreciate you stopping by to see me. I'm sorry you don't have any forwarding addresses on the women."

"Nature of the business," Jody shrugged. "You can't keep up with hookers."

"Hookers," Melody repeated the word as if she'd just comprehended it. "You don't like hookers, Java Jarvis?"

"I like hookers just fine," Java sputtered. "I just don't want one."

Melody's face seemed to crumble. "You don't want me because Jody has made me a hooker?"

"Jody," Java pleaded with the pimp. "Why don't you take your date downstairs and have dinner on the house?"

"That's the best offer I've had all day," Jody crowed pulling Melody to her feet. "Come one Mel, let's order a filet. Java's Place is renowned for their fine steaks and wine."

Java stood to walk her guests to the elevator. Melody pulled her arm forcing Java to lean down as the brunette whispered into her ear. "I will have you," she murmured.

Java exhaled slowly as she watched the elevator door close on her two visitors. The look in Melody's eyes was unfathomable—almost desolate. Java was thankful they

245

had avoided a cat fight. She knew the two women would tangle eventually. Melody had no idea what she was getting into when she confronted Kat.

CHAPTER 53

"I'm going to leave you to lock up," Kat tiptoed to kiss Java. "I need to fill my car with gas. I'll meet you at your place."

"I wish you would wait for me, honey," Java pleaded. "I'm crazy anxious when you're out of my sight."

"Silly, woman," Kat chided. "Surely you know by now that I can take care of myself."

"You did make quick work of those three thugs," Java chuckled. "I'll see you at the lake house."

"I'll have a cold beer and the hot tub ready when you get there," Kat promised.

##

The next morning Chris opened, and customers flooded into the restaurant. The crowd was made up of locals and tourists anxious to try the food they'd heard so much about and meet the restaurant's owner who was a local legend.

"I heard your Java Jarvis single-handedly ended the reign of terror perpetrated on business owners in the French Quarter," one woman engaged Chris in conversation while waiting to be seated.

"She is pretty persuasive," Chris agreed.

"I can't wait to meet her," the tourist enthused. "Is she here?"

"No," Chris frowned. "She's running late this morning."

"What about your blues singer, um Kat Lace?" The woman inquired.

"Kat's first show is at six," Chris responded leading the group to a table.

Chris returned to the hostess stand and looked around for Barbie. The blonde was in the club setting up the bar. "Please take over," Chris asked the maître d. "I need to talk to Barbie."

Before Chris could voice her question, Barbie asked, "Have you heard from Java this morning? It's not like her to be so late."

"I was just coming to ask you that same question," Chris grinned. "I haven't heard from Kat either. I'm going to call Java."

Java's phone sent Chris straight to voicemail. She was dialing Kat's number when the brunette walked in the back door.

"Where's Java?" Kat demanded.

"I just called her," Chris said. "But it went straight to voicemail."

"I can't reach her either," Kat scowled. "She didn't come home last night."

"How do you know?" Barbie chirped.

"We're on the buddy system, remember," Kat smirked. "You two watching each other's back and Java and I teamed together."

"So, why don't you know where Java is?" Chris asked. "When did you see her last?"

"I left ahead of her because I had to get gas for my car," Kat explained. "She was locking up when I left. I fell asleep waiting for her and didn't realize she hadn't come home all night until I awoke this morning. That's when I started calling her cellphone. I was certain she would be here."

"Should we notify Beau?" Barbie asked.

"Do either of you know how to trace a cellphone?" Kat asked.

Two Ways to Die
A Java Jarvis Thriller
by Erin Wade

"No, Java's the MIT grad," Chris scoffed.

"I'm calling Karen and Beau," Kat said dialing Karen's number.

CHAPTER 54

Java lay still trying to determine where she was. No matter how hard she tried she couldn't see anything but total darkness. The rapid dripping of water told her she was in something where water was seeping into a pool or a well. The stench proclaimed the presence of rotting animals. *Probably fell in here and drowned,* Java thought.

She tried to sit up but lay back down when her feet met thin air. Obviously, she was on a ledge. She inched her fingers in one direction and met cold cement. She ran her hand as high as she could ascertaining it was a wall. Sliding her hand in the other direction she soon found the edge of the shelf she was sprawled on. She had no idea how she had arrived at her present location.

She had a splitting headache and raised her hand to find the source of the pain. She whimpered as her fingers touched the back of her head and a knot the size of a golf ball. *I remember,* she thought. *I was hurrying to catch up with Kat. I was locking the door when someone hit me from behind. I never saw it coming. No matter how good one is, when someone gets the drop on you, you're a dead woman. Maybe I am getting too old for this job.*

Lying on her stomach she moved her hand over the edge of the ledge hoping to touch something solid. Instead her fingers plunged into cold slimy water.

"Dammit," she cursed jerking her hand back from the frigid blackness.

She had enough room on the ledge to sit up. The cold dampness made her shake uncontrollably. *It must be early morning,* she surmised. *Hopefully the temperature won't drop any lower and maybe the sunrise will cast some light into this place.*

She searched her pockets hoping to find her cellphone. No such luck. Her wristwatch was missing too. She wondered if she'd been robbed but felt her wallet and ballpoint pen inside the pocket of her leather jacket. *They took everything that would produce any light,* Java thought. *They want me in total darkness to disorient me.*

She fought the desire to sleep. She was certain she had a mild concussion and knew she should stay awake. She kept nodding off and knew this was a battle she would lose. She welcomed the escape of sleep.

##

"We found her Mustang," Beau informed Kat. "It was parked on Harrah's parking lot. Our patrol officers were scouring the town for it as soon as the BOLO went out. Do you have an extra set of keys?

"We towed it to Penny and she's dusting it for prints now."

Kat sat on the bar stool and silently cursed herself for leaving Java alone. In all the years she'd known the blonde it'd never once occurred to her that Java might get into a situation she couldn't get out of.

Java was invincible, only she wasn't. "Who would kidnap her?" Kat squeezed her eyes closed fighting back tears. FBI agents didn't cry. It was an unwritten law.

"She has her fair share of enemies," Beau noted. "The Roche brothers, Jody's no fan of hers. Then there's—"

"You've made your point," Kat interrupted. "Can we talk to Jody Schooley? She was at his place most of the day yesterday trying to find out what they knew about Delores Ruiz and he and his harlot were here last night."

"I'll go," Beau agreed.

"I'm going with you," Kat insisted. "I know Schooley has something to do with this."

251

Two Ways to Die
A Java Jarvis Thriller
by Erin Wade

"You're a bit of a hothead," Beau pointed out. "It might be best if I go alone."

"I'll keep quiet," Kat insisted. "I'll just listen and assess."

"Okay," Beau agreed.

##

The visit to Jody's mansion produced nothing. Jody insisted he'd availed himself of Amanda's charms all night and Amanda confirmed his statement.

"It has to be someone we were getting too close to," Kat insisted as Beau drove back to the restaurant. "Beau, we've never been able to talk to Reverend Driscol Ames. Can we go by the church and see if he has returned from his trip?"

"Works for me," Beau nodded turning his car around. "God knows I have no place to start."

Ames was in his office when the two showed up at the church.

"He's in a meeting," the secretary informed them.

"I noticed Déjà vu LaBlanc's car out front," Kat said. "Is she with him?"

Beau flipped out his badge and ID before the woman answered. "It's a crime to lie to a police officer," he scowled.

"Yes," the rattled woman blurted.

"Good we need to speak to both of them" Kat said.

"I'll tell them you're here," the secretary backed to the door keeping an eye on Beau and Kat.

"Reverend Ames," the secretary opened the door. "There's a policeman here to see you."

"Send him in," Ames commanded rising from his chair.

Beau led the way into the office, flipping out his badge and ID. "Reverend Ames, I apologize for showing up unannounced," Beau's tone was relaxed and nonthreatening. "Miss Déjà vu, what a pleasant surprise to see you too."

Ames extended his hand and shook Beau's. Kat entered the room and Déjà vu puffed up like a spreading adder.

"Please have a seat," Ames gestured toward a sofa across from him. "What can I do for Orleans' finest?" he smiled.

"I'm the lead investigator on The Basher and The Decapitator murders," Beau pulled two photos from his file folder and placed them side by side on top of Ames' desk. "The last two crime scenes have had biblical verses scrawled on the wall. I wondered if you might know of anyone who has a bee in their bonnet over mixed race marriages?"

Ames studied the two photos then read the verses out loud. "These verses would indicate your killer has a problem with mixed race offspring," he agreed. "But I have no one in my congregation with such feelings. Um, is this written on the wall in blood?"

"Yes," Beau affirmed handing the photos to Déjà. "What about you Miss Déjà? Do you have any thoughts on who might be our killer?"

Déjà raised a brow. "You must be desperate, Detective Braxton."

"I am," Beau admitted pulling Delores Ruiz's photo from the file. "This head was thrown in front of Java Jarvis' home. Now Java is missing. We think she's been kidnapped."

"Java, kidnapped?" Déjà scoffed. "She'd never let anyone get the drop on her."

"Do either of you know Delores Ruiz, the woman in this picture?" Beau held up the photo so they could see it clearly.

Two Ways to Die
A Java Jarvis Thriller
by Erin Wade

"She's one of Pender Crane's prostitutes," Ames wrinkled his nose in distaste. "She did attend our Sunday service every Sunday."

"Last I heard she was working for Jody Schooley," Déjà volunteered. "I thought she went home to Mississippi."

"Obviously, she never left town," Beau slid the photos back into his file.

Beau and Kat thanked Ames and Déjà for their time then walked to Beau's car.

"What now?" Beau asked.

"Damned if I know," Kat choked.

CHAPTER 55

Java awoke to a clanging sound. Her headache had ramped up to blinding. Not that it mattered, she was still in total darkness. She held her hand in front of her face to see if she could see it. Her hand covered her face, but she never saw it.

She struggled into a sitting position and leaned against the wall. The gnawing feeling in her stomach reminded her of how hungry she was. Her mouth was so dry she could summon no moisture. Something moved on her left. It didn't touch her, but it was definitely there. Nails scratched against the concrete. She considered extending her hand to touch it but decided she might get bitten by a large rat.

A single beam of light cut through the black and shown onto something akin to a lunchbox about ten feet away from her. Java wondered if it had food in it. Maybe this was her captor's way of feeding her. She slowly stood up the wall careful to maintain her balance.

Once Java felt steady, she began to inch her way toward the light beam. She tried to see if it would cast light on anything else, but it didn't.

When she reached the lunchbox the beam of light disappeared. She slid down the wall and crossed her legs Indian style cradling the box in her lap. Her fingers found the clasps holding the box closed. She took a deep breath and flipped up the clamps. When she opened the lid, she prepared herself for something to leap from it, but nothing happened.

Two Ways to Die
A Java Jarvis Thriller
by Erin Wade

The scraping of nails on concrete reminded her the critter had followed her down the ledge to the box. She prayed she wouldn't have to fight it for food.

She fumbled her way inside the container and felt a sandwich shaped object. It wasn't wrapped in anything only held together by a wooden toothpick. To her delight, she discovered she had a sandwich filled with thick ham, mayo and tomato slices. She had never tasted anything so good in her life. A Ziplock baggie was filled with potato chips. A bottle of water almost made her cry. She slipped the toothpick in her pocket keeping anything that might be useful later.

The varmint whimpered, then growled menacingly. Java tore a piece of the ham from her sandwich and placed it beside her. The animal moved closer and snapped up the meat. Java held her breath as she felt coarse hair graze her arm then the thing moved away from her.

Java munched her potato chips trying to make sense of her predicament. She recalled Penny's proclamation that women in Louisiana had two ways to die. The Basher or The Decapitator. She was certain she was now the prisoner of The Decapitator.

She could hear the critter inching toward her. Its breathing was getting louder. She placed several chips beside her and sat motionless as it moved nearer. Jaws snapped and teeth gnashed as the animal devoured the chips.

Java placed her hand palm down on the cement ledge. To her surprise a soft, wet tongue licked it. A whimper came from the animal.

"You're a dog," Java spoke softly. "How did you get in here?

"Come here, boy. Come on," Java cooed. "Who put you in this hell hole?"

Two Ways to Die
A Java Jarvis Thriller
by Erin Wade

The animal leaned against Java and she put her arm around it. It nuzzled into her side. She welcomed its warmth. She shared the rest of her potato chips with the dog as she felt his back and sides.

Java could feel each of the dog's ribs. He obviously was starving. She was amazed he hadn't attacked her for the entire sandwich. He had short hair and short floppy ears.

"Judging by your condition," Java talked to him, "you can't get out of here either."

Java was shocked that she was getting drowsy. She hadn't been awake very long. She stretched out on the ledge and was surprised when the dog crawled along the edge and stretched out against her body. Java wrapped her arms around him and pulled him against her wrapping her jacket around him. She had a feeling it was the first time both had been warm since their incarceration.

"I'm going to name you Ares," Java mumbled, "God of War because I think we will fight one hell of a battle to escape this place."

##

Again, Java was awakened by the clanging of metal against metal. She tightened her grip on Ares so he wouldn't fall over the edge. When she was certain he was cognizant of his surroundings she relaxed, and he crawled forward until she could sit up.

Once again, the beam of light directed her vision to a lunchbox ten feet away. She pulled herself into a sitting position then pulled Ares across her legs to the other side of her.

She knew the light beam served two purposes: to direct her too the box and to put enough light into the area for night vision goggles to work. Java knew night vision goggles could not work in absolute darkness. They needed a light source no matter how weak.

Two Ways to Die
A Java Jarvis Thriller
by Erin Wade

Java knew she was now being observed like a rat in some cruel experiment. She shook her head. She felt groggy. She struggled to her feet and carefully moved toward the lunchbox.

She moved slowly feeling her way to make certain her foot was on solid cement before moving the other one. When she reached the lunchbox, she sat down and cradled it in her lap. The light beam went out.

Java halved her sandwich and fed Ares half, making him eat slowly. They shared the chips. When she opened the bottle of water Ares began to whimper.

"Are you thirsty boy?" Java purred. "I bet the water in here is vile." She poured the entire bottle of water into the lunchbox and listened as Ares lapped it. He drank until the box was empty.

Java leaned back against the wall and Ares laid his head in her lap. She was surprised when he started making soft snoring sounds. She shook him but couldn't wake him.

They're drugging the water, Java thought. *They probably come in here when I'm knocked out.*

Java knew her captors couldn't see her any more than she could see them. She knew they'd have to turn on the beam to produce enough light for them to see her with night vision goggles. She pretended to be asleep waiting for the sliver of light to slice through the darkness.

CHAPTER 56

"What would Java do?" Kat mumbled out loud as she leaned on the railing of Java's porch. She watched the lazy current carry a plastic bottle downstream. *People think the entire earth is their garbage dump,* she thought.

She had held up all day following Beau around and talking to anyone who might give them a clue to Java's whereabouts. Her profiler's brain kept telling her the answer was in Jody Schooley's mansion. She pulled her cellphone from her pocket and dialed Beau's number.

"Beau, we need to search Schooley's place from top to bottom," Kat blurted when the detective answered.

"Based on what?" Beau muttered

"My intuition," Kat snapped.

"We'll need a warrant," Beau mumbled pulling himself from a deep sleep. "What grounds?"

"Sanitary inspection," Kat huffed. "Those places are always in violation of sanitation law."

"It's after midnight, Kat," Beau pointed out. "No judge will be happy to hear from me about a sanitation inspection this time of night."

"Who's the judge on duty tonight?" Kat asked

"Marilyn Case," Beau replied.

"I'll call her," Kat said. "I've known Marilyn a long time. She owes me a favor."

"Do you need her number?" Beau asked.

"I've got it," Kat replied. "I'll call you back after I talk to her."

"I'll start the paperwork for the warrant," Beau assured her.

Two Ways to Die
A Java Jarvis Thriller
by Erin Wade

Kat pushed the name to dial Marilyn. "Hello, Kat," Marilyn's sleepy voice was as sexy as usual. Kat knew her number was still in the judge's list of favorites.

"I need a favor Marilyn," Kat said.

"Just name it," the judge responded.

"Detective Beau Braxton needs a search warrant for Jody Schooley's place."

There was a long silence before Marilyn answered. "Do you and Beau know what you're getting into?"

"Marilyn, Java has been abducted," Kat blurted. "I know Schooley has something to do with it."

"Tell Beau to bring me the paperwork," Marilyn sighed. "I must be crazy helping you locate the woman who stole you from me."

"That's water under the bridge," Kat mumbled. "We've both moved on."

"Tell Beau he has an hour to get me the warrant," Marilyn said. "I'm not waiting up all night for him. And Kat good luck. I hope you find her."

##

It was four in the morning when New Orleans' finest rang the doorbell of Jody Schooley's mansion. A prim and proper butler opened the door. "Oh," he gasped. "Mr. Schooley isn't here."

"We don't need him," Beau bellowed showing the man the search warrant. "We have a warrant to search this place and everyone in it."

"How many people are on premise right now?" Kat asked.

"Um, let me see," the butler began to tick off people on his fingers. Eleven ladies, six clients, and me."

"Get them all in the great room," Beau commanded motioning to his team to round up the people.

In fifteen minutes, the police officers had herded everyone into the great room.

Two Ways to Die
A Java Jarvis Thriller
by Erin Wade

"What is the meaning of this?" Melody confronted Beau.

Beau gave her a copy of the search warrant then nodded for his officers to commence the search.

"What are you looking for?" Melody demanded.

"Java Jarvis," Kat blurted. "She's missing."

A devilish smile spread across Melody's lips. "As much as I'd like the pleasure of Java's company, I'd never abduct her. It's no fun if all parties aren't willing participants."

Kat took a step toward Melody but Beau's hand on her arm stopped her.

"The anger management classes must have worked," Melody taunted. "I heard you have a vicious temper."

"Miss Rogers," Beau chimed in, "I suggest you sit down and shut up."

Melody cast an angry look at Beau then a taunting smile at Kat. "What makes you think I haven't already been with your woman? She was here for several hours yesterday."

"Java would never touch a whore," Kat hissed.

Melody's face twisted into tears. "You are so quick with your labels. Whore, hooker, they're vile words."

"Kat you should go upstairs," Beau suggested. "I'll question the ladies."

##

Kat was amazed at the cleanliness of the mansion. Every floor was spotless and smelled as fresh as a spring breeze. Each room was tastefully furnished and pleasant.

"Are cat houses usually this clean and welcoming?" She asked one of the policewomen searching the rooms.

"No ma'am," the woman answered. "They usually stink to high heaven and look like an epidemic Petri dish. Everything I've encountered so far has been freshly laundered and there are air fresheners in every room.

"The ladies themselves are immaculate. I mean their hygiene is exemplary."

Kat had to admit that every one of the women looked as if they were going to a debutante ball.

A thorough search of the people and the premises produced nothing that would tie it to Java or her disappearance. It did produce two city councilmen and a council woman. Beau diplomatically looked the other way.

"Since we found nothing," Beau informed the worried politicians, "I won't need to file a report other than nothing was found."

Beau walked Kat to her car. "You got any more intuition calls?" He grumped.

CHAPTER 57

Java had no way of knowing how long she waited for her visitor. Ares began to stir from his drug induced sleep. "Hey boy, you okay?" Java scratched behind the dog's ears and he snuggled closer against her.

"Be still, boy," Java murmured as a whirring noise filled the air. A door opened above her flooding the area with light. Java pretended to be asleep but observed through half closed eyes.

The lunchbox was lowered onto the ledge, ten feet away from her. She scanned the room she was in. It was cavernous. She couldn't see the far side of it but guessed it could easily house several hundred people. As far as she could see, the ledge she was on seemed to run through the entire area. She committed as much of the scene to memory as she could.

The rope was jiggled loose from the lunch box handle and pulled back up the wall. The overhead door whirred closed. Java dropped her head as if sleeping.

A few minutes later the clanging began, and the beam of light sliced through the darkness to highlight the lunchbox. Java surmised her captor was working alone. There had been no coordination of opening doors, lowering boxes and casting the beam. All were done with minutes in between telling her the culprit was moving from place to place.

Knowing her captor was probably observing her through night vision goggles, Java pretended to awaken, and the clanging stopped. *Someone's beating on a pipe with*

Two Ways to Die
A Java Jarvis Thriller
by Erin Wade

a hammer or another pipe, Java thought. *That's just to wake me.*

"Stay Ares," she commanded the dog. If her captors hadn't already seen her new companion, she wanted to keep him hidden. She stood up and walked to the lunchbox.

As she slid her back down the wall and picked up the lunchbox the beam of light went out. "Ares, come," she called the dog.

Ares crawled on his stomach until his muzzle touched her arm then he pushed against her. Java wrapped her arm around his neck and hugged him. She wondered where he had come from. He seemed to be well trained.

Ares sat back on his haunches as Java opened the lunch box. She divided the sandwich giving Ares his half and half the chips. She wondered how long she had been in the cave or whatever it was. She put the toothpick that held the sandwich together into her pocket along with the others.

She'd eaten twelve meals. If her captor was feeding her three times a day, she had been in the tomb four days. *Why hasn't someone found me?* She thought. *Kat's better than this. Why hasn't she found me?*

Java decided to see how far she could walk on the ledge. She counted her steps. She hoped to be on the other side of the space when the beam pierced the blackness again. "That should give them a heart attack," she chuckled.

She knew it would take her captor several minutes to locate her if she was on the opposite side of the cave giving her longer to survey her prison. If she could figure out where she was, she might find a way to escape.

She could feel Ares' nose lightly touching her calf with every step she took. There was something comforting about having him close to her.

She counted a thousand feet and decided her prison was circular or a very long rectangular room. The whirring noise she associated with a visit from her captor started. She lay down flat on the ledge putting Ares between her and the wall.

Light flooded the cave and Java took her time surveying the area. She knew her jailer would be looking frantically for her, but she was on the dark side of the room hidden in the shadows.

Another light source was introduced into the room—a very bright flashlight. Java looked below her and saw an area that was filled with water. She had no idea how deep it was. She scanned a wall lined with old rusting file cabinets and an ancient cold drink machine. Judging by the water level on them she guessed the water to be waist deep.

The bright light moved slowly along the ledge searching for her. Java observed maps of local fallout and natural disaster shelters along with a radiation dosage chart. *Where the hell am I?* She thought. *This place looks like something from the cold-war era.*

The light moved closer to her and ceased movement when it reached her feet. Java turned her face to the wall. The light slowly moved up her body stopping on the back of her head. The light traversed her body several times then went out.

"Now I've done it, Ares," she whispered to her dog. "We didn't get a lunch box."

Java lay motionless as someone scurried across the floor above her. She prayed her captor would open a door and check on her. If she could confront her captor, she could save herself. She wondered if there was an opening above her like the one on the other side of the room.

A screeching sound of metal against metal made her want to clasp her hands over her ears but she lay still. Ares whimpered.

"Shush," she cooed calming the dog. Slowly a shaft of light entered the room as her keeper pried open a sliding door rusted closed from years of neglect. A lunchbox was lowered, and the rope retracted immediately.

Java fought the desire to turn her head and look at her surroundings, but she didn't move. After several minutes the door screeched closed and they were alone in the darkness once more.

"What is this place Ares?" Java talked to her dog as she opened the lunchbox. She located the usual sandwich, chips and water but her hand touched something else—something soft but rough. She grasped it with both hands and explored it with her fingertips. "Burlap—a voodoo doll," she snorted as she fingered the buttons. Her initial reaction was to toss the thing into the stagnant water below her but knew it might provide clues, so she stuffed it into her jacket pocket.

Ares whimpered waiting patiently for his half of the sandwich. They ate their food and Java unscrewed the lid from the water bottle. "I know this is going to put us to sleep big guy, but I'm dying of thirst. I know you are too." She drank half the water and poured the rest into the lunchbox for Ares. He lapped it dry and the two soon fell into a deep sleep.

CHAPTER 58

Kat moaned seductively as she reached for Java. Waking each morning beside the blonde was Kat's favorite thing to do. She moved her hand to touch the soft warmth of her lover then drew herself into the fetal position as her stomach twisted into a knot. Java wasn't in her bed.

She hugged herself as tears streamed down her cheeks. She had loved Java for so long she couldn't imagine life without her.

A week had passed since Java's disappearance. Kat knew that the chances of finding the blonde alive diminished with each passing day. "Dear God, help me," she prayed.

Java's beautiful face filled her mind as she thought about tangling her fingers in golden hair and pulling soft lips against hers. "Don't do this to me, Java," she cried into her pillow. "Please don't leave me alone."

Kat showered, drank a cup of coffee and headed to the restaurant. She wondered how everything could go on the same as always when her reason for living was gone.

She was surprised to see Beau's car in the parking lot of Java's Place. Her heart skipped a beat with the thought of news about Java.

Kat parked and rushed into the restaurant. She stopped when she saw Penny, Beau, Karen and the rest of her team huddled talking softly. Her heart felt as if it would burst from her chest. She closed her eyes against the stinging tears that threatened to announce to the world how much she loved the blonde.

Two Ways to Die
A Java Jarvis Thriller
by Erin Wade

Sirens wailed down the street and the long deep honk of fire engines and emergency vehicles filled the air.

"Java?" Kat cried running to the group.

"We're not sure," Karen caught Kat in her arms. "A druggie found the body this morning. We're going to the scene now. You should ride with me."

"My forensic team is already there," Penny added.

##

Beau flashed his badge to get them as close to the activity as possible but was forced to park a block away because of the emergency response vehicles. The team followed the detective as he held up his badge making it possible for them to walk to the front of the onlookers.

"What the hell is that, Captain," Beau addressed his boss Gary Landry.

"You won't believe me when I tell you," Landry shook his head to indicate his own disbelief.

The team pushed to the front of officers gaping at the scene. A block long section of the street and sidewalks were pushed out of the ground by something huge. It was as if a giant cement submarine was trying to surface from under Canal Street.

"It looks like the Jolly Green Giant's coffin floated to the surface," Barbie scoffed. "What is that, Beau?"

"It's one end of Harrah's parking garage," Captain Landry replied. "Basically, a seven-hundred by one-hundred-foot cement box whose corner has floated to the surface breaking through the street."

Penny rushed to the coroner's truck with Kat close behind her. "Penny, why is the truck here instead of the van?" Kat asked.

Penny pointed to the ladders the fire department had lowered into the hole in the top of the cement. "There's more than one body in there."

"I'm going down with you," Kat declared.

Two Ways to Die
A Java Jarvis Thriller
by Erin Wade

"I don't think you should—" Kat interrupted Penny.

"Please Penny," Kat begged. "I must go with you."

Penny nodded and led the way to the first ladder. "Watch your step."

Penny's team had already set up bright lights so the ME could examine the bodies. Penny looked around her. Two headless bodies were stretched out on their backs.

"Hopefully these will match the heads we have in the morgue," Penny said kneeling by the first body. "Judging from the decomp I'd say these have been here for some time."

The police continued to search the tunnel. "Penny there's another one over here," one of the men called out.

"And I've got one here," a female officer lighted a body with her flashlight.

"Four bodies," Penny mumbled to Kat. "I think we've found The Decapitator's dumping ground."

"Java?" Kat exhaled a ragged breath.

"She's not here," Penny declared.

"Thank God," Kat exhaled loudly.

"We're missing Delores Ruiz's body. Look for one more corpse." Penny instructed her team.

Kat leaned against the wall of the tunnel waiting for her legs to stop shaking. "Were the women murdered and decapitated here," she finally asked Penny.

"No, this is a body dump," Penny concluded. "There's no sign of blood which means they bled out somewhere else and were dumped here."

Kat walked outside the perimeter of the high-beam lights and peered into the darkness. "What is this place?"

"Back in the sixties, the New Orleans City Council was populated by a group that owned a huge construction company," Penny talked as she worked on the bodies. "They railroaded several huge concrete construction projects through the council and made some of the most idiotic decisions imaginable.

"This tunnel for instance. It was a 1.3-million-dollar waste of taxpayer money. This was supposed to be a six-lane interstate tunnel carrying traffic beneath downtown New Orleans and relieving the traffic congestion in the city's business district. Unfortunately, the idea was abandoned after the tunnel was constructed so it became an albatross around the city's neck. It was buried and the city fathers wanted it to stay that way. Out of sight, out of mind, so to speak. Most people have forgotten about it.

"Harrah's is built over the other end of it and uses that section of the tunnel for a parking garage. This unexpected surfacing has to tilt that a little."

"This is in total darkness," Kat pointed out. "Harrah's parking garage is lighted."

"Yes, about half the tunnel was sealed off years ago as water began to seep into it," Penney added. "The thinking was to let this end fill with water to stabilize the entire thing. Harrah's weight on the other end was supposed to hold down that part of the tunnel. As you walk deeper into the tunnel, you'll encounter water."

"I'm going to take Chris and Barbie and search the rest of the tunnel," Kat informed her.

"Probably a good idea," Penny agreed. "Be careful. I have no idea how deep the water gets."

Two Ways to Die
A Java Jarvis Thriller
by Erin Wade

CHAPTER 59

Ares' low guttural growl woke Java. The dog had placed himself between an unseen danger and the blonde. Java placed her hand on his back to let him know she was there. A menacing hiss accompanied by claws raking the concrete alerted Java to the enemy threatening them.

Ares advanced toward the critter. A loud squeal and more hissing ensued as Ares' growl became more hostile. A loud growl and the snapping of strong jaws set off more squealing and scrambling of claws as the unknown visitor retreated a safe distance from the dog.

"Good boy," Java praised Ares as she ran her hands over him to make certain he hadn't been bitten. The dog seemed to grow in stature as Java praised him. She tried to ascertain his breed but wasn't sure. Although he was undernourished, his chest was broad and his back was medium length. He was about eighteen inches tall, and his legs were solid and muscled. Java guessed a Pit Bull.

Although she found no recent injuries on Ares, Java felt numerous scars. "Did they make you fight, fellow?" She said as she lovingly stroked him. "Kat's going to love you. She's the dog whisperer."

The whirring noise above announced the arrival of food. Java pushed Ares' between her and the wall and feigned sleep. The lunchbox landed on the ledge and the rope was pulled back up the wall. Java lay motionless until the usual clanging on the pipes started. The usual light beam highlighted the lunchbox.

Like a trained rat Java stood and walked to the lunchbox, sat down and pulled it into her lap. She

Two Ways to Die
A Java Jarvis Thriller
by Erin Wade

wondered what she was being conditioned for. The same routine every day and like a good subject she reacted the same every day.

As she opened the lunchbox and halved the sandwich the clicking of claws running toward them made Ares ignore his food and whirl to face their attacker. A vicious battle ensued as the dog fought to protect her.

Snarling and snapping were all Java could hear. She couldn't tell who was winning. A mournful howl from Ares ripped through the cavern as dog and attacker went off the ledge. Java cried out as she heard the loud splash below and the pungent smell of the disturbed swamp.

"No," Java screamed, "Ares, Ares come here boy."

She could hear the dog thrashing around in the water. His whines for help broke her heart but she had no idea where he was. She knew he couldn't survive long in the icy water.

"To hell with it," Java hissed as she slid off the ledge and dropped into the slimy abyss.

Java was waist deep in the water when her feet reached bottom. "Thank you, Lord," she shouted out loud. She stood motionless listening for any sound that would tell her where Ares was.

Water splashing on her left led her to the flailing dog. She wrapped her arms around him and hugged him close. He was trembling and whimpering. "It's okay big guy. I've got you. Let's hope there's a way out of this mess."

She moved slowly through the caustic water hoping to hit a wall. She knew she couldn't stay in the freezing water.

She remembered seeing the rusting file cabinets along a wall. If she could locate them, she could shove Ares on top of them and hopefully hoist herself up too. Her captor had gotten her into this nightmare so there had to be a way out of it.

Two Ways to Die
A Java Jarvis Thriller
by Erin Wade

Java sloshed through the cesspool clutching Ares to her stomach. His paws and head rested on her shoulders like a baby. She prayed she found a way out of the frigid water before hypothermia overtook her.

She moved slowly in the darkness knowing she could easily crash into something before she knew it. Holding Ares with her hands required her feet do the searching before moving forward but they were losing feeling fast. Her right foot hit something and she gripped Ares with one arm and reached out with the other to feel what they had encountered.

She had never loved a file cabinet so much in her life. She groped around in the darkness until her hand found the top. She felt the cabinets and discovered there were three of them lined up along the wall. She planted her feet solidly on the floor and lifted Ares to the top of the steel cabinets. *Now to get myself up there*, she thought.

Ares was trembling and whining from the cold. He wanted to follow her but stayed when she gave him the command. Freeing her hands made it easier to feel around in the water. She found something large and solid. *A desk*, she guessed.

She felt her way around the desk praying that she would be able to shove it toward the cabinets. Feeling was leaving both her legs as she reached the other side of the desk. She planted her heels against the floor and her butt against the desk. She shoved with all the strength she could summon. Just as she was about to give up the desk began to move. She kept pushing and praying until the desk slid into the file cabinets.

Shivering from head to toe Java climbed on top of the submerged desk then hefted herself onto the top of the file cabinets. Ares welcomed her with a yelp and a lick on the face.

Two Ways to Die
A Java Jarvis Thriller
by Erin Wade

"Your tongue is the warmest thing I've felt in days," she laughed hugging the dog to her.

The familiar whirring overhead warned her of her captor's return. She pushed Ares behind her and dangled her legs over the edge of the file cabinets. When her jailer failed to find her after carefully shining a bright light along the ledge, the light began to search the filthy water.

Java took in everything the flashlight illuminated. Two metal staircases were about twenty feet from her. *If we can get to the stairs, we can get to the second level and out of the water. I should be able to do that.* She thought then the light flashed on something swimming in the water.

"Son-of-a . . ." Java yelled yanking her feet onto the top of the file cabinet as a huge alligator slammed into the file cabinet where her legs had been moments before.

The flashlight beam instantly bathed her in light blinding her. "What do you want?" She yelled. "Show yourself."

The light went out. Java was certain her abductor was confident she couldn't leave the top of the file cabinet. She waited for the closing of the trap door above and the slim beam of light heralding her lunchbox. Everything happened as usual, but no lunchbox was lowered.

"We're so screwed Ares," Java muttered.

Java reached into her jacket pocket and felt the toothpicks. She counted eighteen of the tiny sticks. "Six days," she hissed. "I've been in here for six days. Where the hell is Kat?"

Java knew her chances of making it to the stairs through the water were slim now that the gator knew she was a meal possibility. She stood up on top of the file cabinet and reached over her head trying to find the ledge. It was slightly above her head.

A chair, she thought. *There was a chair on the other side of the desk when I shoved it against the file cabinets.*

Two Ways to Die
A Java Jarvis Thriller
by Erin Wade

She eased to the top of the desk then dropped to her knees on the submerged furniture. She felt around the edge of the desk until she thought she was close to the location of the chair. Knowing she could pull back a bloody stump, she dragged her hand through the water searching for the chair back. On her third attempt her hand hit the metal object. She grasped it and pulled it onto the desk.

Java was motionless for several minutes trying to ascertain the location of the gator. Failing, she lifted the chair to the top of the file cabinets then climbed up. A loud splash as the gator flapped his tail in the water made her glad she was safely seated on the file cabinets.

Java steadied the metal chair on top of the cabinets. She placed Ares on the ledge then prepared to pull herself onto the ledge. Suddenly a chair leg gave way pitching Java to the left. She scrambled to hang onto the file cabinets and keep from sliding into the water.

Frustrated beyond belief, Java resorted to a primal scream. She wondered if her captor's intent was to drive her mad and then kill her. She wondered if all the other victims had been subjected to the same treatment then murdered.

Taking deep breaths, she calmed her breathing then cleared her mind. Ares whimpered reminding her she now had him on one level and herself on another. She hoped Ares was as smart as she thought he was.

Java slipped back to the top of the desk. She was a strong swimmer but was certain she couldn't out swim a gator. She gripped the twisted chair and flung it as hard as she could then quickly slipped into the water.

The chair hit the far wall and bounced into the water. Java kicked off the desk and swam hitting floating objects and debris. She hoped the gator was after the chair. In a moment of panic, she wondered if she was swimming in the right direction then she hit the metal stairs. She scurried

Two Ways to Die
A Java Jarvis Thriller
by Erin Wade

from the water as the gator slammed his powerful tail into the water making one last effort to catch her.

Java climbed to the top of the stairs and collapsed. She lay still in complete darkness but at least now she was off the ledge and out of the water. Standing she felt her way to the wall on the left of the stairwell. She prayed that Ares would be smart enough to come to her. A whine close to her ear sent a jolt of joy through her soul. The dog had made his way along the ledge and was so close she could hear him panting.

Java felt for the ledge then felt Ares' legs. She put her hands under his shoulders and helped him into her arms. Ares licked her neck and yelped his joy.

Java knew dogs couldn't see in total darkness any more than humans could, but Ares seemed to have a sixth sense when it came to avoiding objects in their way. Java slipped her belt from her soaked jeans and looped it around Ares' neck trusting the dog to lead them to safety.

Ares stopped and began to whine. Java moved around him and ran her hands along the wall encountering a door. She felt around until her hand closed around a doorknob. Twisting the knob, she almost cried when it turned, and the door opened.

Functioning in total darkness with no points of reference was almost impossible. Java felt along the wall and located a switch. She whispered a silent prayer then flipped the switch. Nothing happened.

"It was worth a try," she snickered to Ares.

Java wondered if she was on the same level as her captor. The person had been above her. Now she was above the level she and Ares had been confined to.

"Let's leave the door open and hope our abductor walks past us," Java planned out loud. She and Ares huddled in a corner facing the door. Exhausted from their escape and mental anguish both fell asleep.

Two Ways to Die
A Java Jarvis Thriller
by Erin Wade

Java was awakened by the whirring sound. *There must be electricity somewhere,* Java thought. *That's an electrical sound.*

Java knew she'd have only one chance to surprise her jailer. She crouched in the doorway and waited.

CHAPTER 60

Kat, Chris and Barbie clicked on their tactical flashlights illuminating the old tunnel. "Did you know this was here?" Barbie asked her partners.

"First I've ever heard of it," Kat shrugged, "and I've lived here for twenty years."

"I'm sure the city politicians want to forget about it," Chris theorized, "but it's too big a screwup to go away."

Halfway through the blocked off end of the tunnel they encountered water. Kat flashed her light onto the darkness. "That looks like the wall between this end and Harrah's parking garage," she pointed out.

"We'll need waders or a boat to go all the way to the wall," Barbie surmised. "You want me to get a boat, Kat?"

"No . . ." Kat hesitated. "No, I don't see anything. Just debris and stagnant water."

Penny was finishing up her examination of the last body when they returned to the staging area. "If this thing hadn't floated to the surface, we'd never find these bodies," Penny declared. "I'll let you know if I find anything that will lead us to their killer."

The sun was setting when they finished working the crime scene. "I need to get to the restaurant," Kat said. "The show must go on."

"I'll drive you back," Karen volunteered.

"She can ride with us," Barbie offered. "Chris and I are returning to the restaurant too."

The three discussed Java's disappearance looking at it from all angles.

Two Ways to Die
A Java Jarvis Thriller
by Erin Wade

"I still think Déjà is involved in The Basher killings," Kat shared her suspicions with her teammates. "I don't see her as The Decapitator though.

"We were trying to pull together enough evidence to convince a judge to sign a search warrant for Déjà's home and shop. Java was on to something. I think that's why she's been abducted."

"What?" Chris asked.

Kat told them about the tally marks in Déjà's journal. "Java asked Penny to compare them to the bloody tally at the last crime scene."

Chris drove past the customer parking lot of Java's Place and parked in the back. "It looks like Jody Schooley and Déjà vu are here," she pointed out. "Kat, why don't you take Jody. Barbie and I will double team Déjà vu.

##

Kat looked at her face in the mirror. Dark circles under her eyes evidenced her lack of sleep. Sleep had eluded her since Java's disappearance. The singer carefully applied makeup and fixed her hair. It took her less than thirty minutes to look like a million dollars. She dreaded stepping onto the restaurant's stage without Java smiling down at her from the balcony.

Kat was in automatic mode as the performed her routine. She noticed that Jody Schooley had both Amanda and Melody with him. *Probably trying to drum up business,* Kat thought. *I'll tell Chris and Barbie to watch them.*

Kat finished her set then strolled through the diners welcoming them to the restaurant and signing a few autographs.

"You should join us," Jody invited when she stopped at his table.

"Maybe I will," Kat smiled pulling out a chair between Melody and Amanda.

Two Ways to Die
A Java Jarvis Thriller
by Erin Wade

"I understand you paid me a visit last week," Jody smirked. "Mind telling me what you were looking for?"

"Java," Kat said. "She's missing."

"Java, the queen of cool," Jody snickered. "Someone got the drop on her! Maybe they wanted more than a cuppa' Joe. She is a damn good-looking woman."

Kat stared into Jody's face. "You really are repulsive," she snapped. She stood and walked away from the table.

"You do have a way with women," Melody taunted Jody.

"Shut up whore," Jody growled.

CHAPTER 61

Java slowed her heartbeat trying to hear anything that would indicate another person in the room. She sensed it more than heard it. A sound to her right. Someone was crying. Ares growled and placed himself between Java and the sound.

Java hated the darkness she was operating in. It could be a trick, but she decided she had nothing to lose. "Hello," she called into the blackness.

Sniffing and the crying stopped.

"Hello," Java called again. "Is anyone here?"

"Yes," a woman's voice quavered. "Who are you?"

"I'm Java Jarvis," the blonde answered. "Who are you?"

"Java Jarvis," the joy in the response was obvious. "Java Jarvis it's me, Melody. Where are you? Where are we?"

"Keep talking," Java instructed. "I'll come to you."

"Ares, find," Java held the makeshift leash as Ares led her out of the safety of the room they'd discovered. "Keep talking Melody."

"I'm here. I think you are headed for me." Melody started a stream of chatter. "I'm just going to count out loud until you find me."

Ares led Java to Melody who was sitting against the wall her arms wrapped around her knees. Java touched her head and Melody squealed.

"It's okay," Java assured her. "It's just me. What are you doing here?"

Two Ways to Die
A Java Jarvis Thriller
by Erin Wade

"I don't know," Melody caught Java's hand and pulled herself into a standing position. "It's so cold in here and you're so damp."

"I know," Java huffed. "It's a long story."

"Where are we?" Melody asked again. "How long have you been here?"

"I have no idea where we are," Java answered. "I've been here six or seven days. Someone knocked me out and I woke up here."

"I think I was drugged," Melody mumbled. "I remember having wine with Jody and Déjà vu and I woke up here."

"Do you have a cell phone?" Java asked.

"No," Melody checked her coat pockets. "I have two packs of peanut butter crackers and a half bottle of water."

Java almost drooled. "Would you share. Ares and I haven't eaten in a long time."

"Of course," Melody gasped. "I hope you don't think I'd eat them without sharing. How have you stayed alive?"

"My captor brings food three times a day, but I made him mad and he hasn't brought anything for a while."

"It's a man?" Melody asked.

"I don't know for certain," Java took the crackers Melody pressed into her hand. She ate three of the circular treats and gave three to Ares.

"It's so dark in here," Melody noted. "Is there no light anywhere?"

"None," Java confirmed.

"Wait!" Melody exclaimed. "I have a penlight on my keychain." She searched through her overcoat pockets and sighed with relief when she jingled her keys. She turned on the small light.

Java laughed ecstatically. "Oh, thank God. I was afraid I was blind."

Two Ways to Die
A Java Jarvis Thriller
by Erin Wade

Melody shined the light on Java's face. "You're none the worse for your ordeal," she smiled. "However, you could certainly use a bath and comb."

"May I hold the light?" Java asked. "I have a feel for this place but have no idea how to get out."

Melody handed her the penlight and watched silently as Java flashed the light around the cavernous room.

"What is this place?" Melody whispered.

"I think we're inside the old New Orleans Civil Defense Emergency Operations Center. It's a huge complex of meeting rooms, hallways and dormitories designed to house city officials and law enforcement leaders during a nuclear attack." Java moved the light over the water below. "It's half full of water and at least one gator.

"It was built in the sixties and abandoned after scientists ascertained no one could withstand a direct nuclear blast."

Java led Melody into the room she had discovered. Flashing the light around the room.

"This looks like a storage room," Melody commented. "Look, there are five-gallon jugs of water with cork stoppers."

"And enough K-rations to feed a small army," Java noted, picking up one of the packages. "The packaging is still in good shape."

"What is it?" Melody asked

"It's food the military used for troops in the field," Java explained. "K-rations have a five or six-year shelf life."

"Would it be safe to eat it?" Melody inquired.

"Hopefully we won't have to resort to that," Java gulped. "Let's see if we can find a door."

##

Two Ways to Die
A Java Jarvis Thriller
by Erin Wade

After hours of searching they returned to the storage room. Java and Melody checked the items on the shelves looking for anything that would provide light.

"Flares," Java shouted. "I've found flares."

"We have nothing to light them," Melody pointed out.

"Flares come with their own ignition," Java chirped. "They strike like a match. Keep your fingers crossed they are good after all these years."

Java pulled the cap from a flare and struck it across the flare's end. Nothing happened. She struck it again, harder. A spark flew from the flare. She hit it a third time and the flare burst into flames.

Melody did a little dance clapping her hands at Java's success. "You did it, Java Jarvis."

"Melody, please, call me Java. My last name isn't needed."

"I'm starving," Melody complained. "Do we dare consume your K-rations?"

"I think that would be a bad idea," Java frowned. "They would probably give us food poisoning. Why don't you eat the pack of crackers you have?"

"We can share them," Melody volunteered. "Two for you and me and two for Ares."

"I'd kill for a drink of water," Java choked, "but I'm not sure this water is safe to drink."

"Here," Melody pulled the bottle of water from her coat pocket. "Drink this. I'm not thirsty."

"Are you sure?" Java asked eyeing the water.

"Positive," Melody unscrewed the lid and handed Java the bottle.

Melody sat down on the floor and leaned against the wall. "Do you think they will come back for us?"

"I hope so," Java shrugged. "I'm very tired. I'm having trouble keeping my eyes open."

"Sleep," Melody encouraged. "Ares and I will keep watch.

"Java, Java," Melody repeated the name as if committing it to memory. "Java is a strange name for a girl. It's another name for coffee, isn't it?"

"Yes," Java laughed. "I do prefer it to the other nicknames for coffee."

"What are the other nicknames?" Melody asked leaning her head on the blonde's shoulder.

"Um, there's Cup of Joe, Mud, go juice, jitter juice—"

"I agree," Melody interrupted. "Java is the best of the lot. I like it. It fits you, Java Jarvis."

"Mm-hmm," Java agreed sleep overtaking her.

CHAPTER 62

Light flooded the cavernous room as law enforcement officers pried open the steel door the city maintenance workers had cut through.

"We received several reports of a dog howling in here," Beau frowned. "When workers opened it up, they found evidence of someone being here but no dog or human. I don't know—" A long mournful howl interrupted Beau. "Well damn, there is a dog in here.

"If my hunch is right," Kat yelled standing at the top of the stairs leading down into the bunker, "she should be in here."

Penny and her crew quickly spread high-powered lights around the ledge above the room making every corner visible.

"Jesus, there's a gator in the water," Barbie screamed. "How'd it get in here?"

"Hurricane Katrina," Chris said. "A lot of water creatures are still in places they shouldn't be."

"Spread out," Beau instructed his officers. "Search every nook and cranny of this place. I hope you're right this time, Kat."

"It's just a hunch," Kat replied.

"More of your profiler's instinct," Beau teased.

"Detective Braxton, in here," an officer called.

Kat and her two partners followed Beau into a room where several officers were standing. "It looks like someone's been here," the officer pointed to the recently burned flares.

"She must be in here somewhere," Kat cried.

Two Ways to Die
A Java Jarvis Thriller
by Erin Wade

Kat saw a movement behind a shelf of K-rations. "There," she ran around the shelving and into the jaws of Ares.

"Whoa, big guy," Kat fell to her knees and searched her pockets for anything to feed the malnourished dog. "Do you like granola bars?"

Ares cautiously approached Kat's outstretched offering. "Beau," Kat spoke softly to avoid spooking the dog. "He has Java's belt around his neck."

Ares snapped the bar from Kat's hand and retreated to the corner of the shelving. "Barbie, do you have any snack bars I can feed him."

After taking three granola bars from Kat, Ares allowed her to take hold of the belt around his neck.

"I'll call animal control," Beau offered.

"No," Kat barked. "I'll keep him with me. He's been Java's companion in this hell."

"I've got a blood trail," Penny shouted. "It leads to this room." She pushed open double doors that led to an infirmary. "What the hell!"

They stood in the doorway of an operating room. A bone saw lay on the metal table. Blood covered the floor and the table.

Kat swallowed the bile that filled her mouth.

"It's not fresh," Penny noted. "It's not Java's blood. But I'm betting the DNA in this room will match the bodies we have in the morgue."

The officers spent three hours searching the old bomb shelter but turned up nothing that would lead them to Java.

Kat couldn't hide her disappointment. Her nerves were wearing thin and she desperately missed Java. She walked outside to breathe the fresh air and steady her nerves. She knew she was unraveling.

You've worked much gorier cases than this one, she told herself, *but Java had never been the victim.*

Two Ways to Die
A Java Jarvis Thriller
by Erin Wade

Ares whined and touched her leg with his nose. Kat dropped to her knees and hugged the dog. "You fell in love with her too, didn't you fellow?"

As the sun went down Penny's crew continued to process the crime scene. "You three should leave," Penny encouraged the FBI agents. "There's nothing more you can do here. Kat put your thinking cap on and conjure another location where Java might be."

"Do you want to spend the night with us?" Chris asked Kat as they walked to their cars.

"No, I just want to go home and soak in a nice hot bath," Kat responded. "But I appreciate the offer."

"What're you going to do with that dog? Barbie asked.

"I'm taking him home with me," Kat smiled. "He was the last to see Java."

##

When Kat opened the door on the passenger side of her Benz, Ares didn't jump in. He whimpered as if unsure what to do. Kat lifted his front feet into the car, and he jumped into the seat.

"Looks like you'll be the first one getting a bath," Kat talked to Ares as she pulled her car from the curb.

The drive to Java's lake house was pleasant. Ares lay with his head on the console staring at Kat as if worshiping her.

When they arrived at the house, Ares balked at walking up the stairs. "How long were you locked in that place?" Kat cooed to him encouraging him to take one step and then another. When they reached the porch, Kat clapped her hands and caught Ares' face between her hands looking him in the eye. "You are such a good boy," she praised him.

Kat ignored her growling stomach in favor of bathing Ares. She was surprised at how willing he was to let her lift him into the bathtub. He submerged his body in the water until only is head was sticking out. He playfully snapped at the soap bubbles while Kat scrubbed him.

"Where'd you get these scars big guy," Kat frowned as she gently massaged soap into his hair and around the scars. "Were you abused?"

Ares stood still for Kat to dry him with a towel. When she finished, she stood back and he shook himself from tail to ears fluffing his short hair.

"What a good, good, boy you are," Kat caught his broad head and kissed him between the eyes. "Java will be so pleased to see we've adopted a Pit Bull."

Ares wagged his entire body as he followed Kat into the kitchen. He lay a few feet away from her as she opened canned chicken and boiled eggs for chicken salad.

"We'll have to get you some dogfood," Kat talked to Ares as she peeled eggs and chopped up a tomato. She cut a boiled egg in half and carried it to Ares. He wolfed down both halves as Kat fed it to him. "Good thing I cooked you three eggs," she laughed opening another can of chicken for her companion.

"Only Java could find a starved stray in hell," Kat voiced her thoughts glad to have the dog to bare her soul to. "I envy you being with her these past days. I've missed her so much."

CHAPTER 63

Java floated between sleep and awareness. She snuggled deeper into the soft clean sheets allowing herself to drift back to sleep. *Soft clean sheets*, her mind exploded. *How did I get between soft clean sheets?*

She didn't open her eyes or move as she listened for any sound that would tell her where she was. The room was silent. She moved her hand to brush her hair from her eyes and discovered she was handcuffed to a sturdy metal headboard. She tried to move her legs and realized her ankles were also secured to the bed.

"Ares," she whispered but the dog wasn't with her.

"Finally, you're awake," Melody's voice filled the room.

Java opened her eyes. "Melody are you okay? I thought . . ." She stopped talking as she realized that Melody wasn't bound. She was walking around the bed staring at Java.

"How did I get here?" Java narrowed her eyes trying to think.

"I carried you here," Melody grinned salaciously making Java feel like the main item on the buffet.

"The bottle of water you gave me," Java reasoned out loud. "You drugged me. You're my captor."

"Not captor, my love," Melody hummed. "I'm your savior. The woman you want to spend the rest of your life with."

Which may not be very long, Java thought searching the room for any means of escape. Her gaze rested on the handcuff key on the dresser.

Two Ways to Die
A Java Jarvis Thriller
by Erin Wade

"Where am I exactly?" Java asked.

"The top of the mansion," Melody purred. "This is our honeymoon suite. No one will bother us here."

I was afraid of that, Java thought.

"You carried me up here?" Java raised a doubting brow. "You must be stronger than you look."

Melody grabbed the edge of the comforter and yanked it back exposing Java's naked body. "You look as good as I thought you would," Melody cooed. "Um, I do love making love to a woman with abs and nice round breasts."

"Melody," Java smiled. "Why do you have me handcuffed to the bed?"

Melody brushed Java's hair from her face bending over to kiss her lips. "Because I'm going to fulfill your every desire Java Jarvis," she whispered.

"Right now, my biggest desire is to drink water and take a shower," Java continued smiling. "I'd never make love with you without cleaning up first. I'm filthy."

"That doesn't bother me," Melody traced Java's face with her manicured nails. I've waited a long time to please you, to make your fantasies a reality."

"Just being with you is reality enough," Java tried to keep the sarcasm from her voice. "You're very beautiful."

Melody sat down beside Java. "I think you are gorgeous," she trailed her fingers down Java's neck and stopped between her breast. "I think you will be the most wonderful lover I've ever encountered."

"Don't get your hopes up," Java mumbled. "I might disappoint you."

"I don't think so," Melody caressed Java's breast. "See how your nipples respond to my touch."

Java silently cursed her body for reacting to Melody's fondling. "Don't you want me to hold you and touch you too?" Java reasoned.

Two Ways to Die
A Java Jarvis Thriller
by Erin Wade

"No, I want to make you beg then I want to satisfy you," Melody's smile was almost evil. "Do you beg for Kat Lace, Java?"

"I don't do anything with Kat Lace," Java lied. "She's married."

"Really," confusion danced across Melody's face. "I thought she was your woman."

"No," Java gasped. "Why would you think that?"

"The way you look at her," Melody squeezed Java's breast hard.

"Oh, Jesus, Melody. That hurts," Java cried.

"I'm not wrong," Melody declared. "I study people. I know how to read them, their body language, their looks and the sound of their voices. I know you want to sleep with Kat Lace."

"No," Java shrieked as Melody tightened her hand. "No, honest, Melody. I've been watching you. Wanting you."

Melody relaxed her hold on Java's breast and smiled. "I'm going to fix you something to eat. You must be starving."

"Yes, yes, I am," Java agreed. "May I take a shower while you fix us something to eat?"

Melody trailed her fingers between Java's breasts, down her torso to her abdomen. "I think not," she grinned.

##

For breakfast Kat cooked a steak and cut it up for Ares. "This is the only meat Java has in the house," she apologized to the dog as he gobbled down the delicacy.

"I'm taking you to work with me," she talked as she walked onto the porch with Ares behind her. "Java has some rope under the house. That'll do until I can get you a proper harness."

Ares followed her down the stairs, ran to the grass and rolled around in it. His yelps of joy made Kat laugh. "How long were you in that dungeon, boy?" she rubbed behind his ears and let him run around the yard until he was ready to follow her.

##

Kat stopped at a pet store and purchased dogfood and a harness for the Pit Bull. "You are so handsome," she cooed as she fastened the strap around Ares' chest.

She was proud of how well-behaved Ares was when she took him into the back door of the restaurant. Chris and Barbie fell in love with him and he with them.

"He looks like a different dog," Barbie laughed as she hugged him. "He smells like you."

"I only had my shampoo to bathe him," Kat grinned. "Of course, he smells like me."

"I didn't say that was bad," Barbie explained. "He smells nice just like you."

"Have we heard from Penny this morning?" Kat asked.

Her cellphone rang and Penny's name appeared on her screen. "Speaking of the devil."

"Hello Penny," Kat turned on her speaker. "Please tell me you have good news?"

"I don't know how good it is," Penny quipped, "But I do have news. I found DNA matches in the bomb shelter for all the heads including Delores Ruiz. I don't have her body yet. We're going to make a more thorough search of the facility today in the daylight. Hopefully the killer hasn't had a chance to move her body and it will still be there. The good news is that I did not find Java's blood in that mess."

"Then she's still alive," Kat surmised.

"I think so," Penny confirmed. "I'll keep you informed.

Kat looked at her partners. "What now?"

"Now we open the doors and welcome customer," Chris said.

Two Ways to Die
A Java Jarvis Thriller
by Erin Wade

Jody Schooley and Amanda were the first two customers through the door. "When she has a minute," Jody said after the waitress took their order, "I need to speak with Java."

The waitress relayed Jody's request to Kat. "I'll talk to him," Kat volunteered.

Kat stopped midstride as she noticed the wristwatch Amanda was wearing. It was Java's.

"Java's not here," Kat said as she approached the table. "May I help you?"

"No, I need to talk to her," Jody wrinkled his nose. "It's a business proposition."

"Um," Kat nodded her head as she got a good look at the watch. There was no doubt in her mind it was Java's.

"When she comes in, I'll send her to your table," Kat smiled.

She strolled to the kitchen and pulled Chris and Barbie aside. "I have an idea where Java might be," she whispered. "Amanda is wearing Java's watch. You two keep Jody and his harlot here until I get back. I think they're holding Java in Jody's cat house."

"We should go with you," Chris insisted.

"Call Beau and tell him to meet me there," Kat said. "The best thing you two can do is keep Jody here so he won't call the authorities on me."

"Be careful, Kat," Barbie cautioned.

"Always," Kat muttered as she pulled on Ares' leash. "Come on big guy."

CHAPTER 64

Kat smiled her most endearing smile at the butler who opened the door of Jody's home. "I'm here to see Melody," she winked surreptitiously.

"Miss Melody isn't here right now," the man replied. "Do you have an appointment with her?"

"Not really, just a spur of the moment sort of thing." Kat shrugged. "May I wait on her?"

"This is her day off," the butler countered. "Perhaps one of the other girls can help you. All of them are very good."

Kat looked around the mansion. It was three stories with beautiful balconies overlooking the great room and bedrooms off each balcony. An oversized octagonal cupola topped the third floor forming a huge fourth story suite.

"This is beautiful," Kat complimented. "Do you actually us that fourth level?"

"No ma'am," the butler responded. "It's used mostly for storage."

Kat relaxed her hold on Ares' leash giving him more freedom to sniff around the great room. He seemed to pick up a scent and began whining as he sniffed his way to the staircase and strained against his restraints pulling Kat behind him.

"What's wrong boy?" Kat bent to pet him intentionally dropping his leash.

Ares darted up the stairs with Kat close behind. "I'm so sorry," she called to the butler as she chased Ares up the stairs. By the time the dog stopped at the door entering the fourth-floor cupola Kat was out of breath.

Two Ways to Die
A Java Jarvis Thriller
by Erin Wade

Ares scratched furiously at the door. Kat turned the door handle and stepped inside the room. Ares leaped onto the bed and licked the face of the woman handcuffed to the headboard.

"Java?" Kat cried rushing to her lover. "What have they done to you?"

"Nothing soap and water won't fix," Java beamed. "I knew you'd find me. There's a key on the dresser. Get these cuffs off me before Melody returns."

"Kat Lace," Melody growled the name. "Why are you here?"

Kat turned to face Melody as the woman locked the door. "I've come for Java," Kat said softly.

"Um, no!" Melody shrugged. "but you can join us. Threesomes are such fun."

"Two of us on her while she's chained to the bed?" Kat smirked. "That could be fun."

"Kat," Java croaked. "Don't encourage her. There's something not right with her."

"Because I'm a whore?" Melody stomped to the bedside. "A harlot?" She bent over and kissed Java's lips hard.

In a flash Kat wrapped her arm around Melody's neck gripping her in a chokehold and pulling her backwards away from Java.

Melody backed up crushing Kat against the wall and knocking the breath from her. Kat released her chokehold and dodged as Melody swung her fist toward her face.

"She's strong, Java," Kat yelled as Melody drew back her arm to swing again. Kat ducked as Melody threw the punch and Melody's fist went through the wall.

"Holy. . . what the hell is going on?" Java screamed.

Java watched helplessly as the two women fought all over the room. She had never seen anyone hold their own with Kat and was beginning to worry that Kat might not prevail. Kat's usual deadly blows didn't seem to faze Melody.

Java began screaming and jerking trying to distract Melody. Melody whirled around to glare at Java. "I'll take care of you when I'm finished with your girlfriend," Melody howled. "I've waited a long time to please you."

Kat grabbed a lamp from the floor and swung it with all her might severing Melody's head from her shoulders.

What the hell, Kat thought. The headless body continued to reach out for Java as the lips spoke the words, "Come here baby, I'll show you how a real woman can make you feel." A deep guttural voice came from Melody's head.

Ares growled menacingly putting himself between Java and Melody.

Melody bent down to pick up her head. Kat clasped her hands together and brought them down in the middle of the woman's back sending Melody sprawling on the floor.

Ares jumped from the bed and grabbed the talking head. He caught it by the hair and shook it vigorously. The hair ripped out and the head rolled under the bed. Ares ran after it.

Melody crawled across the floor searching for her severed head. "Kat Lace, I won't simply remove your head" the head roared from under the bed. "I'm going to rip you into tiny pieces."

As Ares played keep away with Melody's head Kat frantically searched for a weapon to stop the nightmare she was fighting.

Kat stripped the electrical cord from the lamp and plugged it into the outlet as Melody jumped to her feet cradling her head in her arms. When Melody charged her Kat rammed the live cord into the head's eye. Sparks flew and crackled as the head's remaining hair caught fire. The head sputtered as it dropped to the floor and the body slowly stopped moving, its arms hanging at its side.

"It's a damn robot," Java yelled. "She's not human."

Kat grabbed the handcuff key and unshackled Java. "I get so tired of fighting the women off you," Kat teased as she wrapped a sheet around her naked lover and held her tightly.

The door burst open and Beau entered with Jody and Amanda in tow. "What the hell?" Beau gasped surveying the destroyed room.

"I warned them this could happen," Jody stormed in picking up the smoking head.

"What exactly has happened?" Beau snapped. "What is this thing?"

"A sex robot," Jody snorted. "It has artificial intelligence and learns quickly. As it interacts with people, johns and other women it learns what each one likes and acts accordingly. The more she was around others the more she learned until it was impossible to tell any difference between her and a real woman."

"I knew Melody was getting smarter by the day. I was thrilled but a little worried too that she might become a free thinker and uncontrollable."

"Or a killer," Kat hissed. "I shudder to think what she might have done to Java."

"How many of these things do you have?" Beau demanded.

"Eleven now," Jody grimaced. "All my girls are AIs. That's why I gave the original women money and a bus ticket to anywhere in the U.S.

"These robots are great. They do anything one asks. They're programed to please. They never get tired or require pay or food. They take care of their own hygiene and do housework. They're pretty incredible."

"If they weren't so deadly," Java commented.

Two Ways to Die
A Java Jarvis Thriller
by Erin Wade

"Obviously Melody had a wire crossed somewhere," Jody shrugged. "I haven't had a moments trouble from the others."

"Did you know you had a problem with Melody?" Beau asked.

"No, I never saw this coming." Jody bowed his head. "I had no idea Melody had set up this suite. I thought we only stored things here."

"I'm sealing off this room," Beau informed them. "I want Penny to go over it with a fine-toothed comb.

"Kat can you take Java home and get her cleaned up?"

"Of course," Kat agreed. "Come on, Ares. Let's take your Mama home."

"May I have some water?" Java pleaded as they descended the stairs.

CHAPTER 65

A sliver of sunlight fell across Java's eyes. She rolled onto her side and threw her arm over the warm woman in her bed and was happily greeted with a good solid lick down her face.

"Ares," she jumped back. "What are you doing here?"

"He hasn't left your side," a soft warm body wrapped around Java's back. "He's worse than a mother bear."

"Um," Java murmured as she turned over and buried her face between Kat's breasts. "There is no feeling in the world like waking in your arms."

"There is no worse feeling than waking in an empty bed," Kat kissed her slowly moving her full soft lips against Java's. "Java I was so scared I would lose you. I don't know what I'd do if I lost you baby."

"I knew you'd find me," Java reassured her. "I was wondering what was taking you so long."

"You can thank Ares for that," Kat kissed Java's lips. "Evidently he went berserk when Melody took you away and howled nonstop until we opened the bomb shelter and found him."

"We can exchange horror stories later," Kat murmured pushing Java onto her back and straddling the blonde. "Right now, I want to hold you and touch you."

"Be my guest," Java whispered.

##

Later Kat left a sleeping Java, turned on the gas fireplace, put on coffee and took Ares outside. It was a cool December morning and the dog frolicked for thirty minutes before running up the stairs.

Two Ways to Die
A Java Jarvis Thriller
by Erin Wade

The smell of fresh coffee and the welcoming warmth of the fireplace pleased her senses. She said a silent prayer of thanks for Java's return as she poured coffee into two cups.

Strong arms slipped around Kat as Java pulled her close and kissed the back of her neck. "I love you," the blonde whispered as she nestled her face in Kat's luxurious dark hair.

Kat leaned back against the woman that was the cornerstone of her world. "I love you so much, baby," she said.

They had breakfast and played with Ares as Java related her experience. "Ares kept me sane," she laughed as she scratched the dog's stomach.

"It's past noon," Kat glanced at her watch. "Is it possible they're going to let us take a day off?"

"Um, that's my idea of heaven," Java beamed. "A warm fireplace, excellent coffee and you."

Both their phones rang at the same time. "And I've conjured the devil," Kat smirked. "I'll take my call in the bedroom."

"Java," the blonde barked into her phone.

"Is Kat with you?" Beau asked.

"Yes," Java answered.

"Good. We need both of you in the briefing room in an hour. Penny's got a hell of a Frankenstein story to tell us."

"We'll be there."

Kat walked back into the living room. "Who called you?" She asked.

"Beau," Java quipped. "And you?"

"Penny. It seems she has quite a tale to share with us." Kat placed their coffee cups in the dishwasher then caught Java's hand as they walked to the bedroom. "We need to get a service vest for Ares," she chatted. "Then he can go everywhere with you."

Two Ways to Die
A Java Jarvis Thriller
by Erin Wade

##

Penny was shining pictures on the white board as the team members filed into the briefing room. She was ramrod straight and smiling. Java could tell the ME was in her element and at the top of her game.

"First I'd like to say how thankful I am that each and every member of our team is safely with us today," Penny smiled. "Java, you had us worried."

"I'm fine," Java blushed as her teammates mumbled their agreement with Penny.

"And we want to welcome the newest team member Ares," Penny continued gesturing toward the dog lying at Java's feet. "Ares saved Java's life."

The door opened and Jody Schooley slipped into the room.

"I think you all know Jody Schooley," Penny introduced the man. "What you may not know is that Jody heads up a federal sex crimes task force. He's deep undercover so feel free to continue to hate him.

"Jody has helped me piece together what has happened and why. First I'll share my findings with you."

"As you know the bomb shelter produced DNA from all our Decap victims. We never found the car belonging to our very first victim, a prostitute known as Classy.

"Melody killed her and stole her car. She kept it hidden in a deserted warehouse on the outskirts of town and only drove it when she killed a woman and needed to transport her body from the fallout shelter to the tunnel.

"Her murders weren't just for fun. There was a reason for them. I'll let Jody share his information with you."

"Thank you. I must tell you that I'm delighted to be able to read all of you in on my task force. Several years ago, the U.S. government underwrote a project to produce artificial intelligence robots to serve as prostitutes or sexbots as we call them. Melody was our very first sexbot.

Two Ways to Die
A Java Jarvis Thriller
by Erin Wade

Her artificial intelligence has been phenomenal, and we were thrilled to see how human she had become. We had no idea she would develop feelings such as jealousy, love, a desire to protect her place in society and general human emotions.

"Sexbots were designed to think and learn. The more they interact with humans the more they become like them. Human sex trafficking has reached astronomical proportions in the U.S. and worldwide. There is such a demand for women in the U.S. and other countries that women are kidnapped and coerced into prostitution. In the U.S. alone, over 20,000 people a year are victims of sex trafficking. Ninety-four percent of those crimes are committed against females.

"The theory behind the sexbots is that they will eventually eliminate the sex trafficking trade as we staff whore houses with sexbots.

"None of our customers realize they are interacting with a robot. That is why we have kept the operation secret. We want to see how accepted the sexbots are. And honestly, I've had no complaints.

"When I was assigned to set up a house for the ladies of the night, I slowly sent the workers home providing them a thousand dollars and a bus ticket to anywhere. As the women left, I replaced them with the sexbots. Five of the women took the money and bus ticket but didn't leave town. They went to work for Pender Crane.

"From Melody's diary," Jody held up a journal, "we've discovered that she thought the women who remained were a threat to her, so she murdered them separating their heads from their bodies. She thought that would make it more difficult to identify them. She had no understanding of DNA. According to her diary, she called Pender ordering a lady and then killing her. Melody was very capable of mimicking a man's deep guttural voice.

"Melody was incredibly strong," Kat noted. "Is there any chance she's also The Basher?"

"No," Jody answered. "Melody was with customers every time The Basher killed."

"According to Melody's diary she was enamored of Java," Jody continued, "and jealous of Kat."

"She had me fooled," Java huffed. "She showed up in the bomb shelter pretending to be a victim just like me."

"I think we can close the case on The Decapitator," Jody continued. "I am trusting all of you to keep my secret. I need to run the mansion for two years to get the data the government needs. There are establishments like mine opening in several large U.S. cities. Houston already has two working houses. Brothels and establishments all over the world are already successfully using the sexbots. Hopefully this will reduce the demand for human females.

"Melody's melt down will be in my report and efforts are already underway to assure nothing like this happens in the future."

"You were our number one suspect," Kat informed Jody.

Jody laughed. "I do act like a total ass. It's all part of the undercover work. It did worry me that Java took me down so easily when I insulted you."

Everyone laughed and continued to ask Jody questions about his operation. After everyone's curiosity was satisfied, they began discussing The Basher.

"I'm convinced Déjà vu is The Basher," Kat insisted. "She's tall enough and strong enough. She has that voodoo thing going on and she's mixed blood."

"I don't think so," Jody argued. "I'll have to check but I'm pretty certain she spent the night at my place on the night one of the crimes was committed."

"Really?" Kat laughed out loud. "You must have a sexbot that looks like Java."

Two Ways to Die
A Java Jarvis Thriller
by Erin Wade

"As a matter of fact, we do," Jody grinned. "Not exactly, of course, but she could be Java's sister and she is Déjà vu's favorite."

"I knew it," Kat hissed

"I'm just thankful The Basher has taken a hiatus," Penny sighed. "I've finally caught up with all the forensics from his crime scenes."

The meeting ended and everyone went their separate ways. "I still think we should pay Déjà vu a visit," Kat insisted.

"I trust your instincts," Java squeezed Kat's hand. "Déjà's place it is."

Two Ways to Die
A Java Jarvis Thriller
by Erin Wade

CHAPTER 66

"Good, she's here," Kat nodded toward Déjà's Cadillac on the parking lot. "We should leave Ares in the car for now. It's cool enough he'll be okay."

"We must be careful," Java advised. "We still don't have a search warrant and Déjà is the high priestess. We don't want to start a race war in Orleans by insulting their religious leader."

"You do the talking," Kat agreed. "I'll be content thinking that she sleeps with a robot while I sleep with you."

"You are evil sometimes," Java laughed.

"Surely you're not just now figuring that out." Kat's sultry laugh sent desire shooting through Java's body.

"Oh, Miss Lace," Java chuckled. "You do tilt my world."

The door chimed as the two agents entered the store and the step-drag cadence of her walk told them Kally was coming from the back to greet them. "Miss Java," she enthused. "We were so worried about you." It was obvious Kally wanted to hug the blonde, but she hesitated, not certain her hugs would be welcome.

"Thank you Kally," Java opened her arms and the young woman practically fell into them, tears streaming down her face.

After a few minutes Kally got control of her emotions and Kat pulled a tissue from her purse handing it to Kally.

"Thank you, Miss Kat," Kally smiled. "Both of you are so kind to me. I don't know what I'd do without you. You've given me a better life."

Two Ways to Die
A Java Jarvis Thriller
by Erin Wade

"You deserve a good life," Java nodded. "We need to see Déjà. Would you tell her we're here?"

"Miss Déjà vu isn't here," Kally sniffed.

"Her car's out front," Kat pointed out.

"I know," Kally nodded. "Reverend Ames picked her up this morning. They're doing a funeral together. Can I help you with something?"

"Nothing important," Java smiled. "We'll catch her later."

##

They drove by the church and were astounded to see the turnout for the funeral. "Must have been someone important in the community," Java commented.

"I suppose we must go back to the restaurant," Kat said gently drawing circles in the palm of Java's hand.

"Oooh lady," Java moaned. "Do you have any idea what you do to me?"

"Maybe," Kat giggled.

Java's phone rang and she pushed the button to put it on the car's speaker. "Java here," she answered.

"Hey boss, is Kat still with you?" Barbie asked.

"Yes. Is there a problem?" Java responded.

"Lindy Rochelle is here," Barbie continued. "She says Kat promised to have dinner with her tonight."

"I did, two days ago," Kat said. "I thought she might have information on Java's whereabouts. Tell her I'll be there on time."

Java groaned as she disconnected the phone call. "So, no returning to the lake house?"

"I'm afraid not, darling," Kat laced her fingers with Java's, "but there is tonight."

##

The next morning Kat dressed silently leaving Java to sleep. She could tell by how quickly the blonde had fallen asleep after their lovemaking that Java was exhausted.

307

Two Ways to Die
A Java Jarvis Thriller
by Erin Wade

She was glad that Ares had slipped onto the bed and was now snuggled against Java's back. She left them sleeping.

She can take one day off, Kat thought as she drove away from the lake house.

Kat stopped by the pet store and purchased a service-dog harness for Ares. *This will allow him entry to any place Java takes him,* she thought pleased with her purchase.

As Kat waited for the red light to change, she wished Java would wake and call her. The squeal of brakes yanked her from her thoughts of the blonde. She watched as a black Cadillac ran the stop light swerving to miss a smaller car.

Looks like Déjà is out today, Kat thought. She decided to follow the vehicle to Déjà's store and talk to the owner.

The car made a jerky stop on the parking lot, backed up to the door, and Kally got out. Kat was surprised to see the girl driving Déjà's car.

Kat waited a few minutes to see if Déjà would come out of the store. When she didn't Kat walked inside.

"Hello," Kat called wondering where Kally had gone. "Is anyone here?"

The usual thump-drag sound that always heralded Kally's approach caught Kat's attention and she pushed aside the beads to enter the back of the store.

"Kally," Kat called.

"I'm back here Miss Kat," Kally yelled. "I'm doing inventory."

Kat followed the sound of Kally's voice weaving her way through the endless shelves of voodoo-oriented trinkets and cheap clothing.

"Déjà," Kat gasped as she spotted the priestess bound and gagged in a corner. Déjà vu's eyes widened in terror at the sight of Kat.

"What's going—" The whoosh of an ax cutting through the air ended Kat's sentence.

CHAPTER 67

"What do you mean she isn't there?" Java controlled her need to scream into the phone. "She left me at nine this morning. I've been calling her for the last thirty minutes. Her phone goes to voicemail instantly which means it's turned off."

Java reread Kat's note. "Love you baby. Call me when you wake." As was her habit Kat had put the date and time at the bottom of the note.

"She never showed up here," Chris reiterated. "Should I call Beau?"

"Give me a minute," Java choked. "Let me check her bank card and see if she stopped anywhere."

A quick check of Kat's card revealed a purchase of gas then a new harness for Ares around nine-thirty. Java called the pet store and learned that Kat had left a little before ten. She called Beau.

"Beau, Kat's disappeared," Java blurted as the detective answered the phone. "Put out a BOLO on her car immediately. She was last seen at the Love My Pets store on Canal around ten this morning. I'm on my way to the restaurant."

##

Her Wrangler was still rocking from the skidding stop when Java's feet hit the pavement. Ares was right on her heels. She ran inside and was greeted by an anxious Barbie and Chris. Beau entered the front door as Java entered the back.

"Have you heard from her?" Java demanded.

"No, not a word," Barbie answered.

"It's been almost four hours," Java dragged her hand down her face fighting back the urge to cry. "Something's happened to her."

"It's just been four hours," Beau pointed out as Karen Pierce entered the restaurant.

"What's going on Java?" the FBI director scowled.

"Kat's disappeared," Java cried.

"How do you know?" Karen asked.

"She left me a note at nine this morning when she left for work."

"Because she spent the night with you?" Karen queried.

"Yes! Yes! Dammit she spent the night with me," Java bellowed. "That's the least important thing on my mind right now. Fire me later. Right now, we've got to find Kat."

Everyone nodded in agreement. "Where should we start looking?" Karen asked.

"Everywhere," Java blurted. "Search Jody's place just in case some rabid sexbot has her. Look at Ames' church. Something's not right there. Check out Lindy Rochelle. I'm going to Déjà vu's store. Keep in touch. Karen you set up the report center. Use my office upstairs. We'll call you as we clear our search locations. Everyone, bring her back alive."

##

Java breathed a sigh of relief as she pulled onto the parking lot of Déjà's store. Both Kat's car and the priestess were there. "Thank God," she swallowed the knot that had formed in her throat and reported to Karen that she had eyes on Kat's car.

"Where's your leash, fellow?" Java patted Ares as the dog insisted on following her into the store. "Maybe the Priestess of the Dead won't mind if you're not on a leash. Stay close."

Two Ways to Die
A Java Jarvis Thriller
by Erin Wade

"Miss Java," Kally beamed as Java and Ares entered the store. She walked around the counter for a hug. Ares moved between Kally and Java as a low guttural growl escaped his throat.

"Ares, down," Java commanded. The dog obeyed but continued the low rumbling.

"I'm sorry, Kally," Java apologized. "He's a little overprotective of me."

Kally nodded. "It's okay. My dog's the same way."

"Kally is Kat here?"

"No ma'am," Kally frowned. "Reverend Ames picked up her and Miss Déjà vu earlier this morning."

"Where did they go?" Java asked leaning against the counter. Ares held his position between Kally and Java.

'To the church, I think," Kally frowned. "People don't keep me informed of their coming and going."

"Are you doing inventory today?" Java asked examining the open journal on the counter.

"Yes ma'am," Kally pulled the journal away from Java. "I just finished counting all these buttons." She gestured toward the bowl of buttons.

"Oh, don't let me interrupt you," Java smiled. "Go ahead and enter your tally."

"Thank you," Kally grinned as she marked four lines then a diagonal line."

"So that stands for five buttons?" Java queried noticing that all the tallies were exactly alike.

"Yes ma'am," Kally beamed.

"I guess I'll catch up with Kat and Déjà at the church," Java strolled to the door. "If I miss them, please ask Kat to call me."

"I will," Kally assured her.

Java returned to her vehicle, Ares jumped in and they drove away.

##

Two Ways to Die
A Java Jarvis Thriller
by Erin Wade

Kally rushed to the back of the store. Gone was the limp she had affected for so long. Déjà watched her through hooded eyes. Kat lay in a puddle of blood. "Probably dead," Kally mumbled. "And I wanted to watch her die."

She picked up the ax she had used to kill Kat and stood over Déjà. "You lied to me," she screamed. "You told me the potion would make me invisible, but it doesn't. They all saw me as they died." She raised the ax over her head. One good hard blow would de-brain Déjà vu.

"Kally," Java screamed, "put down the ax."

Kally turned. "You're smarter than I thought," Kally grinned menacingly. "But, hey, the more the merrier."

"Kally put down the ax, nice and slow," Java reiterated.

Kally hesitated as if confused. "You can see me!" She cried.

"Of course," Java mocked. "Everyone can see you."

Kally swung around to face Déjà raising the ax high over her head. "You're a fake," she screamed at Déjà vu.

"Kally, stop!" Java yelled.

As the ax started its downswing, Java fired her Glock. The shot cut the ax handle in half. A furious Kally turned toward Java. "I can beat you to death with this ax handle," she growled.

Java shot her in the leg, but she continued to advance toward the agent. "Kally, don't make me kill you," Java begged.

Kally lunged forward and Java fired ripping off the arm wielding the ax handle. Kally grabbed her shoulder where her arm had been then stared stupidly at the blood spurting from it.

Java called for an ambulance as Beau and the team burst through the front door.

Two Ways to Die
A Java Jarvis Thriller
by Erin Wade

CHAPTER 68

Java stared into the cold waters of the lake. She couldn't live without Kat. She didn't want to live without Kat. She reread Kat's last note to her. "Love you baby. Call me when you wake." A chill swept over Java like nothing she had ever experienced. She'd never imagined life without Kat.

"Hey, you're going to catch a cold standing out here," a soft voice spoke behind her and Java turned around.

"Oh baby, you're crying." A soft hand caught Java's and pulled her into the house in front of the fire.

"I can't do this anymore," Java choked. "As much as I love being an FBI agent the price is too high."

"That isn't a decision you have to make right now," Kat pulled Java to the sofa and sat down in her lap. "It's because one side of my head is shaved, isn't it?" Kat teased.

Java ran her fingers along Kat's head where stubble was beginning to grow. "Even half bald you're still the most beautiful woman I've ever seen," Java murmured against soft lips. "I don't ever want to lose you."

"I know how you feel," Kat leaned her head against Java's breast. "I thought I would die when you disappeared," she said.

"Kat, on our last case you were shot," Java stroked what was left of Kat's soft dark hair. "You were in a coma for over a month from Kally's ax blow. This job is too dangerous. There are too many crazies out there. Besides I'm certain Karen's demanded meeting with us tomorrow is to request our badges and guns."

"Honey we weren't targeted because we're FBI agents," Kat pointed out. "Melody had the hots for you. She had no idea you were FBI. She truly had a screw loose.

"Kally got her jollies from bashing peoples brains out. She had no way of knowing I was FBI. She started that nonsense to throw authorities off her trail. She was trying to point the finger at Ames. She told the psychiatrist that she had no religious or ethnic reasons for who she killed. They were simply the easiest to get to. Except for Rogers all were poor and didn't even have good locks on their doors. She killed because she loved the sound and smell and the total look of terror on the victim's face just before her ax crushed their skull."

"I know," Java sighed heavily. "But the job is what puts us in harm's way. We wouldn't associate with those people if we were Jane Doe citizens."

"And how many others would have died if we hadn't caught them?" Kat pointed out.

Java nuzzled her face against Kat's neck. "I know you're right," she whispered. "I just love you so much."

"I know baby," Kat kissed her.

##

"You ready for this?" Kat asked as they stood outside Karen's office.

"As ready as I'll ever be," Java faked a smile and knocked on the door.

"Come in," Karen called rising to meet her two best agents. "Kat, it's wonderful to see you looking so good. Java, thank you both for coming."

"Um, you act like we had a choice," Java groused.

"You really didn't," Karen grinned. "I want to thank you both for your exceptional work. I've put you in for the FBI Shield of Bravery. Both of you have earned it."

"Thank you," they chorused.

Two Ways to Die
A Java Jarvis Thriller
by Erin Wade

"That being said," Karen pulled an official looking document from her file folder and slid it slowly across her desk toward Kat and Java. "Please explain this."

Java placed her badge and Glock on Karen's desk.

"It's my marriage certificate," Kat muttered.

"Yes, I can see that," Karen said. "It shows that you are married to—"

"Me," Java interrupted. "We've been married for the last four years."

"I can see that," Karen huffed. "When were you going to tell me about it?"

"Need to know," Java quipped. "You had no need to know."

"If I'd known," Karen glared at them, "I might have been better prepared to protect you. As it is, I'm being forced to remove you from the team."

Java caught her breath. Suddenly it did matter to her that she was an FBI agent and she knew Kat loved the job as much as she. She wanted to beg Karen to let them stay, keep them in the loop, let them catch criminals.

"The powers that be have instructed me to give you your own teams." Karen continued. "Congratulations Agents Kat Lace and Java Jarvis, you are now Assistant Special Agents-in-Charge. ASAC for short. You'll have two teams of four reporting to you. Each of you will be responsible for a team and you can use them together or separately. You will still report directly to me."

Java was speechless. "It seems my wife doesn't know what to say," Kat laughed. "So, I accept our new assignments on the behalf of us."

"What about payroll?" Karen asked. "Name changes?"

"No," they chorused. "Let's keep it simple."

"Um Karen, is there any chance we can have Barbie and Chris," Java found her voice.

Two Ways to Die
A Java Jarvis Thriller
by Erin Wade

"If they put in for transfer, I'll approve it," Karen nodded. "I have a feeling they wouldn't like working with any other leaders anyway."

"We've accumulated a lot of vacation time," Kat said. "We'd like to take a month off before we begin putting together our new teams."

"Effective immediately you are on vacation," Karen grinned. "But only for one week. I need your teams staffed and running by the end of the month."

"A week's longer than I expected," Java huffed.

"I need to fill you in on The Basher case," Karen said. "It seems Kally, her father and brother were all involved.

Kally confessed to everything. She was involved from the beginning. She hated her own mixed family and butchering other mixed families was an outlet to keep from killing her own family. Budro followed her one night and discovered what she was doing. She convinced him to join her in her murderous rampages.

"According to Déjà vu, Kally never had a club foot and was in her early thirties. Her childlike behavior and failure to grasp social norms made her appear to be much younger.

"Kally will spend the rest of her life in the women's prison for the criminally insane. Budro will get lethal injection."

Karen handed Java her gun and badge. "I admire that you were willing to turn these in for the woman you love, but please don't pull that stunt again."

"Karen, do we have to hide our marriage?" Java asked.

"No, I think your team will be proud to know Kat wasn't cheating on her husband and you weren't sleeping with someone else's wife," Karen said. "By the way Kat, who is Marcus Lace?"

"My older brother," Kat laughed.

Java caught Kat's hand pulling her to her feet. "We're on vacation. Let's not waste a minute of it."

Two Ways to Die
A Java Jarvis Thriller
by Erin Wade

They stopped at the door and turned to their director, "Thank you, Karen," they chorused.

"We have one whole week," Java hugged Kat as they walked onto the deck of their home. "Where would you like to go?"

"I'd like to be in my own personal little bit of heaven," Kat tiptoed to kiss her wife. "I'd like to spend the next seven days right here with you and Ares."

"How do you always read my mind?" Java laughed opening the door to their home. She swept Kat off her feet and carried her over the threshold. "Welcome to my world Kat Lace. It was definitely built with you in mind."

The End

Two Ways to Die
A Java Jarvis Thriller
by Erin Wade

A Woman to Die For
By Erin Wade

Good caffeinated coffee is like a fine woman, if they don't make you climb the walls every once in a while, something is missing . . .

Erin Wade from *A Woman to Die For.*

Chapter 1

Katie Brandt wasn't just any pretty woman. She was that woman one dreamed about. The one with long dark hair and flashing brown eyes that danced when a smile spread across her full red lips. She was that woman men and women would die . . . and kill for. She had it all: beauty, wealth and charisma. She even had something she didn't know about, a stalker!

Two Ways to Die
A Java Jarvis Thriller
by Erin Wade

Dr. Shaylor Copeland was the first to reach the woman as she stumbled into the emergency room. She collapsed into Shaylor's arms. Trained personnel moved efficiently to stop the bleeding from Katie's nose and stitch up the gashes across her torso.

##

Shaylor's shift ended at two in the morning. She walked to the cafeteria for coffee. Maybe a cup of the strong liquid would keep her awake until she reached home. She carried the coffee with her as she took one last look at Katie Brandt.

To Shaylor's surprise Katie was sitting up, her head resting on a stack of pillows. Her penetrating eyes were surveying her room.

"You're awake," Shaylor smiled as she approached the woman.

"And alive," Katie scoffed.

"Yes. What happened?" Shaylor pulled a chair to her bedside.

"You are?" Dark Belizean brows accentuated the question.

"Oh, I'm sorry," Shaylor blushed slightly. "I'm Dr. Shaylor Copeland. Everyone calls me Dr. Shay."

A twisted smile played on the woman's full lips as she scrutinized Shaylor. "I'll call you Shay."

"Call me whatever you like," Shay chuckled. "Can you tell me what happened to you?"

"Um, yes. My husband tried to kill me."

Something turned over in Shay's stomach at the thought of Katie being the victim of domestic violence.

"The police will be here in the morning to take a statement," Shay informed her. "You need to file charges against him."

"Don't you know who my husband is?" Katie scowled.

Shay shook her head, no.

"He's Dr. David Brandt, your chief of staff," Katie seemed to shrink into herself.

"Dr. Brandt isn't married," Shay pointed out. "I know because I date him."

"Yes, you and every other female in this hospital. If you'd be kind enough to leave, I'd like to rest."

Shay stood and looked down at the beauty lying back against the pillows. "Why would David try to kill you?"

"I asked him for a divorce," Katie sighed.

Returning to the doctor's lounge Shay tried to sort out Katie Brandt's accusation. Dr. David Brandt was a highly respected physician and one of the kindest men Shay had ever encountered. She had been with the hospital for three years and no one had ever mentioned that David was married. Shay wondered if the woman was delusional. Her wounds were certainly real, but Shay couldn't see David harming anyone.

##

David Brandt walked through his palatial home searching for his wife. It took him fifteen minutes to look in all the rooms and outside. Katie was gone. He wondered where she had gone. How she'd gotten out of the house.

He returned to his den and called the police. "Yes, this is Dr. David Brandt. I need to file a missing person's report."

David waited patiently as he was transferred to the right person. After several minutes a female spoke into the phone.

"Dr. Brandt, this is Detective Beverly Wyatt. How may I help you?"

"Beverly, thank heaven I got you. My wife is gone again. I have no idea where she is."

Two Ways to Die
A Java Jarvis Thriller
by Erin Wade

"Don't worry Dr. Brandt, I'll do a quick check of the hospitals and jails. I'll get back with you."

A call rang in before David could put down his phone. He smiled when Shay Copeland's face appeared. "Hello, darling," he cooed.

"Dr. Brandt we have a patient you must see. Can you come to the hospital right now?"

Shay's doctor voice told David to move quickly. "I'll be right there."

##

Shay was tired but she didn't intend to leave without talking to David. They had been dating over a year and had started discussing marriage. Something that was out of the picture if he was married.

"Honey, what's going on?" David burst through the emergency room doors. "How serious is it?"

Shay motioned for him to follow her to the elevators. "I have a patient I desperately need you to examine," she informed him.

Shay studied David as the elevator glided to the sixth floor. He was extremely handsome. His six-foot frame was slender and muscular like a cyclist. His thick black hair had a hint of silver at the temple. He was every woman's dream.

The ding of the elevator interrupted her reverie. "Room 601," Shay led the way to the patient's room.

Katie was sleeping on her back. The soft sweetness of the woman's face made Shay's breath catch.

David looked at Katie. His eyes darted between Katie and Shay. "Why is she here?"

"Someone brutalized her." Shay watched David's face closely as a darkness spread across it.

"Is she okay? What happened?" He whispered.

Two Ways to Die
A Java Jarvis Thriller
by Erin Wade

"Let's go to the doctors lounge. We can talk over coffee." Shay led the way from the room.

##

They carried their coffee to a table in the corner of the lounge. Shay wasn't certain where to start. David hadn't indicated that he knew Katie and his concern for her as a patient seemed sincere.

"Do you know her?" Shay finally asked.

David stirred cream into his coffee. "She's my wife," he mumbled.

"That seems like pertinent information one should know while dating," Shay scowled. "I mean, what future can one have with a married man? And where has she been? No one seems to know you're married."

"They know," David avoided looking into her eyes. "They just don't talk about her."

"Why not?"

"Katie has some mental problems," David sighed. "She's been in an institution."

"So, you were just going to . . . what . . . marry me and forget about her?"

"No, of course not," David inhaled deeply. "I was trying to tell you. It's . . . it's just not easy."

"She said you tried to kill her!"

"What? No! I'd never do that," David denied.

"David, she's been raped, beaten and stabbed. How did this happen to her? Is she in your care?"

"She was but she ran away. I filed a missing person's report. Check for yourself . . . a Detective Beverly Wyatt is handling the search for her."

"You should call Detective Wyatt and let her know you've found your wife."

David nodded and called Beverly. Shay watched his face as he spoke with the detective. "Yes, of course. No, I'll be here."

"She's on her way," He uttered the misery obvious in his eyes. "Katie said I tried to kill her?"

"Yes," Shay nodded, "and that you raped her."

"I'd never force myself on her," David's loud declaration caused the few people in the lounge to look their way. "Shay this isn't the best place to discuss this. Can we talk tomorrow after we've both gotten some sleep?"

"That's probably a good idea," Shay stood. "I'll leave you to wait for Detective Wyatt."

##

Shay punched the elevator button and scuffed the toe of her shoe on the polished floor as she waited for the door to open. Maudine Trent was on duty tonight and she intended to find her.

"Maudine, can you spare me a few minutes?" Shay leaned over the counter of the nurses' station.

"Anything for you sweet cheeks," Maudine gave her a toothy grin.

"I need a rape kit processed on Katie Brandt in 601."

"It may be too late, hon," Maudine sobered, "but I'll do the best I can. You mind officiating?"

"Not at all," Shay shrugged. "I know rape kits are useless if done after seventy-two hours, but she was admitted thirty-six hours ago, so it will hold up in court."

Maudine gathered her kit and a couple of sheets. "Why wasn't this done when she came in?"

"No one suspected rape and she was in no condition to report it."

"But you suspect it?" Maudine furrowed her brow. "Why?"

Two Ways to Die
A Java Jarvis Thriller
by Erin Wade

"Just a gut feeling," Shay shrugged.

"Yeah, well your gut feelings have saved lives on more than one occasion. You explain to her what's about to happen then call me when she's ready."

Shay slipped into Katie's room and stood for a few seconds watching the beautiful woman sleep. *How could anyone hurt a woman like that?* She thought.

Katie began to tremble violently and cry out. Shay didn't touch her but began talking to her in soothing tones.

Katie's eyes opened wide and darted around the room like those of a trapped animal. "Please, please don't," she cried.

"Mrs. Brandt, it's me, Dr. Shay," Shay turned on the light at the head of the bed so Katie could see who she was.

It took the patient several minutes to calm down and recognize her surroundings.

"Shay," a twisted smile worked its way across sensuous lips. "What time is it?"

"Almost morning," Shay answered.

"Have you been home?"

"No, I've been watching over you," Shay wanted to put her patient's mind at ease. "I need to ask a favor."

"Okay," Katie cautiously agreed.

"I'd like to have the nurse do a rape kit for you."

Silent tears ran down Katie's face. "I didn't say I was raped."

"I know," Shay whispered. "But we need to do this. It's important."

"Alright," Katie sighed. "I couldn't be any more humiliated than I already am."

"I'm going to bring in the nurse now," Shay informed her.

"Could you sit up here by my bed and talk to me during this ordeal?" Katie pleaded.

Two Ways to Die
A Java Jarvis Thriller
by Erin Wade

"Of course," Shay pulled a chair to the head of the hospital bed and took Katie's hand in hers. "Feel free to crush my hand if you need to," she teased.

Katie nodded and squeezed her eyes tightly shut trying to stop the tears that sought release.

Maudine went about her task softly humming as she draped a sheet over her patient. "I'll be taking photos to document trauma," she explained. "Then swab your body for any evidence."

Two hours later Maudine described the final phase of the exam. "I need to be more invasive. This will be uncomfortable and take a while."

Katie gripped Shay's hand tighter and kept her eyes closed tightly. She made tiny mewling sounds when Maudine did the speculum examine, taking swab samples and securing them for DNA testing.

"Do I need to do an anal exam?" Maudine glanced at Shay.

"Please, no." Katie pleaded. "It's not necessary."

"I think you've done your usual thorough exam," Shay tried to hide her exhaustion as she signed off on the many plastic bags containing samples Maudine had collected. "Would you personally make certain Detective Wyatt gets these when she arrives?"

"Sure," Maudine placed her work from the last three hours inside a box, sealed it then signed and dated it.

After Maudine left the room Shay returned to stand at Katie's beside. "Are you going to be alright?"

"Dr. Shay, I haven't been alright for a very long time," Katie murmured.

"We'll take good care of you," Shay promised patting her patient's hand.

Katie clutched Shay's hand. "Please don't leave me alone."

"I won't." Shay said gently.

Two Ways to Die
A Java Jarvis Thriller
by Erin Wade

##

"Did you spend the night here, Sweet Cheeks?" Maudine whispered into Shay's ear.

"Jesus, Maudine," Shay jumped straight up in her chair. A partial imprint of Katie's hand was on her cheek where Shay had rested her face against it all night. "You almost gave me a heart attack. What time is it?"

"Six! Time for me to go home, Doc. I thought I'd—"

"Please stay." The hand she had rested her face against all night caught Shay's arm.

Shay looked down into eyes that could steal one's soul. "I will," she mumbled.

A Woman to Die For

By Erin Wade

A Psychological Thriller coming in the first quarter of 2020

Thank you for reading my book. I hope you enjoyed it as much as I enjoy writing for you. If you enjoyed it, please leave me a review on Amazon.

Learn more about Erin Wade
and her books at
www.erinwade.us
Follow Erin on Facebook
https://www.facebook.com/erin.wade.129142

#1 Best Selling Books
by Erin Wade
Too Strong to Die
Death Was Too Easy
Three Times as Deadly
Branded Wives
Living Two Lives

Two Ways to Die
A Java Jarvis Thriller
by Erin Wade

Don't Dare the Devil
The Roughneck & the Lady
Wrongly Accused
The Destiny Factor
Shakespeare Under Cover
Assassination Authorized
Two Ways to Die – A Java Jarvis Thriller

Coming in 2020
A Woman to Die For
The Devil's Secret
Three Shots, You're Dead – A Java Jarvis Thriller

Made in the USA
Coppell, TX
09 March 2020

16667682R00184